THE CHARLATAN'S CONUNDRUM

and Other Bedtime Stories for Insomniacs

Rich Hosek

Sherman Oaks, California

Visit **BedtimeStories.studio** for more
Bedtime Stories for Insomniacs
and sign up for the Insomniacs Snoozeletter.

The characters and events in this book are fictitious.
Any similarity to real persons, living or dead,
is coincidental and not intended by the author.

Nifni Press
a division of
Paraphrase, LLC
P.O. Box 56508
Sherman Oaks, CA 91413

Read a Book, Read a Mind

ISBN: 978-1-953566-17-1

Printed in the United States of America
First Printing: August 2024

For Zach,

who was there for all
my very most favorite bedtimes.

Also by Rich Hosek

The Dead Kids Club
The Tenth Ride (2024)
Gaston Leroux: The Man Behind the Man Behind the Mask

with Arnold Rudnick and Loyd Auerbach

The Raney/Daye Investigation paranormal mysteries:
Near Death
After Life
Far Sight (2024)

Listen to the

Bedtime Stories for Insomniacs

fiction podcast

Available on all podcast apps and Audible
or visit https://bedtimestories.studio for more information.

Can't sleep?
Don't want to sleep?
Afraid to sleep?

Are the windows closed?
Are your doors locked?
Did you check your closet
and under your bed?
Maybe you should keep a light on
in the hallway… just in case.

Now settle in,
make yourself comfortable,
lay back,
close your eyes,

and let me tell you a story…

TABLE OF CONTENTS

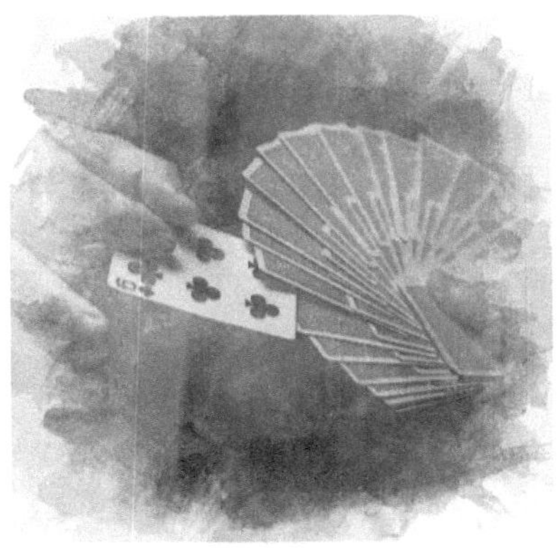

The Charlatan's Conundrum

"Prove that I'm a fake," said the man sitting across from me.

We were in a booth at the diner where I frequently had casual meetings like this one.

"I don't need to. I know you're a fake," I told him.

He dropped his chin in frustration, perhaps even despair. His expression was difficult to read through the layers of fatigue that were present on his face. He also looked as if he hadn't showered for days, which made me glad I was on the other side of the booth.

"I know you know I'm a fake, but I need you to prove it. I need you to demonstrate beyond a shadow of a doubt that I am a charlatan, a phony, a fraud," he begged with pleading eyes shaded under heavy lids.

"What is this all about, Alex?" I asked.

Alex Black was a magician I knew who specialized in mentalism—convincing people he could read their minds. He had started out as a street hustler, doing Three Card Monty and various variations on the Shell Game for tourists on the boardwalk. But eventually, he worked his way into a tiny theater where he did his show every night, with matinées on the weekend. I'd been to the show many times. It was a fun night for out-of-town guests, and Alex was better than most of the performers of his ilk.

He took an envelope out of his jacket pocket. My name was written on it.

"What's that?" I asked.

"It's a check for five hundred dollars," he answered. "I want to pay you to prove that I'm a fake. You know, like how you do on those internet videos you're always making. I want to pay you because I want you to take this seriously. I *need* you to really do whatever you can to prove I'm just another magician."

"I don't want your money, Alex," I protested.

Alex cut me off. "I know," he said with a smile. "It doesn't take a mind reader to know that you're a good friend, but I need you to pretend that I'm someone trying to pull something over on you. And you need to figure out how I did it."

This was something I was actually pretty good at. When I was a boy, I had been a fan of the Amazing Randi, a magician and skeptic who was famous for offering a ridiculously large reward for any psychic who could prove they were real. He had never had to pay out the bounty.

I had taught myself magic from a young age, and learned all the tricks of the trade that I could—especially mentalism, which I found particularly intriguing.

Performers like Alex really made it seem like they had a window into your mind. But in the end—as Penn and Teller so eloquently put it—it was all bullshit. Tricks that used psychology, confederates and sleight of hand to convince the audience—be it a theater full of partially inebriated couples out for a good time or an audience of one—desperate to believe that the person cold reading them really had a pipeline to the afterlife.

When television ghost hunter shows became popular, the internet was flooded with videos and photos of apparitions in various forms.

I had a friend who was a rather good professional photographer who initially helped me debunk a lot of them on my own YouTube channel.

I soon expanded to videos of psychics, demonstrating how I could reproduce everything they did with my own ordinary mind. I had accrued a decent following and had been a guest on a few other channels as well as legitimate TV shows. I had even been involved in a few famous feuds that had had gone viral.

Alex was one of my many resources for the rare occasions when I was stumped. He and I could usually brainstorm the trick the psychic was using in short order, and he even helped me stage some of my debunking videos.

Why he was sitting across this Formica covered table imploring—and employing me, it seemed—to prove somehow that *he* was just another magician was—to say the least—mind-boggling.

"Are you trying out a new bit for your act?" I asked.

Alex slumped back into the vinyl covered bench on his side of the booth and sighed. "No, that's not it at all." He looked away in thought for a moment, scratching the side of his head with dirty fingernails, then returned his gaze to me. "I was hoping I wouldn't have to give you all the details, but perhaps I should start at the beginning."

"Always a good place to start," I said.

"As long as at the end you don't think I'm crazy," he replied.

Now, I was curious. I picked up the envelope between us. It was sealed, and by the feel of it, I could tell there was a check-sized piece of paper enclosed inside. I folded it up and stuffed it into my pocket. "Okay, for whatever good it does, you have engaged me as a professional skeptic, and I will attempt to prove that you are the total fake I've always known you to be."

Alex seemed satisfied.

The waitress arrived, filling our coffee cups and asking if we wanted anything to eat.

Alex waved off her question, satisfied, taking a long sip of his black coffee.

I asked for a slice of pumpkin pie.

Once she departed, Alex began his story. "It started a couple of weeks ago. I was doing my act as usual, setting up the crowd for my first 'read,' the one where I push them into thinking of specific shapes. Most of the audience followed me to thinking of a triangle in a circle—you know the bit—but I could tell from her face that one woman in the crowd had something else in mind.

"I told her she was thinking of a pentagram inside of a rectangle, and although she refused to confirm it, I could tell from her reaction that I was right.

"There's always someone in the crowd who tries to spoil the trick, but usually they're just background noise. I passed it off as blind luck that I guessed what she had been thinking of.

"The next night, I was doing another gag where I do a one-ahead prediction trick. Only I found myself writing down the predictions *before* I got them from the volunteer. I didn't even realize I was doing it. I did my force prediction, and then when I went to write down the first one-ahead, it was already there."

"What are you trying to tell me?" I asked, fearing I already knew the answer.

"I think," he began, suddenly fearful, "I've actually become psychic."

I laughed.

Alex remained stone-faced.

"Is this your shtick now?" I asked.

He shook his head. "I can't turn it off. I'm hearing people's thoughts, seeing glimpses into the future. I'm just waiting for the bending spoons with my mind to kick in," he said, picking up the spoon next to his coffee cup and staring at it.

"Alex, you're a professional mentalist. Cold reading people, playing the odds, creating forcing conditions, it's all second nature to you. You're just in the zone."

He shook his head forcefully, turned his body so he was facing the window we were sitting next to, and gazed out into the street. After a moment, he said simply, "That woman in the yellow dress is going to bump into a lamppost."

I turned my head to follow his gaze and spotted the woman he was talking about strolling on the other side of the street. After a few steps, she paused and fished her phone out of her purse. She continued walking while she had a brief conversation. Then she took the phone away from her ear and started tapping away with her thumbs, her eyes focused on the screen while she continued walking.

Directly into a lamppost.

Alex looked at me as if for an explanation.

"Friend of yours?" I asked.

"No," he answered.

"Easy guess. Most people with a phone are going to be distracted."

"The phone was in her purse when I made the prediction," he countered.

"So … you're telling me you saw it happen before it actually happened?"

Alex nodded.

"That was hardly laboratory conditions," I said, starting to think that maybe this was some kind of con Alex was pulling on me.

"True," he agreed. He closed his eyes for a moment, then said, "enjoy your lemon cream pie."

"I ordered pumpkin," I said.

The waitress returned from behind Alex, carrying a slice of lemon cream pie. "We're out of pumpkin, honey," she said. "Lemon cream work for you?"

I nodded, and she placed the pie in front of me and walked off to another table.

"You saw that they were out of pumpkin in the pie case when you walked in, maybe that they had a couple of lemon cream pies they would probably try to get rid of instead," I speculated.

Alex shrugged. "That's a perfectly reasonable explanation, but you watched me come in. I saw you right when I entered and came straight to the booth. I never passed the pie case."

"You could have stopped by earlier."

Alex sighed, frustrated. "Okay, give me a test. What would you do to verify that someone was psychic? That I can actually read your mind."

I thought for a second. Ideally, if I was trying to test someone who was willing to be tested, I would have a controlled environment with cameras, sound-proofing, a room-size Faraday cage to eliminate any chance of receiving information from the outside. I didn't know how sophisticated Alex was in terms of technologies he might use to augment his act, but I should be able to come up with something off the cuff.

I remembered the deck of cards I always carried with me. As an amateur magician, I always had them at the ready to practice or entertain any kids I met. I took out the deck and gave it a shuffle.

"How do I know you're actually reading my mind?" I asked. "You could just be predicting the future of which card I'll show next."

He laughed. "Yeah, I guess. Let's see what happens and sort it out later."

I picked up a card and looked at it.

"Five of spades," he said.

I placed the five of spades on the table between us.

I drew another card.

"Eight of hearts."

I dropped the red eight on the table and drew three more in quick succession.

"King of spades, two of clubs, seven of diamonds."

He was right on each one.

I stared at him. He was looking straight into my eyes. I smiled and took off my glasses. Obviously, he was seeing the card in the reflection of the lenses. I drew three more cards.

"Queen of diamonds, ten of diamonds, ten of clubs."

I laid each card down as he correctly named them.

Could he see the reflection in my eyeballs? Was anyone's eyesight that good? I turned around. There was no one behind us, no glass panes or mirrors he could be using. I pulled the deck into my lap, keeping it out of his sight and out of view of anyone else. I peeked at the corner of the card on the top of the desk like a blackjack dealer.

"Four of clubs," Alex said.

I dropped the four of clubs on top of the other cards.

"You've gotten better at card tricks, haven't you?"

"It's not a trick," he insisted.

"You understand that's exactly what someone who was faking it would say," I replied.

"Is that your proof that I'm a fraud? That I claim I can actually read your mind?"

"Normally, that would be the first indication," I admitted.

"Picture something," he challenged. "Bring up an image in your mind, something I couldn't possibly guess."

I kept my mind as blank as I could.

He stared at me, silent. Waiting.

I closed my eyes, squeezed them shut and let myself just drift in the darkness, picturing nothing.

Alex remained silent, saying nothing as I continued to keep my mind blank.

The sounds and smells of the diner filtered into my senses. It was more difficult than I expected to keep my mind perfectly blank, thinking of nothing was technically something, but it was like trying to keep from blinking while holding your gaze on a bright—

"A light bulb," Alex said, just as the picture popped into my mind.

I opened my eyes.

"Was I right?" he asked.

"Is that a new force you came up with?" I asked. I tried to think back in our conversation where Alex would have subliminally implanted the suggestion of a light bulb at one or more points, so that the concept would be at the forefront of my mind. It was a common technique.

Alex took a deep breath and sighed again. "This is the problem," he said. "You see me as a magician and mentalist and you think there has to be an angle, a trick."

"Look," I said, "I have to go back to my original thesis. You are very good at what you do. I know you still fend off people who track you after the show to ask you to do personal readings. You're very convincing. After doing it for all these years, it must be second nature."

"So, I am a fraud," he said. "You just can't prove it."

"Well, not sitting at a booth in a diner. If you're really serious, I guess we could set up something more formal, but if you're looking for publicity, trying to take your act to the next level or something, get on TV, I'd prefer you don't use me."

Alex nodded. "I wouldn't abuse our friendship like that," he assured me. "And I do value your opinion."

His words held a tinge of despair. I took the envelope he had given me earlier out of my pocket.

"No, please, you keep that. I asked you to prove that I'm a fake, and that is what you believe I am, so you earned it." He slid himself out of the booth and got to his feet.

"You're phonier than a three dollar bill from China," I assured him.

He looked at me, dropped his head with a sigh, and shuffled out of the diner.

I took a bite of the lemon cream pie, then used my knife as a letter opener to slice through the top of the envelope. I pulled the check out and looked at it.

Five hundred dollars was written in the box for the amount, and his signature was scribbled in the bottom right corner.

And in the spot in the bottom left corner reserved for a memo were the words, "Phonier than a three dollar bill from China."

I ripped up the check, then finished my pie.

Damn, he's good, I thought to myself. *He really should be on TV.*

The Austin Intelligence

"There's a woman in your office, Mr. Bythewood."

"How did she get in there?" Mr. Bythewood asked.

"I don't know. She was here when I arrived," his assistant, Ms. Blackstone, replied.

"What does she want?"

"She didn't say, but she looks very rich."

Mr. Bythewood considered the situation. He was the head of one of the most successful investment firms on Wall Street, and it wasn't unheard of for him to receive inquiries from wealthy people who valued their privacy as much as the returns on their investments. But rarely did they do so in person. Regardless, he would have a word with Junger in security.

"Hold my calls, Ms. Blackstone."

"Yes, Mr. Bythewood," the assistant replied. She sat down behind her desk and started opening the mail.

Mr. Bythewood turned the knob on his inner office door and pushed it open.

Standing in the center of the room was a strikingly beautiful woman. Mr. Bythewood judged her to be in her mid-thirties, but with plastic surgery these days, she could easily have been older.

"Good morning, Ms..." he let the greeting hang in the air between them, hoping she would volunteer her name to complete it.

"You can call me Lina, Mr. Bythewood," the woman said.

"How can I help you, Lina?" Mr. Bythewood asked as he made his way past her to his desk. "Are you looking to make an investment with our firm?"

She nodded. "Perhaps. But I'm a very cautious woman. I like to do my due diligence before I hand over my money to anyone."

Mr. Bythewood smiled. "You want to know about the Austin Intelligence," he said as he sat in his chair and reclined.

Lina again nodded.

"Well, I can't tell you much more than you already know. It is proprietary technology. Trade secrets and all."

"I want to see it," Lina demanded.

Mr. Bythewood waved his hand in the air above him. "It's a cloud thing. Spread out among thousands of servers in dozens of data centers across the globe."

It was Lina's turn to smile. "You and I both know that's not true."

Mr. Bythewood became suddenly nervous. "What do you mean?"

"I mean," Lina began, "that your whole story about a distributed artificial intelligence is a load of—to put it politely—poppycock."

"Oh, I can assure you that the Austin Intelligence is real," Mr. Bythewood said.

"I didn't say it wasn't real," Lina explained, "just that it wasn't a cloud-based AI."

Mr. Bythewood smiled again, this time nervously. "I'm not sure I know what you mean."

"Do I really need to spell it out for you?" Lina asked.

"Please, I'm curious what you think you know."

Lina walked over to a leather couch and sat down on it. She placed her hands on her knees and stared directly at Mr. Bythewood. "Let's begin with your founder, Leonard Austin. He was a singular genius, a man who had the innate ability to see trends in markets and stocks, identify opportunities in derivatives, and apply what can best be described as an uncanny knack for timing to buy and sell at the precise times to maximize returns."

"Yes, Mr. Austin was indeed a bold innovator in the investment field."

Lina nodded. "And he did all that from a wheelchair, without the ability to move on his own, unable even to speak."

"He faced many challenges," Mr. Bythewood agreed.

"He built this company from nothing."

"He had some help."

"From you?" Lina asked. "You did nothing but exploit him. This company is worth nearly ten billion dollars, but Leonard Austin's net worth at the time of his death was a little over two million."

"Mr. Austin was well compensated for his services as a financial analyst."

"Leonard may have had a mind for financial markets, but he did not have a head for business. You took advantage of that. You recognized his talent, and you built this business around him. But you wouldn't have anything if it hadn't been for him."

Mr. Bythewood shrugged. "And he wouldn't have been anything without me. There would be no BA Investments without my foresight."

"And then he died," Lina said.

"Yes, it was very sad, but he was very sick. The doctors said it was a miracle he had lived as long as he had."

"Yet your firm continues making the kind of bold and lucrative deals you were known for when Leonard Austin was alive."

"Because of the Austin Intelligence."

"Which you claim is an AI that was trained via proprietary algorithms to mimic the decision making of the original Leonard Austin. In fact, it does more than manage your investments, it runs the company, everything from payroll to managing your real estate holdings."

"What's your point?"

"The thing is, your AI appears to be much more advanced than any other expert system. It seems to rely on…intuition, acting with a human-like imagination to see opportunities that other AIs, which apply traditional pattern recognition, miss."

"What can I say? That's why people choose BA Investments. We're just better."

"I want to see him," Lina stated plainly.

"Excuse me?"

"I want to see Leonard Austin."

"Mr. Austin is dead. I was at his funeral. I saw them lower his casket into the ground and cover it with dirt."

Lina looked at Mr. Bythewood, staring deep into his eyes. It unnerved him. "You may have buried Mr. Austin, but he's still working for you."

"Don't be absurd. You said yourself that he died."

Lina rose from her seat and started pacing. "When Leonard Austin was first diagnosed with ALS, the doctors didn't think he would live more than six months. But even though the disease rendered his body useless, his mind still worked."

"Yes, I know all this. I was more than just his business partner. I was his friend."

"Then you know about the system he utilized that allowed him to use a computer."

"Of course. It was a prototype device that used machine learning to interpret his brainwaves and translate them into actions on his computer," Mr. Bythewood explained. "Everyone knows that."

"But what they don't know is that, after Mr. Austin died, the interface continued working."

Mr. Bythewood's face became pale. He clenched his jaw and dug his fingernails into the leather surface of the blotter on his desk. "That's ridiculous," he said unconvincingly.

"You may not be aware, but Leonard's neural interface is configured to send regular diagnostic information back to the device's manufacturer. And according to the analytics, he's still hooked up to it. I want to see him," Lina repeated. "Or should I take my one-point-three billion dollars somewhere else?"

Mr. Bythewood said nothing.

"I can almost see what you're thinking, Mr. Bythewood," Lina said. "You're debating whether the commissions that much money could generate are worth sharing your secret." In her hands was a check. She placed it on the desk in front of him. It was made out in the amount of five hundred million dollars. "There's more if you show him to me."

Mr. Bythewood stared down at the check in front of him. The decision was easy. Besides, ever since it had happened, he had been dying to tell someone. He rose from his desk and crossed to a bookcase behind him. It was completely unnecessary to hide The Intelligence behind a secret door built into a bookcase, but when you have a lot of money, you have to spend it somewhere.

He pulled on a book, and a large section of the wall swung open.

Lina walked past the desk to the open passage and stepped inside the room beyond.

It was an office, not as large or opulent as Bythewood's, but impressive, nonetheless.

At the center of it was a desk. Underneath the large, dark slab was a collection of computers connected to each other by a web of cables. On the desk was a system of posts and arms that suspended nine monitors in a three-by-three array pointed at an empty motorized wheelchair. The chair had a halo of sensors attached to the headrest.

Lina smiled at the sight of it. "Hello, Leonard."

She walked toward the chair.

"Whoa, hold on. Stay back. You said you wanted to see. You saw, now step away."

Lina ignored him. She crossed behind the desk and looked at the monitors. A window popped up on one of them. A chat screen.

The word, "Hello," appeared in green letters.

"It's nice to see you again," Lina said.

More words appeared. "Do I know you?"

"Okay, that's enough," Mr. Bythewood said. "You've seen the Austin Intelligence. Time to go."

Lina turned to him. "Why do you call him that?"

"It's not a him, it's an it. The machine learning algorithm in the interface is just mimicking the thought patterns it processed for years. Yes, we tell people it's a massive cloud-based AI because they'd never trust us with their money if they knew it was just a glitching neural interface."

"A glitch?" Lina asked.

"Of course. A happy accident. Serendipity. A billion-dollar bug. What did you think it was? His ghost?" Mr. Bythewood laughed.

Lina did not.

"Look, I'm impressed that you figured out that we weren't telling the whole truth about the Austin Intelligence, but I hope now you understand why."

"Do you know who created the neural interface?" Lina asked him.

"What?"

"Do you know who built this for him?"

Mr. Bythewood shrugged. "Some computer geek."

Lina smiled, suppressing her anger. "It was built for him by an accomplished engineer who devoted her life to the study of neural interfaces for people with ALS, quadriplegics, and other victims of paralysis. And that woman also happened to be his mother."

"You know, now that you mention it, I did know that. Didn't she pass away a little while ago? I think we made a very generous donation to some foundation or something," Mr. Bythewood said. He became nervous. "Did you…know her?" he asked.

Lina didn't respond.

"Look," Mr. Bythewood said, regaining his entitled indignation, "this neural interface is the property of BA Investments."

"You're wrong, Mr. Bythewood."

"I have documentation. All personal property of Mr. Austin reverted to BA Investments upon his death."

"No," Lina told him. "You're wrong believing that it's the interface that's running the computers. Do you have any idea how the human mind works?"

He shrugged. "Not exactly. I mean, who does?"

"It comes down to electrical interactions, and all electric currents create an associated electromagnetic field, and the neurons inside our brains create sequences of pulses that we call brainwaves. It is those waves that the neural interface detects and interprets, translating them into actions on the computer. It does this by creating a symbiotic electronic field that resonates with the mind's activity."

"I know that part," Mr. Bythewood said.

"Without the presence of brainwaves, it's just a funny-looking hat. But when Mr. Austin died, this device trapped those electronic signals in place. So, even though you removed his body, the part of him that persists beyond the lifespan of his physical self remained in place."

"What do you mean, the part of him that persists? Are you talking about a soul?"

"I am."

"And you think that it's trapped in that chair?"

"He is."

Mr. Bythewood crossed his arms. "Look, all of this is very entertaining, but the fact remains that this chair, this computer, and all the financial analysis it provides are the property of BA Investments. You can invest with us or not, but you're going to have to go now."

"I see that you've added redundant power supplies to keep the interface going, but did you know that the symbiotic field can be overloaded with the presence of a second set of brainwaves?"

"What is that supposed to mean?"

"It means that if a second 'soul' were to come within sufficient proximity of the device, it would break the containment effect and release Mr. Austin from your cruel imprisonment."

"That's ridiculous."

"Is it? Leonard loved doing what he did. For him, it wasn't a job; it was a challenge, seeing the patterns and discovering how to unlock their potential. You gave him an opportunity to pursue his passion, and you *did* make him comfortable. I am grateful for that.

"But when he died, you should have let him go. I imagine he's been so thrilled with the fact that he can work all day long without any rest that he doesn't even realize that he's dead. Did you know that—in addition to his physical challenges—he was autistic? That's part of what makes him so good at what he does."

"Look, I don't know what you think you're trying to pull, but if you damage that interface in any way, I'll—"

"You'll what? Sue me?"

"You think a ten-billion-dollar company doesn't have an entire floor of lawyers in this building?"

"Oh, I'm sure you do, but I'm afraid they won't be able to help you."

"And why is that?"

"Do you know what Leonard Austin's mother's name was?"

"Why do you keep answering my questions with more questions?"

"Her name was Angelina Austin."

Mr. Bythewood shrugged. "So what?"

"Lina, for short."

It took a moment for the revelation to hit Mr. Bythewood.

Lina took a step toward the chair.

"I'm warning you. You don't want to mess with the Intelligence," Mr. Bythewood said sternly.

She turned back toward him. Only now, instead of being a woman of thirty-something, she was older, a woman in her sixties. She reached toward the chair with an age-spotted hand.

The monitors attached to the computer flickered.

Then Mr. Bythewood gasped as he saw a figure materialize in the chair.

It was Leonard.

"Hello, my son," Lina said.

"Hi, Mom," appeared on the screen with the chat window.

Lina smiled warmly. "You don't need to use that thing to speak any more, son."

"I don't?" Leonard asked, this time with a voice that appeared to come from his mouth.

Mr. Bythewood's knees buckled, and he almost fell to the floor.

"No, you don't need any of it anymore. You're free." She held her hand out to him.

Leonard lifted his own hand from the armrest and took hold of his mother's. He smiled, excited. "Are we going somewhere?" he asked.

"Yes, but there is one thing I'd like you to do before we go." She placed her hand on the side of his face in a motherly gesture. Something unspoken passed between them.

"Okay," Leonard said, then he looked at the array of computer monitors as a flood of information scrolled by and windows popped open and closed. "All done."

"What's done? What did he do?" Mr. Bythewood asked.

Leonard spotted Mr. Bythewood leaning against the doorway. "Hi, Mr. Bythewood. Did you meet my mom?"

Mr. Bythewood nodded.

"Stand up," Lina said to Leonard.

He reacted with surprise that such a thing was possible, then leaned forward and stood up.

"Come, Leonard. There's so much I want to show you," Lina said.

In the blink of an eye, they were gone.

The computer monitors went blank.

Mr. Bythewood took a moment to regain his balance and push back the blackness that threatened to engulf his consciousness. Leonard was gone. The Austin Intelligence was no more.

He stepped back into his own office. The check Lina had left was sitting on his desk, but when he went to reach for it, it too disappeared. An apt metaphor for the future of his company, he thought. Without the Austin Intelligence, he was nothing.

Ms. Blackstone entered and looked around, confused. "What happened to your guest?" she asked.

Mr. Bythewood sat down in the tall-backed leather chair behind the hand-carved walnut desk and sighed. "I'm afraid, Ms. Blackstone, that your services will no longer be required."

Ms. Blackstone smiled. "He's gone, isn't he?"

Mr. Bythewood was confused by her question. "Pardon me?"

"Mr. Austin. She came here to take him away. I'm glad. You're right. My services are no longer required. I no longer need to watch over him. My job here is done."

Ms. Blackstone promptly disappeared just as quickly and completely as Lina and Leonard had done moments earlier.

"What the hell," thought Mr. Bythewood. "Is everyone who works for me actually dead?" A horrifying revelation crossed his mind. He reached out with one hand and pinched the skin on the back of the other, digging his nails into the flesh as hard as he could. "Ow!" he exclaimed in pain.

Then, relieved, he flipped open the sleek laptop on one corner of his desk. Its operating system recognized his face, and he clicked on an icon in one corner of the device's desktop that simultaneously began selling all his holdings in BA investments, transferring all of his domestic assets to an offshore account and putting in a request to prep the company jet.

Only, that's not what happened.

Instead, the funds were sent to various charities and foundations. Even his offshore accounts were emptied and deposited among several children's hospitals.

Mr. Bythewood sighed in despair. This was just the beginning, he knew. Without the Austin Intelligence—or rather, Leonard—managing their clients' portfolios, the investors would flee. There might even be lawsuits from clients and stockholders, federal probes, stories on TMZ.

A new email message appeared in his inbox.

It was from Leonard.

"Thank you for helping me build this incredible fortune, Mr. Bythewood," it read. "All of the people who will be helped by your generosity will be forever grateful. It was fun working with you. See you on the other side!"

My Bythewood closed the lid of the laptop.

"Sooner than you probably think, my boy," he said.

He opened a drawer in his desk where a gleaming pistol lay, loaded and waiting for just such an occasion as this.

White

The snow came down in large white clumps, so quickly that my footprints were erased as fast as I made them trudging back to the cabin from the woodpile with an armload of logs. A satellite dish perched on my roof was buried in the winter's snowfall and completely useless, but I didn't need some fancy TV weatherman to tell me it was going to be a hell of a storm.

The solar panels were likewise ineffective this time of year, so the television was nothing but a blank frame, anyway. I had plenty of kerosene for my lamps, and the wood kept me warm and cooked my food. There was a shortwave radio for emergencies, but it got all the power it needed from a car battery. My books didn't require electricity, so as long as I had light to read by, the storm could do what it wanted.

I didn't own the one-room cabin. It came with the job. I was a ranger for the National Park Service. But I didn't do the typical ranger stuff, like admonishing tourists about leaving food out for the bears or cautioning them to stick to the trails and stay hydrated. I was a sort of concierge, catering to the hikers and mountaineers who came to summit the mountain. Those who held this post before me had carved their names and the year they were here into the wooden lintel above the door. Curiously, none of them seemed to have held the post for more than one winter.

Ascending the nearby peak, especially in the winter, was a challenge for a lot of alpinists. Its remoteness was particularly appealing for solo climbers, but the National Park Service wasn't too fond of climbers getting lost or injured, so I served as a base camp that was there if they needed help. My visitors jokingly called the simple cabin, The Last Chance Inn.

Normally, I saw a few people a week, some requiring first aid, others needing water or food or some piece of equipment. There was a box of odds and ends in one corner of the cabin that served as a "take one, leave one" collection of climbers' gear that had apparently grown over the years. Ropes, pitons of various shapes and sizes, socks, gloves, hammers, even a pair of crampons could all be found there, probably enough to outfit someone who had come this far with nothing more than hiking boots.

Once the cold set in, I saw maybe a few people a month. They were supposed to get a permit to attempt the summit in the winter, and then check in with me before their climb and after their descent—just to make sure there weren't any bodies wasting away on the peak.

Odds were I wouldn't have any visitors for the next month or two. Hopefully, someone was checking regularly to see that smoke was coming out of my chimney. The stores of freeze-dried meals I had hauled up in the fall would last until the snow melted.

So I nearly choked on the coffee I was drinking when I heard knocking.

I set down my mug, walked the three steps to the door, and opened it.

The man standing there was knee-deep in snow, wearing a fur coat, mittens, and had a knapsack on his back. He wasn't the typical climber who graced my threshold—he wasn't wearing the latest lightweight insulated parka and tinted goggles, nor did he have ropes and carabiners hanging off his belt.

"It's really coming down. You mind if I come in?" he asked.

"Sorry, please do," I replied. "Welcome to The Last Chance Inn."

He smiled at the name. "Last chance in or out," he remarked.

With him came an avalanche of snow. While he started slipping out of his coat in front of the fire, I grabbed the shovel I kept by the door and scooped the drift that had forced its way inside back out into the cold where it belonged.

I closed the door, then crossed to the stove where the coffeepot was keeping warm. "Would you like a cup?" I offered.

He waved off the offer and settled into one of the rough-hewn chairs in front of the fireplace. I picked up my coffee and joined him.

"So, which are you?" I asked.

"Pardon me?"

"Are you coming in or going out?"

He smiled. "Just passing through."

"Don't get many of those," I told him.

"No, I don't expect you do."

"You're welcome to stay the night. I have extra cots," I offered.

"Thank you," he said, in a way that left it unclear as to whether he was accepting my offer.

"You're lucky you found this place. It's really coming down. Where are you headed?"

He glanced at the small windowpane over the tiny kitchen sink, now completely covered with snow. "We get a storm like this at least once a year. There's so much snow that everything stops. The animals and birds hunker down, even the people stay away. It's peaceful," he said, avoiding my question.

"Yes," I agreed. "But I still wouldn't want to be caught out in it."

He nodded. "So you've heard the stories," the man said, staring into the fire.

"Stories?" I asked.

He looked at me, surprised. "About The Beast," he said.

Ah, The Beast.

I had heard the stories, mostly in the context of visitors to The Last Chance Inn remarking that the beast hadn't gotten me yet. The versions I had heard so far described it as a giant bear, or a huge ape, even a wolf that walked on two legs. The one thing they all had in common, though, was that it was as white as the snow and had glowing red eyes.

"Yeah, I've heard them," I said. "The local Bigfoot, huh?"

The stranger laughed. "Bigfoot has nothing on The Beast," he claimed.

"Oh, really?"

"You want to know the real story?" he asked.

I topped off the fire with a fat log. "Sure, looks like we've got all night."

He sat back and stretched out his legs. He was wearing a buckskin shirt and pants, and fur-lined leather boots. Everything looked like it was handmade. His hair and beard were both shaggy and thick, and both almost pure white. He didn't look like he was much over thirty, though. His skin was pale, but free of wrinkles, and his eyes were bright and full of life. I wondered if he had a cabin somewhere in the woods, even more off the grid than this one, and suspected he was one of those crazy preppers who were completely self-sufficient, living solely off the land.

"The stories go back to the first tribes that inhabited these lands. When they arrived here, they encountered The Beast during their first winter. It took one of their women. Three of their best hunters went out to kill it.

"They were never seen again.

"The Beast didn't return for the rest of the winter, and they lived unmolested throughout the spring and summer, and through the next fall.

"But when winter returned, and the first big snowfall of the season stilled the landscape, The Beast came back. One of the elders of the tribe offered himself to the creature. It struck the old man down, then started eating his flesh and bones as the rest of men watched.

"Once it had finished consuming its prey, it flashed its red eyes, then disappeared into the snow, not leaving even the slightest trace that it had been there. They thought it must be a god, and decided from that day on, to honor it by sacrificing one of their number each winter.

"This continued for centuries. But, as the years passed, and the white man pushed the tribe off this land, the tradition was abandoned. But The Beast still demands its tribute, and if you're unfortunate enough to be the one it finds alone in the snow, you'll never be seen again.

"Some say The Beast is supernatural, that it has the ability to assume the shape of other animals and hide in plain sight. It hibernates in its fashion during the heat of the summer, waking in the fall to mark its prey."

I couldn't help but smile. This was certainly the best telling of the story I had heard yet. "Well, nothing's going to be moving in this storm, including me. So, I don't think I have anything to worry about."

The stranger shrugged. "There was one year when none of the elders of the tribe agreed to be the sacrifice to the beast. They hoped it would pass them up that winter. But instead, The Beast stole into every hut where there was a newborn child and took them all.

"The creature has become accustomed to its winter meal. If it cannot find its human victim out in the blizzard, it will find it where it can. If you seek shelter in a cave, it will root you out. If you are a stranded motorist, it will peel open your car like a tin can. If you are in a small, wooden cabin—"

BAM! BAM!

I nearly jumped out of my skin at the loud pounding on the door. Lukewarm coffee spilled onto my lap, and I leaped to my feet. My sleeve got caught on the armrest of the wooden chair and I took a tumble onto the linoleum floor, nearly banging my head against the kitchen table.

BAM!

I scrambled to my feet and looked back at the stranger.

"Do you really think an ancient snow beast would bother to knock?" he asked rhetorically.

"No, but I'm not sure I want to find out who's crazy enough to be out in a storm like this."

"You mean, 'who else?'" he corrected with a smile.

I dabbed the coffee off my pants with a kitchen towel as I crossed the short distance to the door, eyeing the lockbox on the small hutch where I kept a loaded gun.

I opened the door.

A gust of wind blew a torrent of snow into the cabin.

And then I saw a tall figure standing in the doorway. It had fur as white as the snow, and eyes as red as embers.

It entered, peeled back the fur on its head, and raised its hands to those glowing eyes.

Then I realized it was a woman dressed in a white fur parka with red-lensed goggles that she removed to reveal dark, almost black eyes, and equally ebon hair.

"What's a girl gotta do to get out of the cold around here?" she asked.

"Sorry, come on in," I said, stepping aside. For the second time, I shoveled the encroaching drift back outside and shut the door.

The woman slipped out of her parka. Under it she wore what looked like a leather jumpsuit, almost form-fitting. I couldn't imagine that it would keep her very warm unless it had a hidden lining.

"Hello," she said to the stranger in front of the fire, ignoring me completely.

"Can I get you some coffee?" I asked.

She turned and looked me over. "Do you have any bourbon to put in it?" she asked.

I shook my head.

She shrugged and took the seat I had vacated to answer the door.

"Never mind."

I poured myself a fresh cup of coffee, grabbed one of the smaller chairs from the kitchen table, and placed it so I could join my guests around the fire.

"Rough night to be out for a walk," I said, hoping to break the awkward silence that had developed.

"Oh, I love the snow," the woman replied. "I saw the smoke from your fire and thought it might be a good idea to warm up a bit. Oh, my," she said, as if suddenly realizing something she forgot, "you must think me terribly rude. Thank you for letting me in to share your fire."

"No problem, that's what I'm here for," I replied.

"Really?"

"We thought for a second that you were The Beast," the man said.

"The what?" she asked.

"It's kind of a local legend," I explained. "Apparently, there is a creature that stalks these parts during the heaviest snow of the winter in search of a human victim."

She smiled. "I guess I'm flattered that you think I'd have to be some sort of beast in order to be out in the snow."

The man leaned forward. "It is said that The Beast can disguise itself as an animal. Why not a beautiful woman? What better way to lure its victim into a false sense of security?"

She laughed again. "That would be clever." She turned toward the stranger and looked him up and down, and I swear, she licked her lips. "You look like you would make a good meal," she said.

He smiled. "I think you'd find me rather tough." He nodded in my direction. "I think our young host would be much more flavorful."

She turned her gaze to me, her eyes dancing over my body while she bit her lower lip. "Yes, I see what you mean."

"I have some Tabasco in the cabinet, it that will help," I offered.

The woman started laughing, and the odd tension that had developed melted away.

The man laughed, too.

But when he did, I thought I caught a glint of red in his eyes.

Just a reflection from the fire, I assured myself.

"Seriously," the woman continued, "here we are, three strangers in a cabin in the middle of nowhere, buried in snow, talking about some beast possibly stalking us. I'm starting to think I should have stayed home."

"Yeah," I agreed, "it sounds like a corny horror movie."

She turned to the man. "I don't think I've seen you around before. Where do you live?"

"I have a place on the other side of the mountain," he replied. "I don't get out much."

The woman spun around in her seat to face me again. "And you just let him in?"

"Like I said," I explained, "that's what I'm here for. In case someone needs assistance."

"And you're not worried that he's this beast."

"Why would he tell me the story?" I asked.

"A hundred reasons," she replied. "To put you off your guard, to justify his transforming into a giant white creature with glowing red eyes and ripping you limb from—"

"I thought you didn't know anything about The Beast," the man challenged. "I don't think we mentioned anything about what it looks like since you've arrived."

The woman laughed, shaking her head. She held up her hands. "You got me. I'm The Beast. And it looks like I get a super-sized meal tonight," she said, eyeing the two of us as she continued laughing.

I couldn't help but join in. The man seemed equally amused, but assumed a posture that was ready for action. I looked at him, and he met my eyes, then glanced across the room.

I knew exactly where he was looking. At the metal case on the hutch that held my pistol. He surely assumed I was armed living here alone, and the lockbox was the most logical place to keep my weapon.

Was he trying to tell me that this woman actually was The Beast? Could that be possible? Her story about liking to wander around in a blizzard in that ridiculous skintight outfit was a bit sketchy, but did that mean she was an ancient creature driven to eat human flesh?

"Awkward," the woman chimed, a mischievous smile on her face.

Her eyes glowed red.

It wasn't a trick of the light. There was a definite crimson radiance in the back of her eyes. She smiled again, broadly, and her teeth appeared to have grown, her incisors protruding over her lower lip.

"I think I need more coffee," I said, rising quickly. I set my cup down on the kitchen table, but instead of refilling it, I continued walking over to the hutch. The case wasn't locked, but I had to open the latch to gain access to the gun inside. It was loaded, and a round was chambered.

I swung around, and immediately the man grabbed my wrist and thrust it upward, pointing the gun at the ceiling.

Behind him, the woman was no longer human.

She was seven feet tall, covered in fine white fur, with a wolf-like muzzle and fiery eyes.

"What are you doing?" I asked the man.

He was strong. His other hand grabbed my neck. "You know, some people think The Beast isn't some immortal demon, but a creature that lives and dies, is born and gives birth to more of its kind. Which would imply that there is more than one of them, and from time to time, they need to seek each other out… and mate."

I looked at the man.

His eyes assumed the same fire as the beast behind him. In an instant, he was an even taller beast whose razor-sharp claws sliced through my neck, severing arteries and crushing my trachea.

I couldn't breathe.

I fired the gun into the ceiling. Once, twice… then the strength left my hand, and the gun fell free and clattered onto the linoleum.

The Beast let go of my wrist, and I slumped to the floor.

He turned his attention to his mate. They engaged in an act that was brief and appeared painful for both of them.

When they were finished, they ripped away my clothing, then dismembered me and crushed flesh and bone between their powerful jaws until I was completely consumed.

No wonder no one has held this job for more than a year.

As the Tea Leaves

"What do I do next?" I asked the impossibly old woman sitting in the chair opposite me.

She wore a crocheted shawl and had her pure white, wispy hair pulled up into a bun. Her skin looked like an elephant's—an elephant who had been in the bath too long.

She was so devoid of muscle or fat that you could see the contours of her skull and skeleton through her fine, wrinkled epidermis, like the Crypt Keeper on that old TV show.

Her eyes were yellow—both the iris and the sclera—and her teeth, what remained of them, were of a similar tint, the space between them as black as the tea leaves she had used to prepare the beverage that she had carefully poured and set in front of me.

"Drink it," she replied, as if I was a complete and utter idiot.

I lifted the ancient bone china cup to my lips and drank. The water was long past scalding, and the tea—without sugar or milk—was bitter and unsatisfying.

"All of it," the old woman ordered.

I continued pouring the tepid tea into my mouth and swallowed it as quickly as I could. When I was done, I involuntarily shook my head like a baby biting into a sour grape. I set the cup back into its matching saucer.

Madame Pommesfrites picked up the cup and stared into it.

"What does it say?" I asked impatiently.

"Shh!" she replied, not lifting her gaze from the tiny puddle of leftover tea and soggy leaf fragments left in the bottom of my cup.

I was not the type of person to seek advice from a psychic, whether they got the details of my love life and future from a deck of Tarot cards, a crystal ball, or the dregs of an acrid liquid made from dried leaves.

It wasn't my cup of tea.

So what was I doing here? Ah, love makes you do crazy things—as someone (I can't remember exactly who at the moment) once said.

Most of the experiences Julia talked me into were beauty treatments of one sort or another. Sometimes it was the typical mud bath or avocado peel, but on other occasions we indulged in less traditional ablutions and rituals. Things like soaking in a vat of rancid olive oil mixed with pungent smelling herbs, or having butter massaged into intimate places.

But I didn't mind her unusual spa regimens, and even could stomach the occasional chick-flick or vegan restaurant. At least we did those things together.

About a week ago, while we were soaking our feet at a spa where little fish nibbled the dead skin off your heels, Julia suddenly and forcefully insisted that I get my tea leaves read.

"You have to go, and you have to do everything she tells you," she told me, a serious look on her face that crinkled her brow.

"Sure, we'll go together," I suggested. "It'll be fun."

"No!" she almost shouted. She grabbed my arm, her nails digging deep into my flesh. "You have to do it alone. And as soon as possible, or we have to break up."

It seemed like a ridiculous ultimatum to base a relationship on, but, as I mentioned earlier, I was in love. So, I assured Julia that I would arrange to see her tea leaf reader as soon as humanly possible.

She breathed a sigh of relief, let go of my arm, and reclined. A small woman darted to her side from seemingly nowhere and placed two cucumber slices over her eyes.

I did the same, pulling the lever that lowered the back of my chair, but the diminutive cucumber distributor looked at me with disdain and scurried off without adorning me with vegetables.

The appointment was made by telephone. Madame Pommesfrites did not have a website or email address, nor did it seem voicemail, or even an answering machine. Booking a session meant calling repeatedly at intervals during the day until she decided to answer. She gave me a time and day—there were no choices in the matter, no options to pick from—but not surprisingly (she was a psychic, after all) it was an hour that I was free.

Madame Pommesfrites lived in the same neighborhood as Julia. How close Julia lived to the narrow brownstone I didn't know, as I had never been invited to her apartment. She was perfectly happy coming over to my place, and to be honest, I liked that just fine. I never had to scramble to wake up early to get back to my place to shower and change.

Nor did I have to suffer the indignity of a using woman's bathroom. I always found the array of beauty products and devices that were used to crimp, straighten and augment various features intimidating and even frightening. I'd once witnessed a girlfriend deconstruct herself at the end of the day. The makeup was removed, creams applied and curlers entwined. It was a transformation akin to a human being turning into a werewolf—albeit one that smelled really good.

Missing out on whatever rituals Julia performed to look as good as she did was a blessing from my point of view. Such things should always be a mystery to men.

Madame Pommesfrites' home reminded me of the Addams Family. There were antiques everywhere. Some of them seemed like they were really valuable. There was a fine layer of dust over everything, so obviously there wasn't a seven-foot tall butler taking care of the place. The house was extremely orderly and had a precision to it that actually made it all the more disturbing.

She had greeted me at the door with an air of suspicion, as if I was there to sell her something. I told her my name, and that I had an appointment.

"I know who you are and what you want," she said in a creaky voice. She sighed as if I was keeping her from doing something fun and interesting, like changing the doilies on her armchairs. "This way," she said and led me into a parlor, where she directed me to sit in a paisley upholstered chair, its legs ending in intricately carved claws.

I sat down and watched her prepare the tea. She didn't use a tea bag or one of the mesh spheres where you could make your own blend of tea and herbs to suit your taste. She just scooped a mound of dried leaves into a teapot already filled with water. After a while, she poured the cup, and I could see the dark bits of dried fauna mixed in with the brownish-green liquid.

Now she was staring at the pattern the leaves left in the bottom of my cup. I found myself eager to hear what she would discover about me and my future at its bottom.

"You're in love," she said.

I wasn't impressed so far. Why else would a single guy come to an old crone to have his tea leaves read?

"She is very beautiful," she continued.

Again, obvious, considering that I wouldn't be here if Julia wasn't totally out of my league.

"You are going to be married," she pronounced.

Okay, that was interesting news. I had fantasized about a life with Julia, but the idea of marrying her seemed beyond my wildest dreams.

"Will we have children?" I asked?

Madame Pommesfrites looked up from her inspection of my

deepest secrets and darkest future. It was the glare of a thousand librarians trained to silence noisy patrons with their steely gaze. I was suitably cowed by her yellow eyes and the way she pursed her thin lips. She returned that stilling stare to the tea leaves and continued divining my now-and-hereafter at the bottom of the delicate china cup.

"You must buy a house. A large house with at least four bedrooms, an attached garage, a modern kitchen, walk-in closet and a bathroom with a heated floor."

"I must?" I asked, instantly regretting saying anything, as the amber gaze shot out at me from under wrinkled eyelids.

"The engagement ring must be twenty-four caret gold with at least a four caret Marquise cut diamond—not cubic zirconium—with rubies and emeralds embedded in the band."

Without thinking, I reached over to tilt the cup toward me. "That seems awfully specific," I said. Before my fingers touched the china, Madame Pommesfrites smacked them with her bony hand. It stung as if I had been hit by a wooden ruler. I pulled my hand back and rubbed the spot where she had struck me.

"Pay attention," she admonished. "Your happiness depends on what I'm telling you. If you do not do these things, you will not be married and you will spend the rest of your life alone and impotent."

"Why would I be impotent if I don't marry Julia?" I asked, puzzled.

"Do you think this is a game?" she inquired. "I am telling you exactly what you need to do to find bliss, and you question me? Pff! I should keep the rest to myself and let you wallow in sexless loneliness for the rest of your eunuchistic life."

I sat very still and very quiet, hoping to earn the remaining revelations that were apparently essential to my happiness and my manhood.

Madame Pommesfrites made me wait in silence for nearly a minute before she dropped her eyes again and resumed sussing the keys to my contentment. "Oh, my mistake, the ring must be five carets," she said, casting a quick glance to remind me what was at stake.

My hands reflexively covered my groin.

"You will enroll in an MBA program, then get a job in management, eventually rising to CEO of a very successful company. Your wife will have a new car every year, a Tesla—the nice one." She pushed the saucer and its porcelain passenger back to the middle of the table.

I sneaked a peak at the leaves littering the bottom of the cup, but didn't see any five caret diamond rings, or Tesla Roadsters, or walk-in closets there.

"If you are ready to do all those things, you will find happiness. Are you willing to commit to this course for your future?"

I nodded enthusiastically.

Madame Pommesfrites smiled, then she said to me, kindly, "Then go, make your lady happy and you will be happy as well."

I stood, grateful that the experience was over, but also oddly invigorated at the idea that I could be married to Julia. I was eager to go see her and even more anxious to get out of Madame Pommesfrites' eerily unsettling house.

I bumped the small table that held the ancient tea set. The pot was perched on the edge and fell to the frayed rug covering the floor and shattered. My eyes went wide as I saw the broken china and the spilled tea soaking into the tattered rug. I bent down to pick up the pieces, as if my quick action could somehow reverse the disaster. In my haste, I cut a deep gash into the palm of my hand.

I cried out in pain, then stood, holding my hand in front of me as blood pooled in my palm. "I'm sorry, I'll pay for it," I promised.

The old woman didn't seem to hear me or care about the mess on her floor. Her jaundiced gaze was focused on my hand, or rather the red liquid quickly gathering there, threatening to run through my fingers and mix with the tea on the floor. She grabbed the cup that held the remnants of my tea, then gently tilted my hand so that the blood dripped into it. Her skin felt cold and papery, like that of an onion.

"Shouldn't I put pressure on it or something?" I asked, concerned that there was much more blood than I had ever seen before. I started to feel light-headed.

She didn't answer me. Instead, she squeezed my hand, causing the flow of blood to increase until it was about an inch deep in the cup. She let go, not seeming to mind that I was dripping blood on her floor.

Then she did something that nearly made me pass out.

She drank my blood from the cup.

I fell back into the chair, watching as she tilted her head back so that she could extract every drop of my precious bodily fluids from the vessel cupped in her bony hands.

When she could drink no more, she dropped the cup, and it shattered next to the teapot. Her lips were red, coated in my blood, and somehow… fuller.

As I watched, she underwent a transformation. Her posture straightened, her hair darkened and thickened, her skin tightened, and her breasts became firm and full. Her grayish pallor was replaced by a rosy glow. Her eyes brightened and took on a familiar blue hue.

"Julia?" I asked in shock.

The young, vibrant, attractive woman I was madly in love with looked at me and smiled. "Sorry," she said, "you weren't supposed to see this part."

"Are you… are you a vampire?" I asked?

"Oh, heavens no, nothing like that," she replied. "Just think of it as another of my beauty treatments."

"That's a hell of a treatment," I said. "Not quite the same level as a Dead Sea Salt exfoliant."

"Are you disappointed?" she asked, wearing that sad little pout she used to get pretty much anything she wanted from me.

"I'll start with surprised as hell."

She grabbed a small towel from the table and pressed it into my hand. "It's not really that big of a deal. I just need to drink human blood a couple times a month."

I wanted to ask where she got it, but decided that was a question best left unanswered.

"I meant what I said," she whispered, moving her face closer to mine. "I will marry you. If you get me a nice ring, and a house… and you get a better job."

"You will?" I asked. I couldn't tell if it was the blood loss, or the hypnotic effect of those sky-blue eyes, but I felt myself feeling serene and intensely happy.

"Of course. I love you," she promised. "And the best part is that I will always be young and beautiful for you."

"Okay," I replied without much thought.

She lifted the towel, now soaked through, and inspected the wound in my hand. "Ooh, that is deep. We should probably get you to the hospital."

"Hospital," I repeated, feeling sleepy.

"You wait here, I'll go get changed, then we'll get you stitched up and then go ring shopping. I know just the place!"

Julia dashed out of the room.

I heard her footsteps running up some stairs.

Then it sank in. I was going to marry some ancient, blood-sucking succubus who would be eternally young and beautiful.

And I was fine with that.

In fact, I was surprised to realize I was happy, almost giddy at the idea of spending the rest of my life with Julia.

How 'bout that.

The tea leaves were right.

The Yellow Curtain

"You can't possibly have solved the case already," Jeremy White said in utter disbelief. "We just got here!"

"It's obvious," Isaac Black replied in that nonchalant manner that drove Jeremy crazy.

"How can you possibly know who killed this woman without knowing who she is, what she looks like, or how she died?" Jeremy demanded, exasperated. "You don't even know what color the drapes are," he added.

"Her name is Beverly Goldman, tall, brunette, green eyes. She was shot. And the curtains are yellow," Isaac replied without skipping a beat.

"How does he do that?" Detective Brown asked, looking at the yellow drapes, then back at the dark glasses Isaac was wearing. "I thought he was blind."

"Yes, he is," Jeremy confirmed. "But that doesn't mean he can't be an arrogant show-off. Go ahead," he said to Isaac, "let's hear your brilliant deductions."

"Hardly any brilliance is required. We were summoned to this crime scene with great urgency in the middle of the night, indicating this is a case of much concern to someone with great influence. Someone willing to bring in an outside consultant to expedite a matter of great sensitivity. When we arrived, we had to go through a checkpoint. The air outside smells of the East River. We climbed exactly ten wooden steps up to a wide porch to enter, and we're on the second floor of a building that only has two stories.

"Obviously, this is Gracie Mansion, the home of the Mayor of New York, and the woman who was shot is the mayor's wife, Beverly Goldman—who, according to New York Magazine, decided to change the color of all the drapes to yellow to match the outside of the house."

"That is incredible," one of the uniformed police officers remarked.

"Don't encourage him," Jeremy cautioned the policeman, then he whispered to Isaac, "Nobody likes a show-off."

"How do you know she was shot?" Lieutenant Green asked.

"There is an odor of burned gunpowder in the air. A gun was recently fired inside this room. Since there is a dead body, it is no great leap to assume she was at the other end of a discharged firearm," Isaac explained.

The others in the room sniffed to try and catch the scent Isaac had detected.

"And you say you know who did it?" the lieutenant asked.

"Yes, of course."

Everyone waited patiently for Isaac to continue.

"Well?" the lieutenant asked.

Jeremy sighed. "He doesn't know. He's just doing that mind-game thing. Isaac, just tell them what you *do* know so they can find out who killed the mayor's wife."

Isaac walked across the room, directly to an overstuffed, leather upholstered armchair and sat down as if he wasn't completely sightless. Jeremy rolled his eyes as some of the police officers in the room oohed and aahed. The trick was simple. Whenever the two of them entered a room, Jeremy would give Isaac a quick description of the major features, telling him things like, "large wooden desk with body in front of it at twelve o'clock, cocktail cart at two-thirty, overstuffed leather armchair at nine." Issac would then build a map of the room in his mind, so he could navigate it as if could see.

The injury that had blinded him had also ended his career with the police. But after a period of depression and despair, he reinvented himself as a private detective, using his accumulated knowledge, deductive reasoning and remaining senses—such as his heightened sense of smell—to solve mysteries and, as on this occasion, lend support to the police.

Jeremy, his assistant—and also a registered nurse—had long ago stopped being impressed by the various things Isaac did to amaze and confound those around him. He knew the theatrics were part of Isaac's process. A lot of the time, people around him simply volunteered information because they assumed he already knew it. It was effective, but once you'd seen it a hundred times, it got annoying.

"The killer is in this very house right now," Isaac pronounced. "I suggest you make sure nobody leaves."

Lieutenant Green barked orders to some uniformed officers, who passed the commands on through their radios and quickly left the room.

"I want to speak to everyone who has been in the mansion since the time of the murder," Isaac commanded. "Inside and on the grounds."

"Including us?" Detective Brown asked.

"Everyone," Isaac repeated. "Bring them in here."

Lieutenant Green gave a node to his subordinate.

The detective signaled for the people already in the room to gather on one side, then left to retrieve the others.

"What are you doing?" Jeremy asked.

"I always wanted to be an armchair detective," Isaac replied, running his hands along the padded armrests of the chair he was sitting in.

"This is serious," Jeremy said to him. "You've just asked Detective Brown to bring God knows how many people into a room with the mayor's dead wife lying on the floor."

"I know, it's perfect," Isaac replied.

Within five minutes, a dozen more people crowded into the spacious study, various staff of the mayor's residence along with security personnel and the entourage that had accompanied Isaac and Jeremy.

They were all obviously aware of what had happened. But some of them still gasped in surprise when they saw the lifeless form of Beverly Goldman lying on the floor, a hole in the middle of her chest and blood soaking her blouse and the rug underneath her. Some began quietly weeping, and there were more than a couple exclamations of "What the hell?"

Once Detective Brown returned, Isaac crossed his legs and raised his hands in front of him, touching his fingertips together in a contemplative manner.

Everyone turned their attention to him. Someone whispered the question on many of their minds, "Is he blind?"

"Yes, these dark glasses are not just a fashion statement," Isaac said. "I may not be able to see you, but I have other powers that will let me divine the identity of the killer."

"I thought you said you already knew who it was," Detective Brown challenged.

Isaac smiled. "All in good time, Detective. What I need to know from each and every person in this room is their name, and what they had for breakfast, lunch and dinner yesterday. And any snacks."

"What is this, some kind of joke?" one of the policemen asked.

"I assure you, if I was joking, you would be laughing right now," Isaac said. "We'll start with the woman standing there," he said, pointing unerringly at a one of the housekeepers.

Jeremy rolled his eyes. "Show-off," he said under his breath.

"My name is Maria Juarez, I..." the woman began, her voice cracking nervously. "I had toast and coffee for breakfast, a meatloaf sandwich for lunch, and..." She struggled to remember her last meal. "Salmon! I had salmon with asparagus and roasted potatoes. And a brownie. I had a brownie for a snack."

Isaac nodded. "Thank you, Maria." He turned his sightless gaze to the gardener standing next to her. "And you?"

"Jack Hough, um... I skipped breakfast, had a couple burritos for lunch, and a cheeseburger with loaded fries at Henri's on First. Couple power bars for snacks."

"Okay, Jack. Next?"

Isaac went through each person in the room, listening intently as they recited everything they had eaten the previous day. Some of them could barely get the words out, struggling to speak in the presence of the body that was starting to stink. The police were more accustomed to being in the same room with a corpse, but the tone in their voices was resentful for having to be—what was this? Interrogated?

Lieutenant Green only had to admonish the first officer who showed any attitude to get the rest of them in line.

Jeremy engaged in a little game he played with himself, trying to figure out what exactly Isaac was doing. What was it about what they ate the previous day that was relevant to the identity of the killer? He scanned the room, hoping to find some morsel of food that Isaac might have caught a scent of, but nothing was apparent.

Was he just trying to detect stress in their voice? He had always dismissed Isaac's claims that he could sense when someone was lying by the inflections in their words. The detective had a knack for identifying people by their voices. Many blind people had auditory hyperacuity, some to the point of being able to actually echo-locate. Isaac hadn't been able to master that particular skill, but maybe there was something in their tone that was perceptible to him.

More likely, it was something unobvious to Jeremy and the others that was perfectly conspicuous to Isaac, and once he explained it,

Jeremy would feel like an idiot. So, it was his ongoing futile quest to figure out Isaac's reasoning before he could reveal it.

He noticed that Isaac would tap his fingers together during some of the recitations. Was that a clue? Jeremy watched closely, and then at one point in the puzzling examinations, Isaac's fingers rippled in a frantic pattern. Had he sensed something? Was the woman he was listening to right now the one who did it?

Then Isaac turned his tinted lenses in Jeremy's direction and winked.

The cheeky bastard, Jeremy thought.

Once the last person had completed reciting their dietary diary for the previous day, Isaac placed his hands on the armrests and pushed himself up to a standing position. "Detective Brown, please close the door."

The detective, who was standing next to the entrance of the study, grabbed the edge of the door and swung it shut.

There was movement at one end of the room.

Isaac grinned knowingly. "Mr. Heller, I suggest you relax. There's no point in trying to make a run for it."

The mayor's wife's bodyguard stiffened.

Isaac turned in the direction of Lieutenant Green. "You'll find his holster is empty. I doubt you'll find the gun it held, but you might want to have divers check out the river, anyway."

Lieutenant Green signaled two of the uniformed officers, and they all approached Justin Heller. Green knew the bodyguard. They had served together at the Midtown South Precinct years ago. "Hands on your head, Justin," the lieutenant ordered.

Heller shook his head as he complied. "I didn't mean for it to happen," he confessed. "It was an accident."

Green undid the buttons and lifted Heller's jacket fronts to look underneath. There was indeed an empty holster. He nodded to one of the uniformed officers, who took his handcuffs and bound the bodyguard's hands behind his back.

"We... we were having an affair," Justin explained. "She liked to role play. I should have cleared my gun, but before I knew it, she..."

"If you want to make a statement, you can do so downtown. Right now, you have the right to remain silent, anything you say can and will be used against you in a court of law," Green reminded his prisoner.

Detective Brown opened the door, and the uniformed officers escorted Heller out of the room.

"Excuse me," Maria Juarez said, "can we go now?"

Lieutenant Green looked over at Isaac, who granted his permission with a wave.

Most everyone exited the study quickly, anxious to get away from the deceased woman in the middle of the room.

The only ones left were the lieutenant, Detective Brown, Jeremy and Isaac.

"Okay," Green finally said, "can you tell me how you knowing what they ate for breakfast, lunch and dinner identified the killer?"

"Oh, it had nothing to do with it," Isaac replied.

"Of course not," Jeremy said. "I knew he was just playing a game."

"But he identified the killer," Detective Brown countered.

"It was when you closed the door," Green suggested. "He wanted to see—or rather hear—who would react, which of them would feel trapped."

"Good guess," Isaac said. "But did any of you actually see Justin Heller react? You were all, I suspect, looking at the door. And as good as my hearing can be, I had no idea who exactly had made the noise."

"Then how?" Jeremy asked.

"I told you, I knew who had done it the moment I walked into this room and smelled the scent of gunfire. I had encountered that smell moments earlier when we had entered the house on one of the people we passed. So, two plus two equals he was the killer."

"Then what was all the 'what did you eat yesterday' stuff about?" Detective Brown asked.

"Well, I knew that the person who shot Beverly Goldman was someone in the house, but I had no idea what his actual identity was. Fortunately, I managed to bump into him on the way in, and he offered an apology when he saw that I was blind."

"You heard his voice," Jeremy said, finally putting it all together.

"And you needed to hear everyone talk to identify him," Green added.

Isaac smiled that Cheshire grin Jeremy found so irritating. "Jeremy will send you an invoice."

"I'm sure the chief won't have any hesitation authorizing it," Lieutenant Green said. "Thanks for your help, Mr. Black. Again."

"You're welcome, as always," Isaac replied.

Jeremy took Isaac's elbow and led him out of the room, passing the staff from the coroner's office on their way to collect the body.

"You know," Jeremy said, "I was the one who read that New Yorker article about the mayor's wife to you. I don't remember anything about her changing the color of the drapes."

"Yeah, that was a total guess," Isaac said. "Pretty cool that I got it right, though. I'll bet everyone was impressed."

Jeremy sighed as they walked out of the mansion toward the waiting car. "Nobody likes a show-off, Isaac," he reminded his friend. "Nobody."

Interrogation in Room #3

"Tell me again why you killed all those people," I said to the nervous little man sitting across the steel table from me, his wrists and ankles in shackles.

Freddy sucked in a deep breath, then turned his gaze to me and replied, "Because. They were vampires."

I nodded. "Right."

This was starting out to be a bad day.

Chains rattled against the metal chair as Freddy sat back and shook his head. "Why do you keep asking me the same question if you're not going to believe the answer?" he asked.

I mulled that one over.

It was a standard interrogation technique, to keep on asking the same question over and over again. The repetition ate away at the subject's resistance, and eventually—so the theory went—he would be so frustrated he would utter the truth. Usually, when I tried this tactic, the answers would get gradually more detailed. But with Freddy, he had answered the question consistently.

Because they were vampires.

"So," I began, trying a different approach, "you believe in vampires."

"Of course I do," Freddy admitted. "I kill them."

"Is that your job?"

"No one pays me to do it, if that's what you're asking."

"You're just an amateur vampire killer."

Freddy rolled his eyes. "It's not something you do for money."

"Then why do you do it?" I asked. "Help me understand, Freddy." I picked up the folder that was sitting on the corner of the table and opened it.

One by one, I laid out the photos inside in front of Freddy. Crime scene photos of people with wooden stakes driven through their hearts. "They look like ordinary people to me, Freddy. Aren't they supposed to turn to dust, or shrivel up into a mummy or something?"

"Evidently not," he replied.

"You know what I think?"

Freddy shrugged.

"I think maybe you had some other motive to kill these people. Maybe they looked at you funny, stole money from you, got you fired from your job. Then you convinced yourself they were actually vampires, maybe a little voice in your head told you so, and you realized you could be the hero, and you drove those stakes through their hearts and killed them for no other reason than revenge and your own glorification."

He looked at me, one eye black and almost swollen shut, the other one drooping from fatigue. "They *were* vampires. That's how you kill vampires. It's really not that difficult to grasp," he said.

I sat back, staring at the unremarkable man sitting across from me.

Freddy had been killing "vampires" for several months. Of course, the press had a field day with the string of gruesome murders, the victims of which had sharpened sticks pounded into their chests, and he was immediately dubbed, "The Vampire Killer."

He had been amazingly good at evading the police. This was mostly because even though we found plenty of fingerprints and DNA at the crime scenes, Freddy had never been arrested, been in the military or worked at a job where they required his fingerprints to be taken. So, when we ran the evidence through all the available databases, it came back as unidentified.

He didn't own a car, so there was no vehicle to trace, no partial license plate caught by a nearby security camera, nor were any parking tickets issued at an expired meter near the crime scenes.

The one break we did have was an eyewitness.

An old woman who had been walking her Bichon Frise early one morning outside what would later be discovered to be the scene of the third killing. She saw a man across the street from her, and called out a friendly, "Good morning." He looked at her for only a moment, but from that glimpse, she was able to help a police artist create a sketch.

However, it wasn't an anonymous tip generated by the plea for assistance that appeared on the local newscasts that broke the case. Nor was it an eagle-eyed patrolman who spotted him passing by on the street. Four more bodies were found, their hearts impaled by wooden spikes, before Freddy made his big mistake.

They all do, you know. Even the smartest criminals do something stupid, or trust someone they shouldn't, or get caught by some quirk of fate in a situation from which there is no escape.

In Freddy's case, it was an argument with a bus driver.

Since he didn't have a car, he used public transportation to track his victims and then make his getaway from the murders. He didn't use a bus pass like most regular commuters. He dropped the exact change in the old-fashioned mechanical farebox. On one ride—totally unconnected to his string of killings, he was on his way back from picking up a pair of shoes he had resoled—he dropped the coins in the box as usual, but the driver informed him he was a dime short.

Freddy checked his pockets but came up empty. He was in the

habit of counting out the change he needed for his bus trips to the penny and placing the coins in his left front pocket, never bringing more than he needed. He looked at the farebox. He could see the coins at the bottom—they were the only ones there—and they added up precisely to the fare required. He tried to get the driver to count the money, but the woman behind the wheel of the bus was stubborn, and relied solely on the amount shown in red LED numerals at the top of the farebox that said he was ten cents short.

Freddy boarded the bus regardless, but the driver refused to budge until he got off.

He demanded his money back, and the driver handed him a form he could fill out and mail in.

Freddy did not take that well.

He ripped it up and sat down in one of the empty seats. It didn't take long for some of the other passengers to get mad that they were going to be late for work or miss their transfer. One particular man got physical, trying to pry Freddy's hands from the iron grip he had on the pole he was sitting next to. Another passenger joined in the effort to remove Freddy from the bus, but he resisted mightily, kicking out at his assailants, shouting and screaming, demanding the driver drive.

Instead, she called the police.

Freddy and three of the other passengers were arrested for creating a disturbance. He had gotten the worst of it. His nose was bleeding, one eye was starting to swell shut, and he was walking with a limp. So, the police at the station where he and the others were taken were surprised that he didn't want to file any charges.

It was actually a woman who happened to be in the station after being arrested for solicitation, who was the one who pointed at him and said, "Hey, that's the guy from the TV. The Vampire Killer."

Someone dug up the sketch that had been distributed around the city and compared it to Freddy's battered and bruised face. He didn't have any identification on him, but he did have the receipt from the cobbler who repaired his shoes—which had his address on it. Once his fingerprints were matched to the ones that had been obtained at the crime scenes, it didn't take long to get a search warrant for his apartment.

It was there they found a supply of wooden stakes, a two-pound sledgehammer, several cameras and photos of all the people Freddy had killed and dozens more that we assumed were next on his list.

And now he was sitting here, under the harsh glare of the florescent lights, one of the most prolific serial killers this city had ever known.

All five feet and three inches of him.

There was a knock at the door.

I gathered the photos and slipped them back into the folder and exited the interrogation room through the door that led to the adjacent observation room.

"How's it going?" a burly man, nearly six inches taller than myself, asked. He was John Johnson, my partner, John-John for short—which didn't make any sense, since you could just call him John and save yourself the extra John.

"I don't think we're going to get any more out of him," I responded. "He insists it was self-defense. They were vampires. It was them or him."

John-John laughed. "Yeah, either he's smart enough to start laying down an insanity defense or we need to make a reservation for the rubber room."

"He's sticking to his story," I told him.

"I know. I've been watching on the video feed," he said.

"It's working today?" I asked.

"Yeah, I kinda wish the camera was still on the fritz," John-John said, disappointed. "I'd love to have five minutes with him with no one watching."

I nodded. "He is completely unrepentant. And I hear he nearly took down those three guys on the bus."

"Not if I'd been there," John-John replied, staring at the grainy image of Freddy, which made him look even more harmless than his slight frame and balding pate conveyed.

I reached over and pounded the dark gray metal box next to the monitor that recorded everything happening in interrogation room three.

The screen went blank.

I guess they hadn't completely fixed the loose connection that made room three's video so notoriously unreliable. It wasn't surprising. I don't think they had updated the system since the eighties.

John-John gave me a conspiratorial nod.

"I'm going to check on something," I told him. "I'll be back in five minutes."

He opened the door and entered the interrogation room.

I exited the observation room—more like a closet, really—and made my way across the station to the evidence room.

Chuck was sitting behind the thin wire fence that safeguarded all the various incriminating weapons, electronic devices and drugs collected for ongoing cases. "What's up?" he asked as I approached.

"I need one of the stakes from the Vampire Killer case. John-John wants to use it as a prop for the interrogation."

"Really?" he said, somewhat surprised as he got up and crossed over to a nearby shelf and removed a sharpened wooden stake about as big around as his wrist from a box. "I didn't think he went in for that psychological stuff. He's more of a 'tell me what I want to know or I'll beat the crap out of you' kind of guy."

I laughed. "I guess I must be rubbing off on him," I answered.

Chuck handed me the stake. I signed for it and offered a quick salute to thank him.

I twirled it in my hand as I made my way back to the interrogation room, whistling, nodding to the other officers I passed.

I reached room three and let myself into the observation side. I checked that the surveillance system was still showing nothing but static, then opened the door that connected to the interrogation room.

John-John had Freddy in a choke hold, screaming at him, "What were these people to you? Why did you kill them? Tell me, or I swear, I'll break your neck!"

Freddy looked at me pleadingly. "Help," he said weakly.

John-John let loose his grip on the smaller man's neck. "Has it been five minutes already?" he asked, checking his watch. Then he saw the stake in my hand and shot me an inquisitive look in that not-ever-subtle way he had.

I smiled, tapping the pointy stick against my hand like a baseball player testing the balance of a bat.

He walked around the table to where I was and leaned in close, speaking in a low voice. "Are we going to do the good cop-bad cop thing? 'Cause I'm usually the bad cop," he said, eyeing the stake in my hand.

"Yes, you usually are," I said.

Then I took the stake and plunged it deep into his chest.

It went in easily. Although I didn't look it, I was incredibly strong.

John-John's face bore an expression of surprise as he fell to the ground, blood gurgling out of the corner of his mouth as the life drained from him.

I looked at Freddy.

He stared at me, wide-eyed—at least the eye that wasn't swollen shut. "You're… you're a…"

He couldn't seem to finish the sentence he wanted to say, but I suspected it ended with something like "one of them," or "a… a… a vampire!"

"Don't feel sorry for John-John," I said. "He truly was a terrible policeman, and a bit of a racist and a homophobe as well. A lot of the people in this station will quietly thank you for killing him."

"But I didn't kill him," Freddy protested. He looked up at the camera. "Help, help! Somebody help me!" he tried to shout, but his voice was hoarse and weak from his larynx being crushed by John-John's massive bicep. Then he noticed that the little red light that indicated the camera was recording was no longer lit. He shot a glance back at me and swallowed nervously.

"That's right," I told him. "Nobody's going to hear you."

"Why?" he asked. "Why are you doing this?"

"Why did you kill my friends?" I asked.

"Your... your friends?" he asked back.

"Come now. Certainly that conspiratorial mind of yours has put two and two together by now. I'm impressed that you were able to find them, figure out what they were. You must tell me how you did it," I said.

He shrugged. "I... I just get this feeling about some people. It's kind of like a sixth sense, I guess. But I always make sure I'm right. I follow them, see if they kill anyone. They always seem to be weaker right after they feed."

I nodded. "Yeah, you would think it would be the opposite, but a good feast of blood makes you kind of logy."

Freddy looked around, trying to find any means of escape or a way to fight back. But his hands and feet were shackled not only together, but fastened to an eye bolt embedded in the concrete floor.

I pulled the keys out of John-John's pocket and then opened the lock that connected Freddy's chains to the floor. Then, as he stared at me in amazement, I unlocked the cuffs around his wrists.

It was a reckless, chancy move, but Freddy made a dash for the door. His feet got tangled, and he fell directly on top of John-John. He scrambled to a sitting position, slipping in the small pool of blood surrounding the body.

The smell of it made my own blood boil with desire. I could feel my incisors sliding out of my jaw to their full length. My vision became sharper. In the throes of "the bloodlust," I could now see ultraviolet and infrared wavelengths. My hearing became more acute as well, and the rapid pounding of Freddy's heartbeats rang in my eardrums.

Freddy slid awkwardly toward the door.

"You'll get caught," he tried to warn me. "You're in a police station. You'll never get away with this."

"Get away with what? When I got here, I found the two of you dead. For some reason, John-John decided it would be a good idea to uncuff you. You got a hold of the stake he was planning on intimidating you with and killed him." I shrugged. "Maybe you were convinced he was a vampire, too. But before he died, he managed to take you out. He'll probably get a medal."

"Please, don't," he begged. "I won't tell anyone."

"It's not about that, Freddy," I said. "You killed my kind. And it appears you have an ability to detect us that most humans do not. I cannot allow you to share that with anyone."

"I won't," he promised. "I'll plead guilty. I'll go to prison. I'll never tell a soul."

"Like I said, it's not just about telling anyone. It's like if a man-eating lion was terrorizing your apartment building. You wouldn't trust it to not eat you, you'd have to kill it.

You've been, sadly, a very effective vampire killer. I wouldn't be surprised to discover that your lineage goes back to Van Helsing. But that's neither here nor there. The means by which you are able to do what you do is irrelevant to the fact that even though I'm not technically human, I do have feelings.

"And you really hurt them by killing all my friends."

I picked up Freddy by the front of his shirt, lifting him up off the ground.

He closed his eyes tight as I brought him close to me until his neck was inches from my salivating mouth.

I bit deep, and was immediately gratified by the rush of warm, salty blood that flowed into my mouth. I swallowed only a small amount. I didn't want his bloodless body to raise questions.

Then I tore a chunk of flesh from his throat and dropped Freddy back to the ground next to John-John. I took the bloody piece of skin, muscle and sinew from my mouth and placed it in my dead partner's. It was an awkwardly staged scene, but good enough to fool the dolts I worked with.

There was blood on my clothes, but I could explain that by being in shock when I discovered the bloody scene, and careless when I checked to see if—despite the evidence to the contrary—John-John was still alive.

I mussed up my hair, loosened my tie and put my hand on the doorknob.

"Help, help," I screamed at the top of my lungs as I opened the door. "Somebody call an ambulance. Quick! Help!"

I could taste the blood that still covered my lips and chin. I licked away most of it as I felt my fangs retract, then cleaned off the rest with the back of my jacket sleeve just as several uniformed officers came running around the corner.

I fell against the wall and slid down to the ground, feeling the fatigue that followed a feeding—despite not taking my fill. I waved weakly at the door to interrogation room three.

They entered the room, gasping in horror as more officers arrived.

One of them was kind enough to check on me.

"I'm fine," I assured her, "it's not my blood."

But it sure does taste good, I wanted to say, trying my best not to smile.

A vampire killer and a crappy partner, two birds with one stone—or rather, stake.

Guess it turned out not to be a bad day after all.

Sweet Revenge

"Welcome to Gingerbread House Confections. Can I interest you in some of our fine licorice?" the annoyingly cheerful woman behind the counter asked. "We have black licorice, red licorice, licorice twists, licorice laces, licorice nibs, licorice gum, licorice jelly beans—"

"No," said the short, balding man with thick, dark-rimmed glasses and a bushy mustache. "I do not want licorice."

"How about some nice caramels, then?" she offered. "We have hard candy caramels, soft caramels, chewy caramels, salted caramels, sea salt salted caramels, chocolate-covered caramels, caramel covered chocolates—"

"No, I don't want any caramels, either."

"Perhaps a nice truffle. We have maple walnut, dark chocolate key lime, strawberry cheesecake truffles, peanut butter, peanut butter and jelly, caramel peanut butter, coconut cream, caramel cream, raspberry cream, cookies and cream, cookie dough—"

"Please, I am not here to buy candy," the man insisted.

"Oh, of course, I should have guessed a man of your bearing

would be looking for a delicious gourmet cookie. We're famous for our Gingerbread, as I'm sure you know, but we also have snicker doodles, oatmeal raisin, chocolate chip, chocolate-chocolate chip, white chocolate chip, oatmeal butterscotch, lemon coolers, lemon crisps, lemon snaps—"bus

"I am not here to buy candy, cookies, cakes, or confections of any kind," the man pronounced officiously. He opened the satchel that was slung over his shoulder and fished out a sheet of paper. "Your establishment is overdue for a health inspection."

"It is?" she asked.

"It is," the man answered.

The portly woman perched the reading glasses hanging on a chain around her neck upon her porcine nose and looked at the paper. After a moment, she spun it around so it was right-side up for her. "I had no idea I was supposed to arrange an inspection," she said.

"You're not. All inspections are scheduled by the health department."

"Then it's you who is overdue."

The man snatched the paper back and stuffed it into the satchel. "Unfortunately, there appears to have been a bit of paperwork mishandling at the home office. But it doesn't matter who is overdue. The fact is that this establishment is out of compliance."

"Yes, but I didn't know that. How can I be out of something I didn't know I wasn't in?"

"That makes no sense. Even if you didn't know you are not responsible for scheduling the inspection, a responsible businessperson would be aware of the status of all licensure and other municipal obligations and, as such, should reach out to the governing agency to remedy the deficiency."

"Is there a number I can call—if this happens again in the future?"

"No, there is not. We had to turn it off. Telemarketers and calls from online pharmacies kept filling up the answering machine."

"So, how am I supposed to attempt to remedy the deficiency?"

"You could write a letter," the man suggested.

"To which address?"

"The address on the letter."

"Which letter?"

"The letter I just showed you explaining that you are out of compliance."

"But I never received that letter, and you took it back from me."

"Yes, well, I shouldn't have done that."

"Regardless, I didn't actually receive the letter that had the address on it that I could have written an inquiry to if the letter had arrived before I was out of compliance."

"Be that as it may," the man said.

There was a pause.

"Be that as what may?" the woman asked.

"Excuse me?"

"When someone says, 'be that as it may,' they follow it with something that should have been done regardless of the original situation."

"No, they don't."

"Yes, they do. Everyone does," the woman insisted.

"I don't," he replied.

"Then I stand corrected, because you are certainly part of everyone, and if you say you don't say anything after 'be that as it may,' my assertion that everyone does was certainly incorrect. I'm sorry."

"Apology accepted."

"Thank you."

"You're welcome."

There was another long pause.

"Are you sure you wouldn't care for some licorice? Red licorice isn't technically licorice, but we call it that anyway since, even though it's not at all the same flavor, it looks similar apart from the color, that is—"

"No," the man insisted. "I really must tend to this oversight expeditiously."

"Well, don't let me stand in your way."

"Madame, you are quite literally standing in my way," he said, indicating that she was blocking the door to the kitchen with her girth.

"Oh my," she said, moving away from the entrance. But then she stepped back in front of the swinging door. "I'm sorry, but could I see your identification?"

"My identification?"

"Do you have a badge or something? You could be anyone."

"Well, I couldn't be anyone."

"How would I know?"

"I couldn't be Mel Gibson."

"Of course not. You don't look anything like Mel Gibson. He is much taller."

"My point is you tend to make statements that are overly broad exaggerations. We are not starting off on the right foot."

"I see your point."

"I should hope so."

"So, do you have a badge? Or some sort of laminated card?"

The man opened his satchel again and dug through the contents. "Eureka!" he shouted when he had found a hard plastic card holder holding a card that was also plastic, that had a tiny photo resembling the man—though without the glasses and mustache and more hair. He showed it to the woman. "Satisfied?" he asked.

"That doesn't really look like you."

"It's an old photograph."

She took the plastic card holder and studied the card within it carefully, holding it up so that she could compare the image with the man in front of her. "I guess that could be you."

"There's a very good chance of that, since I was the one who sat for the photograph."

"Your name is Grimm?" she asked, curious.

"Yes, it is."

"Any relation?"

"To what?"

"The brothers."

"Which brothers?"

"The brothers Grimm."

"Never heard of them," the man said.

"Really? That's peculiar. Ev—"

"You were going to say '*ev*eryone's heard of them,' weren't you," the man accused.

"I was not. I was going to say, 'hev... a nice day.'"

"I haven't finished my inspection."

"I'm an optimist."

The man sighed with frustration, then pushed his way through the swinging door into the kitchen, snatching the plastic card holder back from the woman's pudgy grip as he did so.

The kitchen was enormous. Mr. Grimm paused to rummage through the contents of his satchel until he found a clipboard. He leafed through the papers that were held fast by the metal clip at the top, making sure he had all the required forms at hand.

"This is quite a large facility. How many people work here?" he asked.

"Oh, it's just me," the woman replied.

Grimm lowered his head and peered up at the smiling confectioner over the top of his dark-rimmed glasses. "You make all of this?" he asked, waving his hand toward the racks of candies and cookies and cakes and cream puffs.

"Oh, yes. I love to bake and make candy. It's quite a passion of mine. Over here we have donuts, both filled and frosted. There is where I pull the taffy—each piece is stretched one thousand times. That's the secret to a perfectly chewy taffy. And of course, the cupcakes are quite popular. We have over one hundred flavors. Red velvet, Black Forest, orange surprise, lemon surprise, lime surprise, grapefruit surprise—which is surprisingly popular—"

Mr. Grimm cut her off. "How long have you owned this business?"

"My goodness, it's been in my family forever."

"Forever is not an answer I can put down on my form," Grimm said sternly. "In what year was this particular establishment put into service?"

"I don't know, precisely, but this expansion was done ten years ago."

"Fine, that will do for my purposes," he said, scribbling the information on the form as he walked through the maze of racks. He eyed the food, looking for any infractions.

Everything looked spotless.

He ran a finger along the underside of one of the racks, and it came up clean.

He came up on a wall of ovens, one in the center having much greater proportions than the others. "That is a very large oven."

"I have a lot of baking to do."

"I don't believe I've ever seen an oven of that scale."

"It was custom made," the woman said proudly.

Grimm walked up to the oven and pulled open the door. It was large enough to fit a person quite comfortably. He pulled out a penlight and shone it on the gleaming interior. "Hmm," he said, as he exchanged the light for a pen and made some notes on his clipboard.

"Do you like your job, Mr. Grimm?" the large woman asked.

The small man peered at her. "Excuse me?"

"You seem to be very good at what you do, but do you enjoy it?"

"It's a job," he replied.

"It's just that I can't image a little boy saying, 'I want to grow up to be a health inspector.'"

"I find the work very rewarding. I feel like in my small way, I'm just as important as a police officer or a firefighter," he said, in a somewhat defensive tone.

"Oh, I have no doubt," the woman replied. "Were your parents health inspectors as well?"

"No," he said, as he continued inspecting the giant mixing machines. "They were teachers."

"Really? What did they teach?"

"Literature," he grumbled.

"And you've never heard of Jacob and Wilhelm Grimm? Grimm's Fairy Tales? They really are quite ubiquitous."

"Yes, so you've told me."

"I just thought with you having the same name, you would have some connection to—"

"Please, I have work to do here. What's in this cabinet?"

"Those are the molds for the holiday chocolates. You know, Easter Bunnies, Santa Clauses, hearts and flowers."

He opened the cabinet and looked over the molds, picking a few of them up and inspecting them carefully."

"Do you know anything about your grandparents?" the woman asked.

Grimm looked at her with a combination of annoyance and curiosity. "Of course I knew my grandparents. What kind of question is that?"

"I'm just curious as to where they were from. Perhaps there is a relation to the German authors?"

"My grandfather Grimm's father was adopted. I'm sure—apart from the name—there is no connection to these brothers you keep on about. Where do you store your perishable ingredients?"

"The walk-in cooler is just over there," the woman replied, pointing to a gleaming stainless steel door." She followed the diminutive inspector as he walked toward the industrial sized refrigerator. "He was an orphan, your great-grandfather?"

"Yes, he and his sister," Mr. Grimm replied. "Now, can we stop this distracting inquiry into my genealogy and get on with the inspection?"

"Of course, of course," the woman said. "Whatever you need. I'm just curious by nature, and your name reminds me of a story from my own family."

"I'm sure that's very interesting, but I really do need to finish my work."

"You do go on, don't let me disturb you. It's quite a fanciful story, anyway, apparently Wilhelm Grimm and his wife, Dortchen, adopted two young children who had murdered someone in my family."

"That is indeed quite fanciful," Mr. Grimm said as he continued examining the eggs, milk, strawberries, blueberries, raspberries, blackberries, gooseberries, peaches, plums, pears, pomegranates and other assorted produce.

"The brothers then convinced everyone that the murder was actually self-defense. They even wrote a story about it, totally mischaracterizing the incident, claiming my relative had kept them prisoner and threatened to eat them. Can you believe that? Outrageous. The truth of the matter was that she was a maker of sweets as I am, and they had robbed her, so she simply kept them confined until a constable could be found to adjudicate the matter. This was back in nineteenth century Germany. It wasn't like you could just pick up the telephone and ring the police."

"No, I don't suppose it was," Grimm said as he finished with the refrigerator and made numerous marks on his clipboard.

"They even claimed she was a witch! Imagine that."

"Indeed," the small man said absently as he checked the electrical connections between the bank of blenders and food processors arrayed on a gleaming counter.

"Well, in truth, she was sort of a witch, but not the sort who would eat children. More like a magician—in the kitchen, of course," she added with a laugh, as if it was the funniest thing anyone had ever said.

"Everything seems to be in order," the health inspector pronounced. "I must commend you on keeping such a pristine kitchen. All the refrigerated items are clearly labeled and dated, your food preparation areas and equipment are clean, no signs of vermin or insects. And your ovens are spotless." He scribbled a few more notes on the forms, then added his signature.

"I'm so pleased to hear that," the woman said. "You know, I was so afraid that someone else would come to do the inspection."

Grimm paused as he was stuffing his clipboard back in his satchel.

"Pardon me?" he asked.

"Well, Maryanne—who works in your office—is a loyal customer. So, when I asked her to misplace my paperwork so that my case would be escalated, I wasn't completely sure the task would be assigned to you."

"Do you mean to imply that you arranged for me to be the one to inspect your establishment? Whatever for?" he asked.

"Why, your name, of course. Grimm."

Mr. Grimm raised an eyebrow. "I'm afraid I'm not quite following."

"It's simple, really. Your great-grandfather and his sister killed my sister," the woman accused.

"Your sister?" he asked, incredulous.

"That's one of the benefits of being a witch. Longevity," she answered. "Time. Time enough to track down the descendants of the miscreants who murdered my dear sister, burned her alive in her own oven."

Grimm looked at her for a long moment. Then he smiled and began to laugh. "You almost had me there," he said. "I thought for a second that you were going to stuff me into your over-sized oven as vengeance." He laughed again. "Oh, that is rich. Quite amusing. I get it now, Gingerbread House Confections, just like the house the witch lived in in the story."

"Which story?"

"Hansel and Gretel," he said, still chuckling.

"I thought you said you'd never heard of the Brothers Grimm."

The man stopped laughing. He clutched his satchel.

"It's taken me over a century to track you down," the woman said, the jolly demeanor evaporating, replaced by a dark, sinister expression that gave the small man chills. "Grimm is a much more common name than you would imagine. And it took me a while to discover that your grandparents had emigrated from Germany to America. This is such a big country to find such a small man in."

She waved her hand and bolts slammed into place, locking the swinging door, while metal shutters rolled down over the windows, sealing them in the large kitchen. The lights dimmed.

Then the large oven roared to life, casting an eerie glow into the darkened room.

"And now," the woman said, tightening her apron strings and pushing up her sleeves, "I shall finally get the justice my sister deserves. You are the last descendant of those vile children. There shall be no one of your line left to terrorize us poor witches."

The witch, despite her size, was quick and strong. As Grimm made a dash for the door, she reached out and grabbed one of his arms, then pulled him back to her and got a hold of his other arm, grabbing him so he was facing away from her, lifting him up so his feet dangled a foot off the ground.

"But I had nothing to do with whatever happened to your sister. I'm innocent," Grimm pleaded.

"Well, since your great-grandfather and his scheming sister are long since passed, you'll have to do," she said without a hint of remorse.

"Certainly, we can work something out," Grimm said. "It was a long time ago. You have a successful business. Murdering me could adversely affect your business plan."

"Honestly, I'll be glad to be rid of this shop. I only set it up so that I could contrive a situation where I could ensnare you, and bestow upon you the fate your ancestors earned."

"You've been waiting ten years for me to come inspect your shop?" he asked, wriggling as best he could to no avail.

"Yes, it's been difficult being so nice and cheerful all these years. Baking and making confections was actually my sister's passion. Once I've finished you off and avenged her, I'll be able to return to my previous vocation."

"What was that?" Grimm asked, curious even as she carried him closer to the waiting oven.

"Mostly potions. Casting a sleeping spell on an unsuspecting princess from time to time."

"That's sounds fascinating," the little man said, the panic rising in his voice. "I'd love to hear all about it," he added, hoping to stall for time.

The witch nodded at the oven and the doors swung open.

A wave of heat hit Grimm directly in the face.

"Sorry, but your time is up," she said. She lifted him higher and pushed him feet first toward the waiting inferno.

Grimm waited until he was inches from the oven door, then pulled back his legs and shot them out so that his feet landed above the oven, causing him to flip over the witch, twisting out of her grasp and landing behind her.

She was surprised that the little man was so agile. "Do you really think you can escape?" she asked.

"Yes, I quite expect I will," Grimm said as he launched a sidekick at her ample buttocks, causing her to stumble forward into the oven.

He quickly grabbed her ankles and shoved her deep inside the cavernous cooking chamber, then slammed the doors shut. He looked around and grabbed a steel ladle and slipped it through the door handles, effectively locking her inside.

"What have you done?" the witch cried from inside the oven. "Let me out! Let me out right now!"

"My grandfather warned me about you," Grimm said. "He made sure I was trained in martial arts in case I ever found myself in this situation. To be honest, I thought he was a little crazy."

The witch ranted and raved for a while longer before she finally fell silent.

Grimm removed the clipboard from his satchel. "Oh my, human remains in the oven. I'm afraid you've failed your inspection after all," he said.

The Haunting of Oscar Morgan

"I think we have ghosts," was the first thing Delores said to Oscar when he entered the kitchen.

Not "Good morning, Oscar," or "Isn't it a lovely day today?" or "The coffee's ready."

"I think we have ghosts."

"We don't have ghosts," Oscar said as he sat at their kitchen table.

"How do you know?"

"Because there are no such things as ghosts."

Delores huffed. She hated it when he dismissed everything she said as unworthy of his attention. "Then how do you explain the voices I hear? The fact that things aren't where I left them. Doors opening and closing by themselves."

"It's an old house, Delores. The neighbors play their television too loud. You're getting old and forgetful," he replied, answering her questions in no particular order.

A voice came on the radio. One of those obnoxious morning dee-jays who thinks ending every sentence with a fart or burp is high comedy. "Why are you listening to this station?" Oscar asked.

Delores shrugged. "It's what was on when I turned it on."

Oscar got up and crossed over to the radio on the kitchen counter. He turned the knob to tune to a different station, but nothing changed. "This thing is broken," he declared. "I'll take it down to my workshop and fix it later."

"You'll never fix it," Delores said matter-of-factly. "I'll just buy a new one." Then she added, "Maybe it's the ghosts."

Oscar ignored her last comment. "No need to spend good money on a cheap radio. I know exactly what's wrong with it." He sat back down, but when he did, it felt like he was sitting in a chair that had been left outside on a cold winter's day.

Oscar entered the living room, surprised to find that Delores had company. She was sitting next to a plump woman wearing some sort of hair wrap that resembled an open-topped turban and an extraordinary amount of jewelry draped around her neck, hanging from her ears and choking her wrists and fingers.

"Oscar, I'm so glad you're home," Delores said. "I want you to meet Esmerelda."

Esmerelda held out a chubby hand. "Pleased to meet you, Oscar."

Oscar grunted and sat down in his recliner, ignoring the gesture.

"No need to be rude," Delores said. She turned to Esmerelda. "I'm sorry for my husband's manners."

"That's all right, dear," Esmerelda said, unperturbed.

"Esmerelda says I'm right," Delores declared proudly. "We have ghosts."

"I'm sure she did," Oscar agreed gruffly. "And how much did that morsel of useless wisdom cost you?"

"Oh, I don't charge for my services," Esmerelda said. "I just want to help."

"If you wanted to help, you wouldn't fill my wife's head with all this haunting nonsense."

"It's not a haunting," Esmerelda informed him. "It's definitely apparitions. A haunting would be like watching a scene from a television show over and over. What you're experiencing is not that. People say they are haunted by ghosts, but the two phenomena are quite distinct. Unfortunately, the term haunting is so misused I'm afraid it's nearly impossible to correct. Regardless, there are definitely beings from a different astral plane sharing this space with you."

"Then why don't they fly off to Fiji and leave us alone," Oscar replied sarcastically.

"It's not that kind of plane," Delores replied, not getting his joke, as usual. "Esmerelda thinks we might be able to communicate with them."

"Why would we want to do that?"

"If we can speak with them, we can discover why they're here and possibly help them move on," Esmerelda explained.

"Great," Oscar grunted.

"Don't you want to help, dear?" Delores asked.

"No, I definitely do not," he said. He glanced out the picture window and was angered to find two children playing on his lawn. "What are those damn kids doing on my grass? I've told them a hundred times to play in their own yard."

Delores and Esmerelda looked out the window. "What kids?" Delores asked.

Oscar looked at his wife with an exasperated expression. "Are you mad, woman? Those kids!" He pointed at the window and looked back outside.

Only they were gone.

It was dark outside. Esmerelda, Delores and Oscar stood in a circle in the middle of the living room.

"Let's join hands," Esmeralda said.

"Let's not and got to bed instead," Oscar suggested.

"Oscar, behave!" Delores said, embarrassed. She reached out and grabbed one of Oscar's hands. "Please, just do this one thing and I won't bother you about it ever again," she promised.

Oscar rolled his eyes, grumbled his dissent, and then offered his other hand to Esmerelda. She took hold of it. Her touch was cool and clammy and caused an involuntary shiver to run down his spine.

Esmerelda closed her eyes and tilted her head back. "Oh, spirits, we call upon you to make yourselves known to us."

There was no reply. Oscar looked around the room. "Maybe they went to the movies," he said.

"Oscar, shush!" Delores scolded.

Esmerelda continued, undaunted. "Please, give us a sign if you can hear us."

The television turned on, then changed channels to one of those computer animated movies Oscar couldn't stand.

"Oh, my," Delores said, shocked.

"You probably stepped on the remote," Oscar said.

"The remote's on the coffee table," Delores told him.

Oscar looked and saw that indeed it was. But that didn't mean that Esmerelda didn't have a universal remote of her own that she activated to fool them. These psychics were all frauds.

"It was the spirits," Esmerelda announced knowingly.

"Can we talk to them? Can we see them?" Delores asked.

"If they allow it and you're receptive," the medium answered.

"Balderdash!" Oscar declared. "There are no such things as ghosts!"

Delores ignored his outburst. "What do we have to do?"

"Spirits don't appear to us through our regular senses," Esmerelda explained. "They make a psychic connection to us, and emotions heighten the strength of that connection." She looked up at the ceiling, "Spirits, I call upon you to share yourselves with us, show us your love, as we will show you ours."

"Oh, for crying out loud," Oscar grumbled.

"I think I can hear them!" Delores declared.

"That's the TV."

"No, it wasn't. I heard voices. And laughter."

"I heard it, too," Esmeralda assured her.

"Are we done yet?" Oscar asked. "I would like to get to bed while it's still dark."

"Concentrate… open your mind…" Esmerelda coached. "Spirits, we are ready to receive you. We are here. Show yourselves to us."

Nothing happened.

"That's it, I'm done," Oscar said. He pulled his hands back and turned to leave.

Delores reached out and grabbed his arm. "Oscar Morgan, you get back here right now. It's your stubbornness that's probably keeping them from showing themselves to us."

"Oh, it's my fault? Look, I only did this to humor you." Oscar's eyebrows slanted, and he pulled his mouth back into a tight snarl as his anger grew. "If you two want to play Ouija board, have at it, I'm going to bed."

Delores let go of him and crossed her arms in a rare moment of defiance. "If you leave now, Oscar, I swear I will divorce you."

Oscar laughed. "Oh, you'll divorce me? I'd like to see you try. You can't even make a decent meatloaf."

"You love my meatloaf!" Delores said.

Oscar's face started turning red. "It's dry, bland, and tastes like shredded cardboard! I only told you I liked it because I was being polite. Why do you think we're always running out of ketchup?"

"You don't have to be so mean," Delores said in a shy, embarrassed tone.

"Mean? I'm the one who was nice enough to go along with this dumb séance," he said, his voice growing louder as his temper flared. "This whole thing is a joke. I don't know what her angle is, but this wannabe swami is up to something, and I'm sure it's going to cost me in the end. I don't want any part of this. There are no such things as ghosts!" he screamed at the top of his lungs.

A woman appeared out of thin air in the doorway to the kitchen. She screamed and dropped the bowl of popcorn she was carrying.

Jane looked at the three ghosts standing in the middle of their living room.

Her husband, Dan, had told her he occasionally heard faint voices, and the children claimed that sometimes when they were playing in the front yard, there was an old man glaring out at them from the house, but she never believed any of it.

Now, there they were, an old couple that definitely looked like the photos that had been left behind in the old house, and another woman wearing some kind of costume.

Dan was on the sofa and the kids were spread out on the floor in front of the TV. They all turned to look at her, then followed her gaze to the hazy apparitions.

Jane looked to Dan and said, "I think we have ghosts."

Light as a Feather

"What would you do if you could control gravity?" Phileas asked.

I had always admired my friend for having a wonderfully unique name. His parents claimed it was a family name and had nothing to do with the protagonist of Jules Verne's *Around the World in Eight Days*. Regardless, he wasn't just another Tom, Dick or Harry. He had a name that was memorable, that stood out. He was always the only Phileas in the room—or as far as I knew, the state.

"How do you mean 'control gravity'?" I asked. "Like Graviton in the comics?" Graviton was a supervillain who could lift buildings into the air and then drop them. Things like that. I think I remember that he had a run-in with the Avengers at one point. As a physicist, I found his origin story absurd. His body had been fused with graviton particles, giving him the ability to control gravity with his mind. That's not how gravity works, folks.

"You know, turn it on and off," Phileas replied.

"I'd go into the satellite launching business," Nemo chimed in. I swear, not all of my friends have the same names as Jules Verne characters, just these two. And Nemo is a nickname. Can't blame his parents for that moniker. "I could charge like ten million dollars per satellite, still cheaper than Space-X, but no overhead."

"Is everything about money for you?" Phileas asked.

"Of course," Nemo replied. "Once you have enough money, you can do anything else. Just look at Elon Musk and Jeff Bezos. I bet if they wanted to, they could become superheroes like Bruce Wayne."

"Bruce Wayne wasn't a superhero. He was an alter ego," I pointed out.

"How can a real guy be an alter ego? Isn't he the origi-ego?" Nemo asked.

"No such word. And it doesn't matter. He's not a real guy, he's a fictional character. Technically, he's Bob Kane's alter ego. He's Batman's secret identity," Phileas said.

"But everyone knows who Bruce Wayne is. That's not much of a secret," Nemo replied.

"It's a secret that he's really Batman," Phileas clarified.

"Why are you asking about the gravity thing?" I asked, changing the subject.

"No reason," Phileas replied. "Just making conversation."

Nemo and I exchanged a look.

"You think you can control gravity, don't you?" I said knowingly.

Phileas shrugged.

"Dude, you always think you have some psychic ability or power. It's all in your head," Nemo said.

"Yeah, that's how psychic powers work," Phileas countered. "Did you guys see that story in the news about all those different volcanoes around the world erupting?"

"Why are you trying to change the subject?" I asked.

"I'm not."

"Sure sounded like it to me," Nemo said. "Go on, then. If you can control gravity with your mind, show us."

Phileas sort of bobbled in his seat. That was the only way I could think of how to describe it. It was as if he was sitting in a chair at the bottom of a swimming pool. He pushed against the armrest and began slowly rising into the air.

"Nice one," Nemo said. "Is this like that 'light as a feather, stiff as a board' thing we used to when we were kids?"

Phileas took a deep breath, then blew out as forcefully as he could. The jet of air propelled him slightly backward, and he slowly drifted over the chair and toward the far wall. This was obviously not some party trick.

He was just floating… weightless.

"How are you doing that?" I asked.

Phileas shrugged again. "I don't know exactly. I just think away gravity and it's gone."

"That's impossible," I said.

"Yeah, I know," Phileas replied. As he neared the far wall, he repositioned himself into a horizontal pose with his feet tucked up under him. Then he pushed off the wall and propelled himself across the room, right between me and Nemo. As he approached a couch on the opposite side of the room, he started falling, then curled up into a ball and crashed into the cushions. "I have to work on my landings," he said apologetically.

"We are going to be so rich," Nemo said. "I have a million ideas of how we can cash in on this. Can you just affect gravity for yourself? Or can you, like, raise a school bus or something? A school bus filled with swimsuit models!"

"How do you know you're affecting gravity?" I asked. "You could just be affecting your own buoyancy somehow—though how either one is possible I can't comprehend."

"It's not just me."

Then I felt as if I had just crested the top of a giant hill on a roller coaster. I was weightless myself. I pushed up slightly with my feet against the ground, and then suddenly gravity was back, and I dropped into my seat.

Nemo obviously had a similar experience, as did several other inanimate objects in the room as I heard things rattle and clatter and

Nemo shout, "Wow, who needs to pay Richard Branson a million bucks to go into space? We'll offer people the chance at half the price!"

Phileas ignored our eagerly entrepreneurial friend. "You didn't answer my question," he said to me. "What would *you* do if you could control gravity?"

Even though he had asked me that precise question just moments ago, it felt like a completely different inquiry at this point. Previously, it was just an interesting conversation starter. Now it was a query with real world implications.

Somehow, some way, my friend since childhood had acquired the ability to control gravity. With his mind.

"I don't know," I answered. "I guess I would want to study the phenomenon, see if there was a way to replicate it in a lab. There are a lot of practical applications, the least of which would be space travel."

"We could ferry people back and forth to the moon! Build a luxury hotel up there. People would pay millions," Nemo said.

Phileas continued ignoring our friend, his attention was focused on me as he got up and walked back to the seat where he had been sitting before demonstrating his newfound powers. "What if you couldn't replicate it, but you wanted to help people?" he asked.

"What do you mean?" I asked back.

"You could totally be a superhero," Nemo suggested. "Gravity Man, Mr. Gravity, ooh, Black Hole," he added, spit balling names.

"How could I use this to make the world a better place?" Phileas asked me.

"Just you? One man with the power to control gravity for himself or a small room."

"What if it wasn't just a small room?"

"Whoa, you can do like a whole building? Or a mountain?" Nemo asked.

"Let's say there doesn't appear to be any limits as to how broadly I can affect gravity. What good could I do?"

I thought about that. Obviously, there was still a significant constraint. Phileas was only one man. And even if he devoted every waking hour to micromanaging gravity to benefit humanity, what could he do? "Do you have to be actively thinking about whatever it is you want to make happen for it to continue?"

Phileas shook his head. He picked up a book from the coffee table and placed it in the air between us. It hung there, spinning almost imperceptibly. "It's like flipping a switch. But it doesn't have to be on or off. Do you have a scale?"

"Like a bathroom scale?" I asked.

"Yeah."

I got up and walked down the hallway to my bathroom. In the closet I had an old scale, the kind with springs and a disc that spun around to your weight. I brought it back out into my living room and Phileas walked up and stepped on it. The numbers swung wildly for a couple seconds, then settled on 182.

"Watch," Phileas said.

Nemo came over to join me, watching the numbers on the scale. The scale started moving, sliding past 170, then 150, all the way down to 100 where it held for a while. Then the numbers spun back up over 200, 250 settling just over 310 pounds.

Nemo and I exchanged a look.

"Forget the lunar hotel idea," Nemo said. "This is the ultimate weight loss plan. That's where the money is."

The scale returned to 182 and Phileas stepped off. He looked at me. "What would you do?" he asked once more, this time almost pleading.

"I hate to admit it, but Nemo's idea of lifting payloads into orbit might be something to consider. We could finish deploying StarLink in an afternoon. Build a space elevator. Construct interstellar craft here on earth and then just lift them out of the gravity well—jeez, what even is a gravity well anymore."

"Why do we have to build all that stuff? We just rent out Phileas to do the job," Nemo said.

"Because we won't always have Phileas. And who knows if anyone else has or ever will have this ability—whatever it is."

Phileas returned to his chair and collapsed into its worn upholstered cushions. "What if I make a mistake?" he asked.

"That's a good point," I replied. "Before you take on anything big, we'd want to do a lot of controlled laboratory experiments and measurements. We may even want to get you up to the International Space Station to start."

"You won't even need a space shuttle," Nemo added. "They can just put you in a space suit and you can float on up."

"What if it's already too late?" Phileas pondered. His voice was quiet, as if he was asking the question not to me and Nemo, but himself.

"What do you mean 'too late'?" I asked.

Phileas ignored my question. "Have you ever read that story, 'Belief' by Isaac Asimov?"

I nodded. It was one of my favorites from the Golden Age of science fiction. In it, a man wakes from a dream in which he was flying to discover that he is actually levitating in real life.

"It started kind of like that, but instead of me dreaming I could fly, I was just lying on my back in the park. There's a hill I like to hike to and then just lay in the grass and stare at the clouds. I was thinking about what it would be like to float among them. I didn't even realize gravity was gone until went to stand up. I accidentally pushed myself into the air and found myself heading straight up."

"An object in motion," I said off-handedly.

"Exactly," Phileas agreed. "I didn't know what was happening, but I knew if I didn't do something, I was going to actually be among those clouds. Then the next thing I knew, I was about fifty feet in the air… and falling.

"I realized too late that I wasn't actually flying. I was subject to the laws of nature—well, not all of them, obviously, but I don't have negative gravity, I can't like repel myself away from something else. So even though I was no longer accelerating toward the ground, I was moving fast enough to hurt myself."

"What did you do?" Nemo asked. We were both literally on the edge of our seats.

"I scrambled. I tried to orient myself so I could at least land on my feet. The best way I could describe it was that I was swimming in the air—well, the equivalent of a doggy paddle at least.

"And I started slowing down."

I slapped my hand against the coffee table in front of me. "Of course. Whatever you're doing, you essentially are canceling your mass—or east least how it applies regarding the force of attraction."

"What are you talking about?" Nemo asked.

I slipped into "professor" mode. "The force of attraction is an equation that derives the attractive force between two objects as proportional to the product of the masses divided by the square of the distance between them. If one of those masses is nothing, it zeros out the equation, and for that body, there is no gravity."

Phileas nodded. "I continued trying to 'swim' my way against the direction I was moving. And then a gust of wind kicked up, and suddenly I was like a dandelion seed floating on a breeze. After a while, I was able to direct myself to a spot where I could make a landing without breaking my neck. I—" he looked at me as he started to adopt my theory of his abilities, "—added back some of my mass so I wouldn't just bounce off the ground. It hurt. My shoulder was sore for days, but I survived."

"Obviously," Nemo added.

"After that, I confined my experiments to an indoor setting. And I discovered that I was not only able to control my own mass, but the mass of other objects." He looked at the book he had previously set floating in the air, and it fell back toward the coffee table with a thud.

Nemo seemed deep in thought. "Okay, so you can't actually fly, but we could outfit you with some kind of jetpack, right? With no mass, you should be able to move around pretty easily. Or maybe we could engineer some kind of wings for you."

"What are you talking about?" I asked him.

"The superhero thing," Nemo answered. "He may not be able to zip around like Superman, but we can definitely work with this mass controlling thing."

"I don't want to be a superhero," Phileas stated.

"But you said you wanted to help people," Nemo countered.

"Not like that. I was thinking bigger."

I suddenly became gravely concerned. Phileas had not come to us with the excitement of someone who had learned they could do handstands or shoot a spitball fifty feet with dead aim. Something was wrong. Asking me what I would do was not merely a question… it was an apology.

Our eyes met, and I could sense I was right. There was something Phileas wasn't telling us.

"How big?" I asked.

He slumped back in his chair, took a deep breath and let it out as a sigh. "I pulled out some old physics books and started looking at what I could do with this power. All sorts of things are affected by the force of attraction equation. Aeronautical lift, friction, fuel consumption…

"What if, I thought, I could reduce the energy required to do all this work on Earth? What if planes and cars didn't require as much fuel? People could have just a little extra pep in their step?"

"You didn't," I said, as the implications of what he was saying suddenly hit me.

Phileas didn't answer. He just looked down at his hands as they gripped the armrests of the chair.

"Didn't what?" Nemo asked.

"Change the mass of the earth," Phileas confessed. "It was just a little." He looked toward me as if for absolution. "I didn't know."

Nemo signaled with his arms that he was at a loss as his gaze shifted between me and Phileas. "Zach, what's he talking about?" he asked me.

Phileas continued to avoid my stare.

"Everything has changed," I answered.

"That doesn't help," Nemo replied. "Somebody tell me what the hell is going on."

I turned to Nemo. "Phileas thought he could solve our energy crisis by making it so that most everything we did would require less of it. Do you remember seeing the old video of Alan Shepard hitting a golf ball on the moon?"

"Who's Alan Shepard?"

"Doesn't matter. The point is, you can hit a golf ball for miles on the moon because the moon has less mass and the force of attraction between the moon and the golf ball is less. So, the same about of energy imparted into the ball by hitting it with a golf club will send it sailing."

"I wouldn't mind adding a few yards to my drive," Nemo said.

"The thing is, that's not the only thing that would change. By changing the mass of the earth, you affect all the forces acting on it internally. Magma would be facing less pressure and could more easily make its way to the surface."

Nemo turned to Phileas. "Hey, didn't you say something about a bunch of volcanic eruptions?"

I continued. "The orbit of the moon would shift, affecting tides, causing earthquakes as the tectonic plates suddenly were able to move just a little bit easier."

As if to punctuate my point, the house began to shake.

"Was that an earthquake?" Nemo asked.

"And it would affect the earth's orbit around the sun."

Phileas raised his head and looked at me, begging for forgiveness I couldn't give him. "I put it back as soon as I realized," he said.

I shook my head. "It doesn't matter. It's all different now." I laughed, thinking about the flood of outrageous conspiracy theories that had been floating around the internet recently. How the tide charts were suddenly wrong. The moon was rotating, after millennium of showing the same side to the earth as it revolved around us. The sun was dimmer.

At the time, I thought it was all some kind of fad, people making scientific deep fakes trying to sucker others into believing the world was coming to an end. How many other people had disregarded the warnings as a bad joke?

Maybe they were the lucky ones.

They didn't know the world was about to end.

"Is this bad?" Nemo asked.

"Yeah, Nemo," I said. "This is really bad."

Nemo's demeanor shifted from his usual upbeat self to uncharacteristically worried. "Can't he just, you know, put it back?"

I shook my head. "That's not how his ability works. Anything he would try would create greater perturbations in the system. It would just make things worse."

Another earthquake shook the room. Pictures fell from the walls. Car alarms were wailing outside on the street. The power went out.

"Worse than this?" Nemo asked.

"I'm sorry," Phileas said.

"Sorry?" Nemo asked. "What the hell, dude. You, like, broke the world."

"I just wanted to help," he explained.

I almost felt sorry for him.

A crevice opened up beneath my house. The floor fell away.

We all sat floating in the air, defying gravity.

I looked at Phileas. "What's the point?" I asked.

Phileas looked to Nemo, who finally grasped the gravity of the situation. He nodded grimly.

Far below us, magma flowed. I could feel the heat rising up.

Phileas shifted his gaze to me, and I nodded as well.

He closed his eyes.

"Next time you want to help," Nemo said, "maybe write a check to UNICEF."

And we fell.

The Time Cop Paradox

As usual, I was the first one to arrive at work. I liked this job. It was much better than tending bar for the neighborhood gin joint down the street, but nothing at all what I expected working at a think tank to be like.

The National Institute for New Ideas—or NIFNI—wasn't anything fancy like the Rand Corporation, staffed with dozens of the top people in myriad fields. It was me and five other thinkers who mostly solved problems for our eccentric billionaire boss. The others were incredibly smart people with stratospheric IQs. So what was an ex-bartender doing working with a roomful of geniuses?

Well, they hired me to fill the void for the one thing they were all deficient in: common sense.

We all worked in a giant communal office, in the middle of which was my desk. I set down the newspaper I picked up on my way in and opened it to the comics page.

A minute later, Worm entered. Worm was short for Bookworm—essentially a nickname for a nickname. He was a legacy Jeopardy champion, from before the days they let the winners keep going past five wins. In that era, he was the top money winner, but it always bugged him they had changed the rules, and players like Ken Jennings became huge celebrities—and much to Worm's horror, the host of his beloved Jeopardy. He spent a good portion of his day petitioning the game show to reinstate the restriction and revoke Jennings' illegitimate wins.

"Good morning, Worm," I said.

He ignored me and sat down at his desk in the corner, picked up a book from one of the several stacks surrounding him, and started reading. He was, of course, a speed reader, and spent three or four seconds on each page before flipping to the next.

"A real page turner?" I asked.

Worm paused to peer at me over the top of his reading glasses. "That joke wasn't funny the first hundred times you said it," he muttered.

I smiled. He was right, of course, but it always amused me to see him react.

The next person to enter was Suzy—or rather, Dr. Suzy. She had more advanced degrees than there were *Fast and Furious* movies—including the *Hobbes and Shaw* spin-offs.

"Good morning, Suzy," I said.

Suzy smiled at me as she set the cardboard box she was carrying on her desk. "Good morning, Jack," she replied. "How's today's Wordle coming?"

"Oh, I gave up on those," I answered.

"Sudoku?"

"Boring."

"Crossword puzzle?"

"Takes too long."

"Jumble."

I nodded. "I like the pictures that go with it."

"Of course you do," she said politely, yet condescendingly.

"Hey, there may be a cute cartoon, but it's still very challenging," I said.

She started pulling items out of the box and assembling them on her desk. One of her degrees was in Electrical Engineering, but she was also a Chemical Engineer, Structural Engineer and an accomplished theoretical physicist, so whatever she was building could be anything. It was interesting to watch her work, but even more entertaining to watch Worm watch her work.

Her activity had distracted him from the thick book he was now halfway through. I could tell that as she removed items from the box and set them on her desk, he was growing increasingly perplexed and frustrated.

Finally, he couldn't keep silent any longer. "What in the world are you building?" he asked.

"A time machine," Suzy replied without looking up from her work.

"Did you say 'time machine'?"

"I did."

"Time travel is impossible," Worm said.

"Says the guy who can quote every line from *Time Cop*," I interjected.

"*Time Cop* is Jean-Claude Van Damme's masterpiece," Worm replied, defensively. "Both he and Ron Silver deserved Oscars for that movie."

Suzy and I sighed simultaneously. Worm's love for books was rivaled only by his love for Jean-Claud Van Damme movies. Personally, I preferred Jackie Chan's work in the genre, but Van Damme was a close second.

"But," Worm continued, "I like it because of the flawless pairing of thrilling action with witty dialog—not because of the science."

"Exactly," Suzy agreed. "You don't need to drive a high-speed sled into a brick wall to travel through time."

"You can't travel through time at all," he insisted.

"Correct," Suzy affirmed. "Technically, time is traveling through you."

He scratched his head. "That doesn't make any sense at all," Worm countered.

"It does if you're smart enough."

Worm stuttered and stammered for a moment.

"Besides," Suzy added, "if two versions of the same person from different timelines were to touch, they wouldn't meld together into a CGI blob like Ron Silver did in Time Cop."

"Of course not," Worm agreed. "The energy from the time differential would create an instantaneous explosion equivalent to a small yield tactical nuclear bomb."

Suzy laughed. "There's no way that would happen."

"How could it not? Which ever way you travel through time, you need to impart energy into the system to make that happen, so when that differential is bridged, it has to go somewhere."

"Are you going to believe some silly action movie, or an actual theoretical physicist?" Suzy asked.

Worm stared her down.

Suzy stared back even harder.

Worm blinked first. "It's not silly," he said in his defense.

Suzy smiled and continued plugging various components into each other. "You know," she said, "it also doesn't make sense for someone who changes their own past to retain the memories from their previous timeline. In fact, it doesn't make any sense for them to return to their new present. They would simply cease to exist, and the alternate version of themselves would take their place."

"Not necessarily," Worm replied. "The person who was in the timeline before could be the one who ceases to exist."

"Wow, so Van Damme essentially killed the version of himself that was leading a perfectly happy life so that the other version that had caused the death of his family could alleviate his guilt. Nice."

"Do not mock Van Damme!" Worm warned.

"I'm just saying, either way, the movie is horribly flawed. Real time travel isn't anything like that."

"That's because there is no real time travel."

"I'll remember you said that when you want me to take you back in time to challenge Ken Jennings in the Jeopardy Tournament of Champions."

Worm grunted, then returned his attention to his book.

I got up to take a closer look at what Suzy was doing. "So, if you have a time machine, how come you haven't traveled back in time to buy a lottery ticket or something?" I asked.

"It's not finished yet," she replied.

"What do you need?"

"I don't know."

"You don't know?" I asked, surprised that Suzy would admit there was actually something she didn't know.

"I have no idea what it needs. But I'm ninety-nine percent done."

"Flux capacitor?" I suggested.

Suzy shrugged. "Could be."

"There's no such thing as a flux capacitor," Worm said from behind the pages of his book.

Suzy ignored him. "I'll figure it out eventually," she said confidently.

"Why are you working on it now if you don't have all the components you need?" I asked.

"Well, when I do figure it out, I'm going to finish the machine, travel back in time and give myself the part so I can use it in the future to travel back in time."

"Oh, for the Pete's sake and a box of snakes," Worm said loudly. "Now I know you're messing with me. You can't build a time machine by expecting you'll solve the problem in the future and sending yourself the solution in the past so that you have it in the future! That's not even a paradox. That's just ridiculous."

"Says the man with zero PhDs," Suzy replied casually.

"I don't need some fancy letters after my name to know what you're saying is complete and utter nonsense."

"To a small minded person who doesn't understand how to disconnect cause and effect."

"You can't have the effect before the cause!" Worm shouted.

"If you say so," Suzy replied, continuing connecting the various parts of her time machine together.

Worm was fuming.

Suzy gave me a surreptitious wink.

"When do you plan on giving yourself this mysterious missing part?" I asked.

Suzy snapped the final pieces of her device together, then looked at her watch. "Now would be good."

All of us—Worm included—looked at the door to the office expectantly.

Nothing happened.

"Ha!" Worm exclaimed. "I knew it. I knew you were messing with me." He slammed his book shut and slammed it on his desk. "Yes, I was right. You were wrong!" He did a sort of dance—more like a jig—around the office. "I was right, you were wrong," he sang. "There's no such thing as time travel!"

He danced his way over to the door. "Did you really think I would fall for that? That I would believe that some future version of you was going to show up and hand over some magical part that would light up your mythical time machine? How stupid do you think I am?" Worm asked.

A second Suzy appeared in the doorway. "About as stupid as a sea cucumber with a lobotomy," she answered.

Worm was so surprised, he tripped over his own feet and tumbled to the ground. He recovered and got up, acting as if he had meant to do that.

"But... how... this..." Worm sputtered.

"You're late," the original Suzy said to her future self.

"This watch you bought us is slow," future Suzy replied.

"Did you bring it?" now-Suzy asked.

"Of course, I'm not as addle-brained as our friend here," future-Suzy said, nodding in Worm's direction.

"This is impossible," he said, taking off his glasses and cleaning them. But when he put them back on, there were still two Suzys.

"Is one of those books on your desk a dictionary? Because maybe you need to look up the definition of that word. I do not think it means what you think it means," future-Suzy said, quoting Mandy Patinkin from *The Princess Bride*—my favorite movie.

"What is this?" Worm asked suspiciously. "Some kind of holographic projection?" He reached out and touched future-Suzy.

She was solid. He touched her arm, her shoulder, her hair.

"Careful," now-Suzy warned. "That's the most physical contact he's had with a woman in years. He might think you two are engaged if you let him keep doing that."

Worm looked back at now Suzy and rolled his eyes. "For your information, I had a date last week."

"Really? What day? What was her name? Remember, I have a time machine now. I can go back and check," she said.

Worm swallowed. "I'm not going to tell you. That's private information," he insisted.

"Was her name Bette?" future-Suzy asked.

"Bette you spent the night alone watching a Jean-Claude Van Damme marathon," now-Suzy added.

Both Suzy's laughed, the same exact five-note chuckle that ended in a smirk.

Future-Suzy pulled out a small circuit board with a mysterious glowing crystal set in its center from her pocket. "One time crystal, ready to use," she said to now-Suzy. She started walking toward her younger self.

"Wait, stop!" Worm yelled. "Don't touch her!"

We all looked over at Worm. His eyes were filled with panic.

"The time differential! Don't let her touch you!"

"Don't be ridiculous Worm," now-Suzy said. "This is not *Time Cop.* I'm not going to explode or meld with myself if we touch. That's just a cinematic fantasy."

"Are you willing to take that chance?" he asked.

Now-Suzy and future-Suzy exchanged a look, then shrugged.

Future-Suzy tossed the time crystal to now-Suzy, who caught it in midair. She turned it over in her hands, admiringly. "I did a good job on this."

"Yes, you did. Now, can you plug it in so I can justify existing in this timeline?" future-Suzy asked.

"Of course," now-Suzy replied.

"But where did it come from?" Worm asked.

"I brought it," future-Suzy explained.

"You're giving her a device that already existed in the future, so she can use it now. But when was it actually built?"

"Right now," now-Suzy replied.

"No, that's imposs—that doesn't make sense. You didn't build it. You can't just pluck things out of the future without them having an origin at some point in the past."

"Right," now-Suzy agreed. "And now is my future self's past. I don't understand why this is so difficult for you to comprehend. It's happening, so obviously it's possible."

"I see that it's happening," Worm agreed. "But..." He looked in my direction. "Does any of this make any sense to you?"

"Well, like she said, it's happening right now, so obviously it must be what she says it is."

Worm shook his head. "No, no, this can't be real. I must be dreaming. That's it. I'm still at home in bed. This is a dream. Of course." He seemed relieved. "Phew. For a second there, I thought I was losing my mind." He laughed. "I need to remember this one and tell you guys about it when I get into work."

Future-Suzy reached over to Worm and pinched him as hard as she could on the arm.

"Ow!" he exclaimed.

"Still think you're dreaming, genius?" she asked.

Worm's relief evaporated, and dread crept into his expression. "I'm not dreaming?" he asked, rubbing the spot on his arm future-Suzy had pinched.

"Maybe I'm the one dreaming," I offered.

Worm ran his fingers through his hair, muttering to himself, trying to come up with some rationale that would mend his shattered world view.

"Well, thanks for stopping by," now-Suzy said.

"No problem," future-Suzy replied. She crossed over to her past self, arms outstretched.

Now-Suzy smiled and opened her own arms to accept her future self's embrace.

"No, don't!" Worm shouted. He ran out of the office, screaming. "Evacuate the building! Everyone, get out!"

His voice faded as he got further and further away.

The two Suzys hugged.

Nothing happened.

They didn't meld together into an unstable blob.

They didn't explode.

"Do you want to introduce me?" I asked.

Now-Suzy stepped back, sharing a conspiratorial smile with herself. "Jack, this is my sister, Lucy."

Lucy offered her hand to me. "Nice to meet you, Jack."

"Twin sister, I assume. I didn't even know you any siblings at all."

"Yeah, we don't tell people. Makes it easier to pull pranks like this."

"I admire your dedication. You're like Christian Bale in that move, *The Prestige*."

"Yeah, we told Christopher Nolan he could use the idea as long as he never gave us credit."

"You know Christopher Nolan?" I asked.

"Not as far as you know," Lucy answered. She turned to Suzy. "By the way, you're still on for going to that charity thing with my husband this Saturday, aren't you?"

"I'll be there. Totally worth it to see Worm running out of the building, thinking he was going to die in a time explosion."

"No sex with him this time," Lucy warned.

"I won't make that mistake again," Suzy promised. "Later."

Lucy looked me over. "This one is cuter than you let on," she said to her sister.

"One-twenty," Suzy replied.

Lucy nodded knowingly. "Ah. Still…" she added, looking me over lasciviously. She strutted out of the office.

I turned to Suzy. "One-twenty?" I asked.

"Your IQ. We don't sleep with anyone under one-fifty. Sorry."

I shrugged. "Good to know."

Suzy swept all the pieces of her "time machine" into the box she had brought them in, then sat in front of her computer and started scanning emails while browsing the web.

I returned my attention to the Jumble puzzle on the comics page. I chuckled to myself as I read the clue, "A martial arts vehicle blocking a river is called a…"

I filled the letters in the space provided.

"Van Dam."

The Tiny Little Man

"You're a what?" Buck Harris asked.

"An homunculus," replied the tiny little man. His voice was barely audible, not only because he was only about three inches tall, but also because he was trapped under an upside down pickle jar.

"A homoncu-lunk?"

"*An* homunculus," he repeated, shouting as loudly as he could. "If you let me out, you can hear me better!" he suggested.

"No way, I'm going to be rich when people get a load o' you," Buck said excitedly.

"Possibly," the homunculus conceded. "But if you keep me under this jar, I'm going to suffocate shortly and that will severely cut into your potential earnings."

Buck considered the miniature man's point. He looked around to see if he could spot the lid from the jar, but it was nowhere to be found. So, instead, he grabbed the menu for the local Chinese restaurant from the fridge where it was held in place by a magnet shaped like a piece of bacon. The paper was fairly stiff, so he was able to slide it between the overturned jar and the counter. The homunculus had to dance around while he did so. Once it was in place, Buck righted the jar, spilling the small man onto his butt as his glass prison flipped from top to bottom.

"You could have given me a little warning there," the homunculus said. "I'm not some cockroach or mouse."

Actually, that was exactly what Buck had originally thought he was. He had discovered that some of the food packages in the cupboards had holes in them—particularly the cookies. He had set out a bunch of mousetraps, but none of them had been tripped, and the roach motels remained vacant.

So, Buck had made a plan to stay up and see if he could catch the critter in the act. He had borrowed a pair of night-vision goggles from his neighbor, Randy, and set a package of Almond Windmill Cookies on the counter (they seemed to be the food thief's favorite) then sat himself on a chair in the middle of the kitchen with a couple cans of Red Bull handy in case he got tired.

It was shortly after midnight when Buck heard a rustling noise coming from somewhere under the sink. The cabinet doors opened slightly, and then something slipped out. It was tiny. He couldn't make out exactly what it was through the distortion of the night-vision goggles. At first, he thought it was a big bug. It leaped up onto the framing part of the cabinet door, then reached for the dish towel that was hanging off of the handle, climbing along the terry cloth until it could grab a hold of the edge of the countertop and climb up.

It started moving toward the toaster, which was underneath one of the upper cabinets, but then caught sight of the cookies. It changed direction and approached the bag and used some kind of tool to cut a hole in it.

Buck thought that was odd, even for a big bug.

He got up slowly and silently and stepped toward the counter. As quickly and smoothly as he could, he grabbed the empty pickle jar, slid the Almond Windmill cookies package away, and placed the jar over the critter.

"Gotcha!" he shouted.

"Let me go!" it shouted back!

Buck nearly jumped out of his skin.

He backed away toward the kitchen door and reached for the light switch.

Big mistake turning on the lights while you're wearing night-vision goggles.

Buck was instantly blinded.

He ripped the goggles off, then blinked until his eyes readjusted and the big blue spots he was seeing faded away.

Under the jar on the counter was what looked like a tiny little man. He was naked except for a tiny loin cloth fashioned from a scrap of fabric and some string. Tucked into the string was a tiny red plastic sword—a novelty toothpick Buck collected from a local bar. The creature's eyes were big, and were either completely black, or just had large pupils. He had pale white skin and long, dark hair pulled back into a ponytail. His ears were somewhat pointed, like the elves in *The Lord of the Rings*.

He was pushing on the side of the jar, moving it, inch by inch, toward the edge of the counter.

Buck rushed forward and grabbed it, moving the jar back to the middle of the counter, knocking the small man off his feet.

The creature within looked up at Buck, disappointed. He sat down and crossed his arms.

"What are you?" Buck had asked.

Which catches us up to now.

The tiny little man paced anxiously around the inside of the now right-side up jar.

"So," he said, the jar serving to amplify this voice a bit. "Here we are. You caught me. Now what?"

"I don't know," Buck admitted. "Not much I can do in the middle of the night. I guess I'll wait till morning and call my Uncle Pete. He used to work for the local TV station. He might know someone who can help me figger out what to do with ya."

The homunculus looked at Buck skeptically. "That's your big idea?"

"Jeez, cut me a break. I didn't think I was going to catch a homuncul-acallit."

"Homunculus," he corrected.

"Whatever. I thought you were a big bug."

"Do I look like a big bug?"

"No, of course not, not with the lights on. What are you doing in my house?" Buck asked, trying to regain control of the conversation.

"Did you think this was just an empty lot when you dug that giant hole and built this monstrosity here? This was my land and my family's home for centuries before you showed up. Technically, you're in my house!"

"How was I s'posed to know that?" Buck asked.

"That's the trouble with you humans, you just blunder in wherever you want, with no regard for the natural order and think you own the place just because you're the biggest and loudest thing around. You know, there was a beautiful, natural world here before you came along. My family planted the apple trees you dug up to pour your foundation."

"That's not my fault," Buck said. "You should have said something."

"Oh, so it's my fault?" he replied. "And what would have happened if, when you brought in your big digging machines and concrete and lumber, I'd come out and said, 'Excuse me, this is my home, go find your own space'?"

Buck shrugged. "I dunno."

"I'll tell you what you would have done. You would have slapped a jar on top of me and sold me to the highest bidder."

"You don't know that," Buck said defensively.

He folded his arms and looked up at Buck from his glass prison.

"Okay, maybe," Buck confessed. "But it's not like I wouldn't cut you in on the deal."

"Oh, really? Now you want to be partners?" he asked.

"I'm thinking about it. You're right. If you were here first, you got rights."

The homunculus seemed shocked. "Well, thank you for recognizing that," he said. He looked up expectantly. "So, aren't you going to let me go?"

"No, of course not. I said I'd cut you in. If I let you go, then there won't be nothin' to cut you in on."

"You're smarter than you look," he said. "But then again, you'd have to be."

Buck could sense he had just been insulted, but couldn't figure how. "People will pay just as much to see a dead hobuncle as they would a live one," he warned.

A smile appeared on the homunculus's tiny face. "You really have no idea what you're in for, do you?"

"What d'ya mean?"

"Well, first off, I'm a sentient being—that means I can think and communicate," the homunculus said.

"I know what sentiment means," Buck told him.

"Yes, of course you do. You've heard of animal rights activists, haven't you?"

"Yeah, sure, they're those nuts who feel sorry for chickens and cows getting eaten."

"Yes, in a manner of speaking. So imagine how they'll feel about you keeping a thinking, feeling being captive in a jar."

"I don't have to keep you in a jar," Buck said. "I can get you like a doll house you can live in. And some real clothes."

"Oh, so a nice prison."

"Yeah."

"Here's the thing. No matter how nice you make it, someone's going to think you're mistreating me, and they'll file a lawsuit. Do you know a good lawyer?"

"No," Buck replied. "But my cousin, Paul, fights his own traffic tickets."

"Paul, sadly, will not be good enough. You'll have to hire an attorney who will charge a minimum of five hundred dollars. An hour."

"No way," Buck said, surprised at the amount.

"And that doesn't include the retainer. Do you have that kind of money, Buck?" he asked.

"Hey, how do you know my name?"

"I've been living in your house ever since you built it. I know all about you."

"What's your name?" Buck asked.

The homunculus let out a noise that sounded like something Buster—Buck's dog—would yelp if someone stepped on his tail.

"What kind of name is that?"

"Do you think we homunculi have been speaking English for millennia?"

Buck became curious. "Why do you speak English at all, and how come you talk so funny?"

"I learned your language by watching PBS. You tend to fall asleep with the television on, and it's no challenge to operate the remote control to change channels to something more edifying than the fishing channel, even at my size."

"So that's why Sesame Street is on when I wake up in the mornin'," Buck said. "Well, I can't pronounce whatever it was you said, so I'll call you Homer."

"Clever. Homer the homunculus. Regardless of what you choose to call me, my point remains. You're not thinking this through, my friend."

"Well, the way I see it, it don't matter how much some fancy lawyer costs, 'cause I'm gonna make millions offa ya."

"Perhaps. But you won't see that money. There will be injunctions filed, your accounts will be frozen, you'll go broke before you ever put your hands on a penny of it."

Buck looked at him. Most of what the tiny little man said didn't make much sense to the backhoe operator. "You're trying to trick me," He said, grabbing a cookie from the package on the counter.

Homer shrugged. "Look, I know you don't trust me, and you probably think I'd say anything to get you to let me go."

"That's right."

"But, on the other hand, you've got me. If you were to screw a lid on this jar, there would be nothing I could do about it. I would suffocate and die. I am completely at your mercy. So, it is in my own best interest to make sure you do this right for the sake of my own survival."

"So what's all that fancy talk mean?"

"It means if you intend to exploit me, I might as well ensure that you do it in a manner that accrues the most benefits to myself."

Buck opened a Red Bull and took a sip, then grabbed another cookie, trying to take in everything the tiny little man was telling me. It sort of made sense, but at the same time he had that nagging feeling that Homer was trying to pull one over on him.

"So whatcha thinkin'?" Buck asked.

"A formal arrangement. A contract. An agreement that will forestall any do-gooders from trying to interfere. I will grant you the rights as my representative to promote and publicize my existence, arrange for revenue generating events and appearances and to license my likeness for merchandise and promotional purposes."

"Huh?"

"You'll be my agent," Homer said.

"And we'll split everything fifty-fifty?" Buck asked.

"Well, a typical agent-client relationship is ten percent to the agent—"

"Only ten percent?"

"But in our case, we can adopt a less traditional split. That is, of course, if you want to forgo the wishes." Homer replied.

"Wishes?" Buck asked.

"I'm a mythical, magical creature. Of course there are wishes involved."

"If you're so magical, how come you were so easy to catch?"

"Obviously, I can't use the wishes myself. That's not how magic works. Otherwise, I wouldn't be three inches tall and sitting at the bottom of a jar."

"How many wishes do I get?"

"Just the three. Don't get greedy, Buck."

Buck grabbed another cookie and bit off the top of the windmill. He'd always wondered why these cookies were in the shape of a windmill. But he had an idea they wouldn't taste the same if they weren't.

"Why didn't you mention these wishes in the first place?"

"You were so caught up in the making money thing. I didn't want to discourage you."

"Yeah, but I can wish for money, right?"

"You can."

"What's the catch?"

"No catch," Homer assured him.

"If I wish for a million dollars, it's not gonna be 'cause I got my legs chopped off by a helicopter."

"Well, I'm not quite sure how that would happen, or why you would get a million dollars from it, but I assure you, there is no catch. Are you sure you only want a million dollars?"

Buck reconsidered. He nervously tossed another cookie into his mouth. "What's the limit?"

"No limits," Homer said. "It's a wish. You can have literally anything you want."

"So, a billion dollars is okay."

"You have to say, 'I wish I had' for it to work."

"Oh, right," Buck said. He closed his eyes and crossed his fingers. "I wish I had a billion dollars." He cautiously opened his eyes and looked around.

Homer laughed. "Did you think there would be a pile of money on your kitchen table?" He paused to catch his breath, then laughed some more, literally rolling on the bottom of the jar. "You should have seen the look on your face! Priceless! Three wishes, I can't believe you fell for that."

Buck was not amused.

He grabbed another cookie and viciously bit into it, staring down the title little man until he stopped laughing.

The homunculus looked up at Buck. "My apologies. It's a flaw. I couldn't resist."

"I'm startin' to think none of that stuff you told me about being your agent and all was for real," Buck said. He felt a pang in his stomach and reached for the Red Bull to wash down the latest cookie he had consumed. "I'm startin' to think I should take my chances to see how much I can make off a dead hornbuckle."

"Oh, come on, Buck," Homer replied. "I'm sorry, truly I am. Let's start over."

Buck got up from his chair and started looking through the trash for the lid for the pickle jar.

"Don't do what I think you're doing, Buck. You'll regret it."

"You're gonna regret ever trying to steal my cookies," Buck said.

Homer laughed again. "Is that you what you thought I was doing?"

Buck stopped picking through the trash. A spasm hit his gut, causing him to double over.

"What's the matter, Buck? Tummy ache? Feeling a little lightheaded, perhaps a little weak?" Homer asked.

The pain in his gut was increasing. He'd never mixed Windmill Almond cookies with Red Bull before. He usually enjoyed them with a cold glass of milk. But this was worse than indigestion. His head started to ache, and he became dizzy. Suddenly, it felt like his knees were going to give way. He reached for his chair and sat down before he collapsed.

"What's happening to me?" he asked, almost panting.

"Nausea, headache, confusion, weakness, difficulty breathing… sounds like acute cyanide poisoning to me."

"Cyanide?" Buck asked, his breath becoming labored.

"Yes, like the type I've been extracting from apple seeds I procured from the few trees you kindly left behind when you razed my orchard. I've been collecting it for several months. I wanted to make sure I had enough to give you a lethal dose."

"Why would you want to kill me?"

"I did explain the whole 'you built your house on my land' thing, didn't I? I hope you're not that out of it yet. I was hoping you wouldn't die without realizing why."

Buck looked at the half eaten package of cookies.

"Yes, that's right. I wasn't stealing your cookies, I was poisoning them. Nice of you to have a fondness for almond cookies. I was afraid you might smell the cyanide, but obviously you didn't notice."

Then, the burly man dying on his kitchen chair smiled.

Homer saw the grin, and his own amused expression changed.

Buck laughed. "Guess the joke's on you," he said to Homer. "You're going to rot away in that jar." He took a few last gasping breaths. His eyes rolled back in his head and he slid off the chair into a heap on the kitchen floor.

The homunculus tried to peer over the edge of the counter, but the angle was such that he could only see the top of Buck's head. He took a step back, then ran the short distance from one side to the jar to the other. His momentum caused the jar to tip a bit. He repeated the maneuver several times until the jar fell over onto its side with a clink.

He stepped out of the glass container and walked over to the counter's edge, peering down at the dead man lying on the floor. To his sensitive nose, the body was already beginning to reek, the stench mixing with the scent of bitter almonds from the cyanide.

He lowered himself to the cabinet handle that the dish towel was attached to and shimmied down its length to the floor. He cast one last look back at his deceased nemesis. "Maybe you should have wished for a long life," he said.

Homer the homunculus knew that Buck had a dog, but the creature was always asleep during his nocturnal missions in the house. He was always cautious to avoid the old hound even though it spent most of its day and all of its nights asleep in the raggedy dog bed in one corner of the kitchen, or sunning itself on the front porch.

But all the commotion from Buck falling to the floor and the jar tipping over had awoken Buster from his slumber. The sight of the creature moving along the counter, then down the towel, reminded the old dog that he was perpetually hungry. He slowly and silently got up and padded toward the sink.

When the homunculus paused to look back at Buck, the dog snatched him into his jaws and crushed him between his yellow teeth. After a few crunches, Buster swallowed the creature, returned to his bed and fell back asleep.

Everything Must Go

"I hate garage sales," Nancy said as she watched the slow-moving parade of bargain hunters wind their way through the maze of folding tables that displayed the various items that had been cluttering the house since her father had died.

"Why?" her friend, Barb, asked. "I think it's a great way to have other people pay you to take away your junk."

"Yes, that part's nice. I just don't like all these strange people around."

"Well, honey, you only have to put up with them for the weekend," Barb replied in her deep, raspy, smoker's voice.

"I know," Nancy replied. "Are you sure you can't stay and help me out? I'll give you fifty percent off of anything you want."

"No thanks, darlin'. In fact, I'm going to bring some of my stuff tomorrow to try to unload. Thank goodness this town has a high population of hoarders. You'll be fine. Just remember, everything must go, so no price is too low."

"Right. It's just..."

"It is what your father wanted you to do. I mean, the man actually put it in his will, for heaven's sake."

"Okay, okay. I guess I can suffer through a couple of days of strangers in my driveway."

Barb gave her friend a parting hug and started off across the lawn to where her old Mercury was parked.

Nancy watched her go and instantly became anxious. A few people looked her way, and she managed to smile, masking her discomfort.

The instructions in her father's will were peculiar, to say the least. He had made her inheritance, his home and the remainder of his estate—with portions of it bequeathed to various charities and foundations—conditional on her holding a garage sale on the weekend after his funeral. It was specific about which newspaper she was to advertise it in, which community websites to list it on, and even the hours it was to be open. She was instructed to sell the contents of her father's basement—mostly books, old records, and various obsolete electronics—the tools she didn't want or need in the garage, the contents of his closets and the knickknacks that had adorned his study—specifically one particular item he had singled out.

A black wooden box.

Many of the items were of a mystical nature. Nancy's father collected books and artifacts related to witchcraft and necromancy, a hobby Nancy's mother had always found disturbing. On Halloween, he would deck out the house and yard, transforming their home into the most popular trick-or-treat destination in town.

Nancy's mother had passed away several years before.

Her father had blamed what he considered his wife's premature death on one of the town's local celebrities, a new-age guru who owned a yoga studio and sold all types of homeopathic remedies, crystals and candles. When Nancy's mother had been diagnosed with cancer, instead of relying on the advice of her doctors, she was convinced by the guru that becoming a vegetarian, buying an overpriced salt lamp and meditating would cure her.

It did not.

Her death had devastated Nancy's father.

He started a personal vendetta against the man he blamed for misleading his wife, causing her to trust the alternative therapies to the exclusion of traditional medicine. A decision that cost her her life. There was a drawn-out legal battle between the two men, with the guru ultimately winning a sizable judgment and a cease and desist order against Nancy's father.

Failing to achieve any sort of justice in the courts, he decided to pursue a different course of action. His interest in the occult grew, and he devoted his time and a good deal of the money that remained after the verdict against him, finding a way to exact vengeance on his rival. He'd researched curses, voodoo dolls, spells and other mystical methods to damage the guru's reputation and business.

But Nancy's father had died without seeing his goal realized. The guru had outlived him. Nancy had always found her father's positions on his mother's decision to pursue alternative cancer treatments and his belief in the occult contradictory. It seemed to her that the new-age beliefs he blamed for her mother's death were similar to the mysticism he had become so devoted to.

But all of that was irrelevant now. Her father's obsession had died with him. His death was sudden and unexpected, and Nancy had no desire to pursue her father's preoccupation with exacting a price from the guru for her mother's death. She was the type of person who liked to keep to herself, which made her father's final request all the more difficult to fulfill.

She stood behind the card table where she kept the cash box she had stocked with coins and small bills. Garage sales were a cash business, and as Barb had reminded her, customers were more likely than not to haggle—even though she had tried to price everything at a ridiculously low amount. Maybe she would sell out the first day and she could cut the uncomfortable experience short.

Although a lot of the items were spread out along the length of the driveway, Barb had persuaded her to set some of the smaller and more stealable bargains on a table just inside the open garage where Nancy could keep an eye on them. A few people had perused the baubles. One woman had made an offer on a pair of bookends that Nancy accepted. As far as she knew, they were worth hundreds or even thousands of dollars, but the point of the sale was not to make money, it was to satisfy her father's last wishes.

Everything must go, she reminded herself.

There was that one item on the table, however, that her father had requested be sold at a specific price, and Nancy could not sell it for a penny less without breaking the terms of the will. It was a box made of a very dark wood, almost black. It was about four inches on each side and heavier than it looked. There was obviously something inside. If she shook it, she could sense that it contained something solid.

There was no obvious way to open the box. There was no hinge, no latch. There were seams visible where the grain abruptly changed direction, but despite those imperfections, the surface was smooth.

The price was 1000 dollars. An extraordinarily expensive item for a garage sale, but her father's instructions had been clear on the matter. 1000 dollars and not a penny less.

Some of the customers had been curious about the box, but when they spied the small sticker with the amount written on it, they quickly set it back in its place and moved on to more affordable items. Nancy wasn't sure what the point of trying to sell this expensive box at a garage sale was. If it was some sort of lesson her father was trying to teach her from beyond the grave, the point of it was completely lost.

It was shortly after noon on the first day when she spotted him.

Her father's nemesis pulled up in a Tesla roadster. He wore dark glasses, but the obnoxious bun of gray hair atop his head, and the pure white Kaftan he wore, betrayed his identity, regardless. Some of the people at the garage sale recognized him, a few were brazen enough to say hello.

Nancy froze.

What was he doing here? Was this one last dig at her father? The last thing she wanted to do was to perpetuate their feud.

He wandered through the maze of tables, his hands clasped behind his back, carefully scrutinizing the items for sale as he sauntered by, occasionally looking in her direction.

Nancy wasn't sure if he recognized her. They had met before. He had had the audacity to make an appearance at her mother's funeral, and she had been present at her father's home when the two men had engaged in a very loud argument for which the police had been called.

Eventually, he made his way to the table of knickknacks just inside the open garage. She could tell that he was interested in the box—but was trying not to make his desire known. He made a show of picking up all the items around it, looking at the price tags, and then setting them down. When it came time to inspect the wooden box, once he felt its heft, his eyes widened, and he unconsciously licked his lips. He looked at the price tag, then over at Nancy, an expression of surprise on his face. He carried the black wooden box over to where she was standing.

"Pardon me, I think there's a mistake on this price tag. It says 1,000 dollars, when I think you meant to put a decimal point in the middle. Shouldn't it be ten dollars?" he asked.

"No, that's correct. 1,000 dollars," Nancy assured him. The words came much easier than she expected.

He laughed. "Surely you can't honestly believe that anyone would pay 1,000 dollars for this… box. Do you even know how to open it?"

"No, I don't. But it will cost you 1,000 dollars if you'd like to take it home and try."

"I'll tell you what," he said affectionately. "I'll give you 100 dollars. Judging by the prices on the rest of the items, you are more interested in getting rid of this… junk than profiting from it." He pulled a money clip out of a pocket in his Kaftan and made a show of peeling off a crisp, new hundred dollar bill. He placed it on the table before her."

"If you have nine more of those, you can take it home," Nancy said. She was starting to enjoy this interaction. All morning, she had been the one acquiescing to people's low-ball offers, it was nice to turn the tables on someone, and doubly satisfying that it was the guru her father had hated so much.

He laughed again. "All right, I'll make it 200, but I'm afraid that's as high as I'm willing to go." He laid a second hundred dollar bill on the table.

"Okay," Nancy said, plucking the box out of the man's hands, much to his surprise. "If that's as high as you'll go, I'm afraid I cannot sell it to you. We have some fine belts and shoes you might be interested in," she offered, knowing full well a man who wore Kaftans and sandals would have no interest in such items.

The guru glared at Nancy, then looked down at the box now held tightly in her grasp. "Look," he said, "I will confess, I am very intrigued by that box, but 1,000 dollars? I don't think you'll find another person willing to spend the 200 dollars I just laid on your table. That said…" he produced two more hundred dollar bills.

"The price is 1000 dollars," Nancy said. "There's still an assortment of neckties in excellent condition available," she offered. "Those might be more in your price range."

The guru snatched up the bills and stormed off.

Nancy was surprised to discover how much she enjoyed stymieing the guru. Perhaps that was the reason her father had insisted she demand such a high price for the box. He knew it would knock her confidence up a notch or two. *Thank you, Dad,* she thought to herself. It almost made the whole experience worthwhile.

The guru, meanwhile, made his way down the driveway toward his car. He would take a few steps, pause, look as if he was going to turn around, but then continue on his way. He eventually made it all the way back to his convertible in fits and starts, looking over his shoulder, eyeing the other patrons, occasionally casting a glance back at Nancy. He got to the Tesla, opened the door, then slammed it shut without getting in and instead strode directly back to the garage, a determined look on his face.

Nancy had to try not to smile.

"All right," he said. "I'll give you 600 dollars for that box. Surely that's ten times what it's worth."

"Perhaps," Nancy agreed, "but the price is 1,000 dollars. I'm afraid I'm quite firm on that. Have a nice day." She took the box and placed it back in the center of the assorted knickknacks on the card table.

The guru stared at it, taking deep breaths, struggling to contain his obvious anger. If his clientele could see him now, they would be shocked at his lack of composure.

"Tell me," he said to Nancy, "why are you so intransigent on the price for that box?"

She considered explaining the circumstances of her father's will, but then shrugged and replied, "No reason. It's just a really nice box. And I'd like 1,000 dollars for it."

"750," he countered.

"1,000," Nancy insisted.

"800."

"1,000."

"Nine—"

"The price is 1,000 dollars, sir. Thank you for coming."

The guru looked like he wanted to shout at Nancy. His face turned red, and he clenched his fists. He looked at the box, then back at Nancy.

She smiled.

"Oh, all right," he said. He slammed ten 100 dollar bills on the table.

Nancy picked them up and carefully counted them, then held them up to the sun to inspect the security strip and watermark. "It's yours," she proclaimed, and stashed the money in her jeans pocket rather than the cash box.

The guru's demeanor instantly changed. "Ha! Yes! Thank you, kind woman!" He picked up the box and turned it over and over in his hands. "You don't know what this is, do you?"

Nancy shook her head. "Whatever it is, it's yours now," she said.

"Yes. Yes, it is. I am the owner, the possessor, the master of the box and everything within."

"If you can open it," Nancy reminded him.

It was the guru's turn to smile. He held the box by opposing corners between the thumb and middle finger of his left hand, then squeezed another pair of corners with the fingers of his right hand.

There was a click.

A gap appeared around the center of the box. He set it down, savoring the moment.

"This, my child, is not just some nice-looking box. It is a soul chest. There are only a few of these known to be in existence. Legend has it that when a person gazes at the crystal within, it captures their soul, their very essence, leaving their body an empty husk."

"Are you sure you want to open it?" Nancy asked.

The guru smiled again. "That is, of course, unless there is already a soul within. Then the owner of the box becomes the master of that soul, and can command it to do whatever he wills."

"That doesn't sound very useful," Nancy remarked. "I mean, what can a disembodied soul do? It's not like it's a genie and will grant you three wishes."

"You can command it to tell you things. Reveal secrets, stuff like that," he replied defensively.

"My Alexa does that," she countered.

He laughed. "You don't recognize me, do you?"

"Oh, no, I absolutely do. You're the new-age nut my father had a feud with for all those years."

"You're his daughter," the guru said, surprised.

"Yes, and I guess my father gets the last laugh, because he got you to pay 1000 dollars for a silly little puzzle box."

"Ah, we shall see who gets the last laugh."

He opened it.

There was a perfectly round, clear crystal inside.

He stared at it, perplexed. "That's odd, it's supposed to turn red when it contains a—"

Then his face went blank.

He stood frozen in place, not even breathing.

Then the crystal in the soul chest glowed red.

Nancy slammed the lid shut. She heard the hidden mechanism lock it closed with a series of clicks.

Then she fulfilled the other mysterious request of her father's will, to be executed if this particular situation were to arise.

From a box under the cash table, she removed a second small wooden soul chest, this one made from white wood with the same expert craftsmanship. She followed the steps the guru had performed to open it, holding it by the corners and squeezing.

The box clicked and whirred, and a gap appeared around the middle. She positioned it on the cash table in place of the other one, and opened it, facing the guru.

The crystal sphere in this one was glowing red. But only for a moment.

It dimmed, and then the guru blinked his eyes and took a breath. He looked at Nancy and smiled. "Well done, my dear. You are as clever a girl as there's ever been."

The phrase was familiar to Nancy, they were her favorite words of praise from...

"Father?" she asked.

The guru smiled mischievously. "Yes, Nance, it is I," he said. The voice was still the guru's, but the words were definitely her father's. He was the only one who shortened her name to a single syllable like that. "Nance."

"I don't understand," she said.

"It's quite simple, after I had exhausted all the legal remedies available to me—and lost quite spectacularly—I devised a plan to take absolutely everything from this devious phony," he explained.

"You mean what he said about the soul chest was true?"

"Well, I didn't hear what he said. I was in the other box. But what he likely didn't know was that a soul in an already occupied box could move into the body from which the spirit had been captured by another soul chest.

"I knew he was a notorious garage sale addict, and I was absolutely certain he couldn't pass up this one. I had made it known to mutual acquaintances that I had acquired a soul chest, and that when I was ready to die, I was going to transfer myself into it. And then I did so," he said, carefully closing the box to avoid any additional inadvertent soul sucking. "What our unsuspecting friend didn't count on, however, was that I had two such chests, and in his arrogance, he would assume I was inside the one I instructed you to sell for 1,000 dollars."

"That was quite a big gamble to make," Nancy said.

"Yes, well, I didn't have much to lose. And now I have gained everything. I not only have his fortune, but the massive sum he extracted from me through the courts. Don't worry, you can keep the house."

"I don't care about the house, I'm just glad you're back—though this will take some time to get used to," Nancy confessed.

Nancy's father patted his belly, then put a hand up to the top of his head where his gray bun was mounted. "Yes, I'll have to do a bit of working out, but first things first. I must get to a barber. Then buy some proper clothes." He pulled the Kaftan away from his chest and peered inside. "And some underwear." He searched his pockets and found the empty money clip. "Could you loan me a few dollars, my dear?" he asked Nancy.

Nancy took the 1,000 dollars out of her pocket and handed it to her guru-father.

"Thank you, Nance. I knew I could count on you," he said, then pulled Nancy into a hug. She hoped purchasing a bottle of cologne was on her father's to-do list. The combination of incense and body odor the guru emitted was quite unbearable.

He pulled a key fob out of another pocket and looked up and down the street. He pressed the button and saw which car chirped back at him. "Nice. I always wanted a convertible."

Nancy watched as he walked happily through the tables filled with the remnants of his old life, on his way, apparently, to a brand new one.

Then he stopped, looking around for something.

"You didn't happen to already sell my golf clubs, did you?" he asked.

Nancy shrugged. "Everything must go," she answered.

Her father smiled and nodded, then got into his Tesla and drove away.

Howl

Alan Chaney woke to a dull ache in his right shoulder and that side of his neck. He tried to open his eyes, but the light in the room was too bright. He squeezed them shut and turned his head away. The movement caused that dull ache to erupt into a storm of fiery pain, reaching deep into his flesh.

"Don't move," a voice told him. A woman's voice, one he didn't recognize.

"Where am I?" Alan asked. His voice sounded hoarse, his throat was sore.

"Here, drink this," the voice offered.

He opened one eye into a slit and saw that there was a straw in front of his face. Alan instinctively opened his mouth and then felt the straw touch his lower lip. He closed his mouth and sucked, drawing the ice-cold water over his parched tongue. The first swallow was painful, but the more he drank, the easier it became. The straw was pulled away.

"Easy, you don't want to drink too much."

Alan took a deep breath and found that simple act was painful as well. Was there any part of him that didn't hurt? "Am I in a hospital?" he asked.

"Yes," the woman responded.

"What happened to me?"

"You don't remember?"

Alan tried to bring up his most recent memories. He had been heading home after a late night at the office. He had taken a shortcut through the park. It was a nice summer evening. He had passed a couple walking in the opposite direction, but aside from them, he seemed to be alone. He recalled looking up at the full moon. It was unusually big and bright and cast pale shadows across the neatly manicured grass from the trees and lampposts and benches that lined it.

But beyond that, he couldn't remember anything else.

"Was I shot?" he asked, thinking maybe he had encountered a mugger. He had been held up before at knifepoint, but in that instance, the thief was satisfied taking his watch, wallet and phone and leaving Alan alive—though emotionally shaken.

"No. You were attacked by an animal," the woman told him.

That was probably the last thing Alan had expected to hear. There were no wild animals in this part of the state, let alone the city. You'd see the occasional stray cat or a rat rummaging around a dumpster, but what could have put him in a hospital?

"An animal? What kind of animal?"

"The doctors think it might have been a large dog. The policeman who came to your aid described it as a wolf."

"A wolf?" Alan asked. His voice cracked, and he started coughing.

The woman—Alan could now see she was a nurse, clad in pink scrubs, wearing pink Nitrile gloves, a colorful cap that hid her hair and a disposable surgical mask over her face—offered him the straw again. He leaned forward slightly to suck up a couple of mouthfuls of water, then laid back again.

"There aren't any wolves in the city," Alan said.

The nurse shrugged. "I'm just telling you what I heard."

"How long have I been here?"

"Just under a day. You had surgery to repair some of the damage to your shoulder and you've been asleep since then."

"Surgery?"

"Nothing too major. The wounds weren't as deep as they could have been. Apparently, you were wearing a thick leather jacket, and that protected you from any serious damage."

Alan remembered something else from the previous night. A sound, something disturbing. And even though it was a pleasant summer's evening, he had felt a chill, and had turned up the collar of his motorcycle jacket. "My jacket," he said weakly.

"I'm afraid you won't want it back. It was completely soaked in blood. By the way, my name is Jillian. I know you've been sleeping all day, but you really should try to rest. Your body needs to recuperate."

Alan looked at the nurse. Her name was printed on a tag attached to her scrubs. He looked around. Evidently, his injuries had earned him a private room, his was the only bed.

He had been in the hospital a few times before. Once was when he had passed a kidney stone. That pain had been intense, like someone slowly pushing an icepick into his back and twisting it. Another time he had been dehydrated and had passed out on an unusually hot fall day running through the very same park he had been attacked in the previous night. On both of those occasions, he had had to share a hospital room.

He could see an infusion pump mounted to an IV stand that had a large bag of saline and a couple of other smaller bags attached to the loops of metal at its top. Alan looked over at the whiteboard where he expected to see his name, vital stats, meds and information about his doctor. But it was blank.

Then he noticed something else. At the foot of his bed, his ankles were bound in padded restraints. He tried to sit up, but something was holding him to the bed. He tried to raise his hand to pull down the blanket to see what it was, but he couldn't move his arms. They, too, were fastened to the rails of the bed with leather straps.

"Relax, Mr. Chaney," Jillian said in a soothing voice.

Alan was instantly anything but relaxed as he suddenly felt an intense panic, and the rush of adrenaline that accompanied it. "Why am I tied down?" he asked. "What's going on?"

"This is for your own safety," the nurse told him.

"Safety? What are you talking about?"

Jillian sighed, then tried to smile reassuringly. "There is a small chance that you may have gotten… an infection," she said.

"An infection? What kind of infection would—" Alan instantly assembled all the information he had been given in the last few minutes into one terrifying conclusion. "Do I have rabies?" he asked.

The nurse placed a comforting hand on his uninjured shoulder. "No, no. It's not rabies. You were given the vaccine and a dose of HRIG, but purely as a precaution. Besides, you wouldn't be exhibiting symptoms this soon after a bite."

Alan breathed a sigh of relief. He knew there was no cure for rabies once you had symptoms, so it was reassuring to know he had been treated.

But it if wasn't rabies…

He looked over at the nurse. "Then why am I tied down?"

"Oh, I did that," Jillian confessed.

"What?"

"I need to keep an eye on you. So, I managed to get you transferred to the psych ward. You know, the doctors never read the forms you ask them to sign at the end of a shift when they want to get out of here. And the transportation guys don't ask questions, they just follow the instructions the computer spits out."

"Why do you need to keep an eye on me?" Alan asked, suddenly fearful.

"Because the infection you might have has no cure. And if you do start exhibiting symptoms, I don't want you to hurt anyone."

Alan was confused. "Is that why you're wearing a mask and

gloves?"

"No, not at all," Jillian told him. "I'm wearing these so in case you are not infected, you won't be able to describe my face and so I don't leave any fingerprints. By the way, my name's not really Jillian," she added in a whisper. "And I do hope I'm wrong. I really do."

"Wrong about what? What do you think I have?"

"Lycanthropy," she pronounced carefully.

"What?"

Jillian took a deep breath and squeezed his shoulder gently and compassionately. "I believe you may have been attacked by a werewolf," she said.

Alan looked into Jillian's eyes. She didn't look crazy. "A werewolf?" he asked.

She nodded.

Alan started to laugh, but his laughter quickly turned into a cough.

Jillian offered him the ice water once more.

He sucked at the straw, then cleared his throat. He smiled at her. "Did Jerry put you up to this? Is this some kind of joke?" He looked around the room and spied the private bathroom in one corner. "You can come out now, Jerry, you got me! You got me good!"

No one emerged from the bathroom.

Alan looked up into the consoling eyes of the nurse.

"You're crazy. You're like one of those angels of death."

"No, I'm not like them. I don't go around killing otherwise healthy people. I would never do that. I took an oath," she assured him.

"That doesn't mean you're not crazy," Alan replied.

"No, I guess it doesn't. You're just going to have to trust me," Jillian said. "If it turns out you're not infected, and you don't transform into a wolf tonight, then I'll make sure you're returned to the recovery unit so you can life a long, healthy life—though you might have to give up any dreams you might have had of being a major league pitcher."

Alan tried not to laugh again. She didn't seem crazy, but there was a seriousness to her demeanor and the way she spoke that he didn't find reassuring. "That's good news," he said. "That means you'll be letting me go in the morning because there is no such thing as werewolves."

Jillian shook her head. "That's what they want you to think," she said. "The fact is, there has been a rash of killings over the last few months. People disappearing, body parts being found, corpses that have been eaten. All around the full moon."

Alan could not take her seriously. "Listen, I know crime in the city has been on the rise, but I'm sure if you look at every day of the month, there are people who are killed or go missing. And if there were really people who had been eaten, we certainly would have seen it on the news."

The nurse shook her head. "I've seen the bodies. It's true," she said.

"Look, I work with numbers and statistics every day. I see facts bent and twisted to support all types of conclusions, many times completely contradictory ones from the very same data. Werewolves cannot be responsible for whatever pattern you think you're seeing, because they don't exist. They're a fiction dreamed up by Hollywood."

Jillian looked at Alan, her eyes focused and unblinking, staring at him over the paper mask. "Werewolves are real," she said, with more sincerity than Alan had ever heard from anyone about anything ever before.

It gave him chills.

"My sister was killed by one. She had her throat torn out, flesh ripped from her face, her chest, her abdomen. The creature had eaten her heart and her liver. I was the one who found the body. I could see in her eyes the terror she had experienced, the horror she had witnessed.

"Don't tell me werewolves don't exist, Mr. Chaney. Because I know they do."

Alan swallowed painfully, the soreness he had felt earlier returning as his mouth dried out. He felt urine flowing as his bladder released its load, but he didn't sense any warm wetness on his leg. Instead, he heard it start to fill a bag attached to the catheter that had been inserted into his urinary tract.

Jillian looked down at the bag. "Good color, no blood," she said out of habit, as if he was any other patient—not someone she had strapped down in a quiet corner of the psych ward.

"Help!" he shouted. "Someone, help me!"

"Oh, Alan, you seem like a smart man. You know that won't accomplish anything. Half of the patients here are paranoid, and these rooms are quite soundproof."

Alan stopped his shouting and looked into the eyes of the strange nurse once again, trying to discern just how crazy she might be. "You're really going to let me go if I'm not a... a werewolf?" he asked. The word felt odd on his tongue.

"I promise," Jillian said, nodding reassuringly.

"Okay." Alan looked out the narrow window next to the bathroom. It was dark outside. He turned his gaze to the nurse. "Well, it's already dark and I'm still human," he said triumphantly, with a smile. He took deep breaths of relief. "I'm human."

"The moon hasn't risen yet," Jillian replied. She checked her watch. "But we'll know in a few minutes."

"Well," Alan said confidently, "I'm sure if I haven't exhibited any symptoms by now, I must be okay."

"Perhaps," Jillian conceded. "Do you feel itchy at all?"

Alan tried not to think about feeling itchy, but of course just the mention of it sparked an itch on the tip of his nose.

"No," he lied.

"How about your joints? Any discomfort?"

"You mean aside from the ache in my shoulder from getting bitten by a dog?"

Jillian inspected the morphine pump across from her on the other side of Alan's bed. "Could be the painkillers are suppressing it," she thought out loud. Then her eyes widened. "When was the last time you shaved?" she asked.

"Yesterday morning, I guess," he answered.

The nurse looked at the hospital room window.

Alan looked over as well.

There was just the edge of the full moon visible, creeping slowly into view.

Suddenly, Alan felt his hands itch. He looked down.

They were covered with a soft, downy layer of brown fur that was slowly thickening. "Oh my God!" he exclaimed. "Oh my God!"

Alan looked at Jillian, who looked at him with now sorrowful eyes.

"No, no, this can't be real. Werewolves are not real. This isn't happening."

Jillian reached into a bag that was sitting next to her on the floor.

"What are you going to do?" Alan asked.

"You're a werewolf, Alan. If I don't stop you, you will change into a horrific beast and kill people."

"Stop me? Stop me how?"

"With a silver bullet, of course," she answered, pulling something out of her bag.

"You're going to shoot me?" he asked. "They'll hear it. You'll never get away. They'll catch you."

Jillian showed Alan a transparent pouch containing a cloudy liquid. "Not that kind of silver bullet," she said as she calmly walked around the bed to the IV stand. She hung the bag on one of the loops at the top, then connected a tube to an opening at the bottom.

"What is that?" Alan asked.

"Colloidal silver," Jillian explained. "Some people use it because they believe it boosts the immune system—which is questionable. But it actually is very good at treating wounds and burns. Fun fact, if you take too much of it, you'll actually turn silver. In your case, though, I'm afraid it will kill you."

"Don't," he begged. "You don't have to do this."

"Yes, I do," she said, and released the clamp that allowed the fluid to mix with his saline line and flow into his veins.

The transformation was progressing faster now. The fur covering his skin was now a thick coat, mostly brown with white patches on his ears and around the muzzle that now protruded from his face.

His bones started to change, reconfiguring themselves into the skeleton of a predator. His teeth thickened and became longer and sharper. His hands and feet transformed into paws, ending in talon-like claws.

The werewolf howled.

Then, its frantic struggle just stopped. It lay still. The heart rate monitor that had been reporting Alan Chaney's vital statistics let out a steady tone.

Jillian switched it off.

She looked at the body strapped to the bed and let out a tear. He hadn't fully transformed, and she could see what remained of his humanity in his eyes. Those frightened eyes set in the face of a horrifying beast.

Surely, when they discovered his body, they would take the anonymous tips she had made to the police more seriously. There was a werewolf on the loose.

Likely more than one.

Jillian scratched at her arm.

There wasn't much time.

She grabbed her bag and stuffed the pouch with the remainder of the colloidal silver into it. She scanned the room for anything else she might have left that could identify her and opened the door to peer into the hallway.

It was empty.

She started walking briskly past the elevators to the stairwell, bounding down the steps two at a time, nearly stumbling as she felt her bones begin to bend and twist. She had learned she could postpone the transfiguration, but not completely stop it.

At the bottom of the stairs was a doorway that let outside to the summer night. She tossed the bag into a nearby dumpster and ran.

With each step, her body changed.

Dark gray fur covered her skin, the shoes she wore split as her feet grew larger and razor-sharp claws sliced through the fabric and laces. The shredded sneakers fell away, discarded among the detritus in the alley.

The scrubs also were torn into shreds as her body changed and grew.

Her face burned in agony as her mouth transformed into a snout. New, enticing scents filled her animal nose and instinct took over.

By the time she reached the end of the alley, she was fully a wolf.

The woman no longer had control over her actions, but she remembered everything as if she was watching a horrifying movie play out in front of her.

She could remember the previous night when she had attacked Alan in the park, her attempt to administer a killing blow thwarted by the thick leather of his jacket.

She could remember the night she had killed her sister.

The wolf turned to face the moon, lifted its head, and howled into the night.

A girl screamed.

The creature turned and saw a pair of humans across the street from her, the female clutching her mate in a panic. He tried to turn, to run away, but the girl's frantic actions caused them both to fall.

The beast snarled, then sprang toward the pair, eyes wide and mouth open.

The Jade Dragon

"Why is it called a drawing room?" Jeremy White asked, as he and his companion entered the wood-paneled chamber, richly appointed with antique furniture, portraits with gilded frames and an enormous Oriental rug. "It doesn't look like anyone does any drawing in here."

"It's derived from the term 'withdrawing room,' a place people withdrew to when they wanted to be alone," Isaac Black explained, as he adjusted the dark glasses that obscured his sightless eyes. "These days, a drawing room is generally used to entertain guests."

"The question was rhetorical, Isaac. There's no one here yet to be impressed," Jeremy told him. "Save the trivia. I've already heard it all."

"You didn't know why it was called a drawing room," Isaac pointed out.

As the rest of the people from the dinner party filed in, Jeremy described the room to Isaac in a low voice. Isaac's hearing was especially acute, and he took in the information his assistant gave him and built a mental map of the room in his mind. He could also hear the others enter the room engaged in conversations carried over from the dinner table. Once Jeremy had finished giving him the lay of the land, he walked across the room, stopped in front of a cushion covered sofa, turned around and sat down, adjusting the cushions behind him.

The performance had the desired effect. A few of the people in the room muttered, "did you see that?" and "I thought he was blind!"

Isaac tried to pick out the sound of his host's voice, David Sorrel. He was the reason Isaac had been invited to this rather exclusive dinner party by way of another one of the guests, Lydia Rosenblum. She was the president of the Amaranth Foundation for the Deaf and Blind, an organization that provided rehabilitative services for the newly disabled.

The organization—and specifically, Lydia—had literally saved Isaac's life. He had been a detective with the Chicago Police Department when he was shot in the head while pursuing a suspect. Miraculously, he had survived, but the injury to his brain left him totally blind. He was in the throes of depression, and seriously considering suicide when Lydia got word of his situation and made available to him all the services required to teach him to live a fulfilling and independent life—including introducing him to Jeremy White, who was initially employed as his nurse, but now functioned more as Isaac's assistant.

To repay her kindness, Isaac began helping Lydia out with her "little mysteries," as she called them. Certain problems that she and her staff, certain donors and beneficiaries of the foundation had, which could be solved by Isaac's particular talents. During his career with the CPD, he had been the detective with the highest clearance rate. And even though he could no longer see, his mind was still as keen as ever. Isaac even asserted that his ability to discern clues that other people overlooked was heightened without the distraction of sight.

David Sorrel was one of the top benefactors to the Amaranth

Foundation, but it didn't matter who it was Lydia asked him to help, Isaac was forever in her debt and thus always at her disposal. She had given him the short version of the problem her donor needed help with. A missing statuette of some sort that was causing quite a rift in the Sorrel household.

Isaac had picked up part of the story during dinner, and even more of the context concerning the relationships between the members of the family. Any sighted person would likely have been able to see the disdain people held for others by the look on their face, but Isaac found he was able to discern even more by the tone in their voices, and especially who talked to whom—and who didn't.

During the dinner, he had answered a few polite questions addressed to him, but for the most part he listened, and by the time dessert was served he had a pretty good idea of the dynamics at play. And in his experience, that was usually where the answers lay.

At the end of the meal, Isaac rose to his feet and clinked his wine class with the edge of his knife. It had the desired effect. The conversations around him abruptly ended, and everyone shifted their attention to him. "Mr. Sorrel, I want to thank you for your kind invitation and the wonderful meal."

"You're quite welcome," David replied.

"I was wondering if this would be a good time for me to help you with the situation Lydia has brought to my attention. Might I suggest we adjourn ourselves to your drawing room?" Isaac didn't wait for an answer. He stepped away from the table and held out his left hand. Jeremy got up and stepped in front of Isaac, positioning his elbow to guide him.

"Uhm, yes, I think that would be fine," David replied.

"Which way?" Jeremy asked.

Their host nodded toward a short hallway and Jeremy began leading Isaac in that direction. It wasn't until they were almost out of sight that the other guests started rising from the table to join them.

And now there were a dozen people crowded into the modestly sized drawing room, most of them forced to stand.

Isaac was alone on the sofa, with only the cushions for company. He turned his gaze, obscured by dark lenses, in the direction of the desk that Jeremy had indicated was to his left, hoping that his assumption that David Sorrel would sit down behind it was correct.

It was.

"I understand something is missing," Isaac said.

Sorrel nodded, then realized he was answering a blind man and said, "Yes, it's a jade statue of a dragon."

"About four inches tall," Isaac told him.

"Precisely," Sorrel said, surprised.

"And the last place you saw it?"

"Right here on my desk," he said, pointing, then added, "on the far right corner."

Isaac nodded.

Sorrel went on. "While I was having a conversation with my brother," he added disdainfully. "About money, of course."

The last statement was obviously a dig, as evidenced by the grunt that came from Sorrel's sibling, Peter.

Isaac ignored the family drama for now. "And when did you notice it was missing?"

David Sorrel had to think about that one for a moment. "It wasn't until the next day, I guess," he admitted.

"Is this jade dragon valuable?" Isaac asked.

"It's priceless," Sorrel stated. "It was a gift to my great-grandfather from the emperor of China."

"I can understand why you're so upset by its disappearance," Isaac said.

He turned to face the direction the indignant grunt from Peter Sorrel had come from earlier. "How long have you been living here with your brother?"

Peter shifted uncomfortably. "I came to stay in the *family* home a month ago. I'm currently making a change in my career and thought it would be a good idea for the children to spend some time with their aunt and uncle," he said.

"The freeloader lost his job," David translated.

The conversation shifted to a well-rehearsed argument between the brothers, with Peter enumerating the generous offers he was considering from various financial firms, while David listed all the failed investments that had left Peter in need of his brother's largess.

Isaac let the conversation play out as he reached out with his left hand and squeezed one of the cushions he was sharing the sofa with, pulling gently on the silk fringe along its edge.

The squabble between the Sorrel brothers quickly faded to silence.

Isaac cocked his head in different directions, trying to determine what had happened to end the quarrel.

"Isaac, the cushion," Jeremy said to him, softly.

"Hmm?" he asked. Isaac actually knew exactly what Jeremy was talking about. He had heard Meredith Sorrel, David's wife, bragging to Lydia about her collection of antique cushions in the drawing room, and he wanted to see if his careless handling of them, let alone his presence on the sofa—which was essentially just an exhibit for them—would dominate any other conversations in the room, no matter how intense.

It did.

Isaac let go of the fringe, gave the cushion a pat, and put his hands in his lap, smiling apologetically.

"I'm sorry, Mr. Black," Meredith Sorrel said, sheepishly. "It's just that those cushions are very old. No one usually sits on that sofa."

Isaac leaned forward to stand.

"No, please," Meredith continued. "It's all right. Just do be careful."

Isaac nodded his understanding and settled back down on the sofa, careful not to scrunch the cushions too much.

"Auntie, Auntie!" came a cry from the doorway accompanied by the patter of children's feet.

Two children wearing pajamas rushed into the drawing room, a boy and a girl who looked to be very close in age.

"Cassie hit me," the boy said.

"Did not," Cassie replied.

"Children, you're supposed to be in bed," Peter Sorrel said. Then, to the rest of the guests, he added, "My apologies. They think they're on holiday. I'm afraid I've been quite indulgent since their mother passed."

Meredith bent down to talk to the children. "You know you're not supposed to be in here. Go back to your rooms and maybe I'll read you a story when we're done."

"Okay, Auntie," Cassie said, the accusations between her and her brother seeming to have been forgotten. They left the room, scampering away just as quickly as they had arrived.

Once they were gone, Meredith addressed the room. "It's so nice having children in the house."

Many of the guests offered statements of agreement.

David grumbled from behind his desk.

"Mrs. Sorrel," Isaac said, "why did you hire a new maid this week?"

Meredith raised a hand to her mouth in surprise. "How on Earth did you know that? She just started on Tuesday. Did you tell him, Lydia?" she asked her guest.

"How could I have known?" Lydia asked back.

Jeremy sighed. This was the part where Isaac got to show off, listing the tiny observations he made during the course of the evening that led to the conclusion that Meredith Sorrel had hired a new maid. It was something Jeremy had seen a hundred times before, so he was quite immune to being impressed by it.

"You had to correct her several times during the dinner service. She obviously doesn't know all of your preferences yet, like an experienced maid would. From what little I heard her speak, she accidentally used the wrong name—I assume she was still used to addressing her former employer. And when you greeted your guests at the beginning of the evening, you apologized to several of them that you couldn't find a photo of your recent vacation that you wanted to show them. I'm guessing she might have placed it in an unfamiliar location after dusting."

"That is remarkable," one of the other women said.

"I told you he was special," Lydia Rosenblum added proudly.

"I assume your last maid had to leave suddenly because of an illness in her family."

"All right, how did you know that?" David asked. "I know for a fact we haven't told anyone why Alice had to leave. Her mother is undergoing chemotherapy, and she decided she needed to go take care of her."

"Because the only suspect you have for the disappearance of your statue is your brother. If it had been the recently replaced maid, I wouldn't be here, so it must have been a personal matter of grave circumstances that called her away," Isaac answered.

"In other words, he guessed," Jeremy said.

"Quite an outstanding guess," a man leaning against the far wall nursing a glass of whiskey said.

"I assume you conducted a thorough search of the house," Isaac said, returning the conversation to the subject at hand.

"Yes, indeed. We've been over every inch of this house," David said, exhausted at just the idea of it. "Alice looked everywhere before she left, and Irene did the same since she arrived. Fresh set of eyes, you know." He looked over at Peter. "I haven't been allowed to search my brother's rooms, though."

"I searched them," Peter answered.

"Yes, so you say. Is one of those supposed job offers you have guarding a henhouse?"

"Careful with your slander, brother. I did not steal the statue. Although, I don't remember father leaving it explicitly to you in his will."

"Father wouldn't have trusted you with his used socks," David declared.

"David, Peter," Meredith said. Her words immediately silenced them as effectively as Isaac's transgression of fondling the cushions had earlier.

"I believe you, Mr. Sorrel," Isaac said, directing his sightless gaze at Peter. "You did not steal the Jade Dragon."

"How can you possibly know that?" David asked. "You've been here all of two hours. You don't know him the way I do."

"Because," Isaac replied simply, "I know exactly where it is."

"You do?" Meredith Sorrel asked.

Isaac nodded.

Everyone waited with anticipation.

"Don't expect him to just say where it is," Jeremy cautioned everyone. "We're not going to get out of here that easy."

"I don't understand," Peter said. "You come into this house, having met everyone for the first time this evening, not being able to see a thing—if Mrs. Rosenblum is to be believed—and you say you know where the Jade Dragon is?"

"That's right," Isaac said.

"Well, as appreciative as I am for your belief in my innocence, I'm afraid I cannot return the favor. I don't for a second believe you know where it is. There's no way you could know."

Isaac answered by reaching under his leg and pulling out the Jade Dragon, holding it up for all to see.

Some of the guests actually applauded, as if it was a performance.

Jeremy rolled his eyes, knowing the reaction would only serve to further inflate Isaac's overblown ego.

"How in God's name did you find that? Where? When?" David asked, utterly surprised.

"It was rather simple," Isaac said.

Jeremy knew that from Isaac's point of view, that was true. And, once he explained himself, everyone else would wonder how they had missed his obvious deductions, but at the moment Jeremy was as lost as the rest of the dinner guests.

"I knew three things coming here tonight. One, that something of great value was missing. Two, that every effort had been made to find it before Lydia engaged my help. And three, since it hadn't been found, it must be somewhere no one had looked."

"Of course it was somewhere no one had looked," Jeremy said. "Otherwise we wouldn't be here."

"Precisely."

"I don't understand," Meredith said, confused. "We've only been talking about it for the last few minutes. I can't for the life of me figure out when you could have deduced where it was, let alone find it and be holding it in your hand."

"You gave me the answer, Mrs. Sorrel," Isaac replied.

"I did?" she asked.

"During dinner, I heard Lydia ask you about the cushions. You were very proud of them and even mentioned how you personally carefully clean them yourself—I assume to make sure they aren't damaged."

"Yes, that's right."

"And I further assume your maid, Alice, and now Irene, were instructed to leave them out of any cleaning routine they did. In fact, I wouldn't be surprised to learn that they weren't allowed to touch them under any circumstances. I sincerely apologize for my actions earlier when I did so. I had to confirm my theory."

"What theory is that?" David asked.

"That the criminals were someone living in this house."

"Criminals? Whatever do you mean?" Meredith asked. "You said it wasn't Peter, and I know it wasn't myself or David."

Jeremy was the first one to catch up with Isaac. "The children," he said, frustrated that he hadn't seen it earlier.

"They were also a topic of conversation at dinner," Isaac explained. "You expressed how delighted you are by their presence, Mrs. Sorrel."

"But the children know not to play in the drawing room," she insisted.

"Exactly," Isaac said. "I don't know about you, but when I was a kid telling me not to do something was a surefire way to get me to do it. I suspect they were playing in here at some point between David and Peter's argument and when the dragon was discovered to be missing. It is one of the few things that would catch a child's attention in this room."

"You still haven't told us where you found it," Peter said.

Isaac smiled. "I found it exactly where I find most of the things I lose in my own home." He spread his arms out. "In between the sofa cushions."

"You must be joking," Jeremy said. "Tell me you're joking."

Isaac turned toward his assistant. "When you described the room to me when we entered, I realized that the only place that no one would have thought to look was the one place that everyone would not even have considered.

"I presumed that the children had been playing in here, the dragon had been either tossed or fell into the sofa—which they knew was even more off limits than the drawing room—and both of them were too afraid to admit what they had done, especially considering the strife the statue's disappearance had caused among the family.

"So, when I had the opportunity, I went directly to the sofa, sat down and slipped my hand between the cushions, found the statue tucked between them, and slipped it under my leg. "

"And made your overly dramatic reveal to impress all of us," Jeremy added.

"I didn't think it was overly dramatic," Isaac said. He rose to his feet, walked over to the desk where David Sorrel was sitting, and placed the statue precisely on the back right corner.

"You must be able to see a little bit," one of the guests accused.

"I can assure you, it is medically impossible for Mr. Black to see anything with severed optic nerves," Jeremy confirmed.

"Thank you," David said.

Peter cleared his throat.

David turned to his brother. "I'm sorry I accused you, Peter. It was wrong of me," he said humbly, for all to hear.

"Apology accepted," Peter replied.

"This has been a most remarkable evening, Mr. Black." David said to Isaac. "I can see why Lydia speaks so highly of you. You made it sound so obvious, but I quite think no one would have ever discovered where the children had left it until after Meredith and myself had passed, and maybe not even then. Not only that, I would have resented my brother for the rest of our lives. I am truly grateful. There must be something I can do to repay you."

Isaac turned to Lydia. "Just keep writing checks to the Amaranth Foundation."

"You can count on it," David assured him.

"As for me, Jeremy mentioned that you have a cocktail cart in this room, and I heard you talking during dinner about a fifty-year-old single malt Scotch Whiskey you had recently acquired. I'm not sure I'll ever have another opportunity to try something like that."

David smiled proudly. He rose from his leather chair, and crossed to the cocktail cart, where he picked up the ornate bottle of The Balvenie Scotch, pulled out the cork and poured a couple ounces into a crystal glass. "Ice?" he asked.

"Is that a trick question?" Isaac asked back. "I'll take it neat."

"Good answer," David said, deeming the detective worthy of drinking it.

Isaac held out his hand and David placed the glass in it. He lifted it to his lips, then paused to allow the aroma to drift into his nose. Then he took a sip, savoring the experience, slowly drinking and enjoying every drop.

They stayed a while longer while Isaac received compliments and praise from the guests, and a particularly strong thank you from Peter, who seemed to carry himself with a renewed sense of pride.

As they were walking out toward their waiting Uber, Jeremy said to his friend. "You know that was a fifty thousand dollar bottle of Scotch."

"Fifty-seven thousand, three-hundred and fifty dollars. And ninety-seven cents," Isaac corrected.

"You could have just asked for a check. We do have bills to pay."

Isaac nodded. "George Bernard Shaw once said, 'Whiskey is liquid sunshine.' And that's the closest I've come to seeing sunshine since I…"

There was no need for Isaac to finish his sentence. Jeremy knew exactly why he had accepted a meager shot of fine whiskey over any amount of money. There were moments, even since he had reinvented himself as a private detective and put the worst of his depression behind him, when he became acutely aware that there were things he would never see again.

Likely, the entrance of the excited children was one that especially hit home.

"Just don't start singing John Denver tunes," Jeremy warned. "Hearing you try to belt out 'Sunshine On My Shoulders' would spoil the moment."

Isaac laughed. "Deal," he said as they got into the back of the Town Car and rode away.

Draw Me a Picture

"You want me to do what?" George asked the tall, unpleasantly gaunt man standing in the hallway just outside his apartment door.

"I need a portrait made," he replied.

That's what George thought he had said. "You want me to draw a picture of you?"

"No, no, not me," he said with a tone of desperation in his voice. He pulled a framed photograph from one of the deep pockets of the long, dark overcoat he wore and offered it to George. "Her."

George took the photo and looked at it. It was of a strikingly beautiful woman clad in an elegant white dress—perhaps a wedding dress. Her hair was a radiant auburn, more red than brown. Her eyes were green, framed by long, dark lashes. And her skin was nearly pure white, bejeweled by a spray of freckles across her cheeks and the bridge of her nose, with more speckling her bare shoulders.

"I don't do portraits, I draw comics," George replied, handing the photo back to the man. "I'm sorry."

"Please," he replied. "I must have a portrait of her, immediately.

And you're the only artist I know—well, know of. I overheard you talking about what you do in the laundry room once or twice." He extended a hand. "My name is Ambrose. Ambrose Hilton," the man said.

"I'm George," George replied. "Nice to meet you."

Ambrose nodded anxiously. "I can pay you," he said, getting back to the subject at hand. "Surely you can do a simple portrait."

"Well, I would love to help you, but I'm in the middle of a big project. I really don't have time to take on any commissions right now. I'm sure you could find someone online who does this sort of work."

"No, no," Ambrose replied vehemently. "That will take too long. It must be done immediately. I will pay you one thousand dollars."

George paused. A thousand dollars would come in handy. He had a small stream of income from his online supporters, but the bulk of the money he had raised to crowdfund the project he was working on wouldn't be available for a couple weeks. And more than one bill was currently overdue.

Ambrose grew impatient. "Two thousand dollars," he said, his tone now approaching panic."

George considered the offer. Two thousand dollars would give him the breathing room he needed to really devote the time his current graphic novel demanded.

But before the artist could reply, Ambrose almost shouted, "Five thousand dollars. Please. I need your help."

George was flabbergasted. Five thousand dollars? He'd never made more than a few hundred dollars from anything before. He saw the desperation in Ambrose's eyes, and wondered if the man might go higher, but he also felt a little guilty and somewhat sorry for whatever circumstances had driven him to make such a desperate offer.

"Okay," George said, as he carried the photo over to his desk, where his computer and digital drawing tablet were. He set the photo next to the monitor. "Give me a couple of days. I'll see what I can do."

"No, you must do it today. By midnight," Ambrose insisted.

"By midnight?" George asked.

"And you can't do it on that thing," the tall man added, waving his hand at the computer. "You have to paint it. On this." He stepped out into the hallway and returned a second later dragging a large rectangular item draped in a sheet—almost too tall to fit through the doorway—into the apartment. Ambrose leaned it against the wall next to George's desk, then pulled the sheet away.

It was a large framed painting of an empty room.

George looked at the massive canvas. It was oddly hypnotic, almost photo realistic, as if you could step into the room it portrayed. It looked like a library—at least there were shelves of books in the background. Also, a table littered with various arcane items. An ornate Persian rug covered the floor.

"I don't paint," George said. "I thought you knew that. I'm a digital artist. I work on my computer."

"You must know how to paint," Ambrose replied.

George had taken several painting classes in art school, but that was almost ten years ago. "Kind of," he admitted. "But even if I could, I don't have any supplies, and it's been years— "

"I have everything you'll need," Ambrose assured him. He disappeared out into the hallway again and returned with a large trunk, which he dragged into the middle of George's apartment. He closed the door, then fished a key from a pocket on the inside of his overcoat and turned it in the lock, securing the chest. He flipped open the lid, then pulled out a set of extending drawers, like the tackle box George's father had once owned. There had to be a hundred small jars of various pigments all lined up in chromatic order. There was also an assortment of brushes, an artist's palette and tins of paint thinner.

George stared down at the assortment of supplies. It looked ancient, not at all like the paints he had used that you squeezed out of a tube. The brushes' handles were ornately carved, the bristles he could tell were some sort of animal hair. "Mr. Hilton, I appreciate your very generous offer, but I don't think I'm the man for the job."

"Seven thousand dollars," Ambrose said. He pulled a stack of cash from yet another pocket and placed it on George's desk. "Here's one thousand now. I'll bring you the rest tonight. You must help me. You must," he implored. "The artist I originally hired backed out on me and this has to be done before midnight."

George looked at the stack of money on his desk. His bank balance had never been that high. He could afford to get a new computer, a new tablet, and pay his rent and overdue utilities for months with that money. But a full size portrait? In oil paint? By midnight?

"Please, try," Ambros begged. "I have faith in you. You can do this."

George glanced at the painting of the empty room, then at the photo of the woman on his desk, then back at the painter's chest. There was something about the collection of paints and brushes that called to him. He picked up one of the brushes and held it in his hand. There was an almost iridescent sheen to the bristles. What kind of hair was it?

"Thank you," Ambrose said, as he started heading for the door. "I have so much to do before midnight. I do have one request, though. I want to watch you finish it. I want to be here when you apply the final brush strokes. It's very important to me that I be present when it is completed."

"Okay," George replied without looking up. He held the brush as he would if he were painting with it, and an almost electrical sensation traveled through his hand and up his arm.

"Thank you, thank you, thank you," the tall man repeated as he let himself out of the apartment.

George looked at the painting. He could almost see the woman standing there, one hand resting on the desk, the other gently caressing the golden locket that hung around her neck just above her breasts.

He set the brush down, then extracted the photo of the woman from the wood and glass enclosing it and taped it to the frame of the large painting.

He was suddenly filled with confidence.

Yes, he could do this. He checked the chest and was glad to see there was plenty of white paint he could use to render the dress and her porcelain skin. He opened one of the jars and scooped out some of the bright pigment with a thin, flat blade and plopped it onto the palette. He scanned the other colors and picked the ones that he knew—he just absolutely knew—where the right ones to capture the hues in her hair and eyes.

Then he picked up the brush again, and that same electric feeling shot through him, energizing him.

If he had been watching himself work, or viewing a recording of it, George wouldn't have recognized himself. It was as if he was possessed. Like someone was standing inside him, guiding his arm, choosing the right brush for the right stroke in the right place.

Before he knew it, he had painted her entire body and most of her head. Her elegant form took on the same photorealistic depth as the background. Her hair looked as if it was almost subtly moving in a gentle breeze. Her lips were slightly parted in a mischievous smile, and her perky nose was perfectly symmetrical, and made even more beautiful by the band of freckles splashed across it.

He painted the eyes last. Those hypnotic green eyes.

George forgot all about Ambrose's request that he be present when he finished the portrait. There was nothing that could have stopped him. He was compelled to complete her.

Two perfect dabs of the darkest black paint created pupils in those entrancing eyes, pupils that opened into something beyond the ebon pigment.

The artist lost himself in those eyes. They were so real. Beyond anything he had done before. He glanced at the clock.

It was almost six.

He had been painting for nine hours straight, and although he was hungry, it was sleep he needed more. He picked up the sheet that had been draped over the painting previously, covered the portrait, walked the eight steps to his bed and fell asleep the moment his head hit the pillow.

George awoke with a start. Had he heard a noise? He got up, his hunger now insisting he get something to eat. He made a pit stop in the bathroom, then shuffled to the kitchenette in one corner of the apartment, yawning and stretching. Then he opened the fridge and stared at the collection of condiments, grabbed a can of Mountain Dew, pulled the tab and took a long, satisfying drink.

He opened the freezer, pulled out a Hot Pocket, and stuck it in the microwave.

Something was wrong. There was a nagging feeling in the back of his mind, something he had seen out of the corner of his eye. He turned around and looked over at the canvas leaning against the wall next to his desk.

The sheet was gone.

And the canvas showed a painting of an empty room.

George dropped the can of soda and a green, fizzing puddle grew on the floor.

"What the hell?" he exclaimed.

Had he dreamed it all?

No, it had been real, *so* real, *so* powerful. He could still remember the feeling of the paint dragging across the canvas, the smell of it on the palette.

He saw the sheet balled up on the sofa. How had it gotten there? He glanced at the clock over his desk. A few minutes past nine. There was no way he could finish before Ambrose's deadline. He'd have to give the money back.

George snatched the sheet off the sofa.

The woman he revealed gasped.

George screamed.

The woman screamed.

They both screamed.

The microwave beeped.

"Who are you? What are you doing here?" George asked as he stepped away from her. His bare foot hit a patch of Mountain Dew and he slipped and fell hard.

"Am I in hell?" she asked

"Hell?" George asked back. He looked around the apartment. It was a little messy, but still.

"I am dead, am I not? I remember dying. I remember wasting away in a hospital bed and closing my eyes for the last time," she said. "And then I woke up."

The woman uncurled herself from the fetal position she had been balled up in on the sofa. She sat up, then stood, cautiously.

George couldn't believe it. It was her. The woman from the photograph. The woman he had painted. Here, in the flesh.

She wore the same white gown, the golden locket hung around her neck, her radiant hair fell lightly on her shoulders and those eyes… those beautiful green eyes. He even recognized every tiny freckle he had meticulously applied to her milky skin.

Had he done this? Had he brought her to life? Was there some kind of magic in those brushes? Those paints? Had Ambrose known this would happen? Is that why he was so insistent that he be here when George finished?

"Who are you?" the woman asked.

"I'm George," he replied. He got to his feet, rubbing his tailbone. "Who are you?"

"My name is Jessica," she said. "How did I get here?"

"I think I painted you here," George confessed, turning his gaze to the painting of the empty room.

"That's where I woke up," Jessica said as she crossed the room on long, slender legs that seemed to barely touch the floor. She reached out toward the painting, expecting her hand to pass right through, but it stopped when it hit the canvas. "How is this possible?" she asked.

"I don't know," George answered. "But I think you and me both have a lot of questions for Ambrose."

Jessica gasped. "Ambrose? He's behind this?"

"He must be. He's the one who hired me to paint you, and brought that canvas and the paints."

She became alarmed. "He mustn't find me. You have to protect me."

"From what?" George asked. "He's a little weird, but he didn't seem dangerous to me."

"But he is!" Jessica insisted. "Whatever he has done, it is only so he can possess me. To own me. He was my lover, once."

"Ambrose?" George had a hard time picturing the tall, gangling, plain man with such a beautiful woman.

"Yes. At first he was kind, but then his true nature came through. He kept me a prisoner. I wasn't allowed to see anyone else. He was so jealous, so mean." She started to sob.

George didn't know what to do. He took a few steps toward her, then she closed the distance and threw her arms around him, squeezing him tight as she cried. George put a hand on her back and gently patted it. "Don't worry, everything is going to be all right," he promised. What else was he going to say?

Jessica withdrew and wiped away her tears with the back of her hand.

George quickly grabbed a couple of tissues from the box on his desk and offered them to her.

"Thank you," she said as she dabbed at her cheeks. "Where is he?" she asked, suddenly afraid. "Is he nearby?"

"He's probably downstairs in his apartment. He lives on the basement level. I don't really know him that well. We've shared an elevator a couple times, but he honestly didn't seem like—"

"You don't know him the way I do," she cautioned.

"Well, that's true," George agreed. "I guess this explains why he wanted me to wait for him to come back just before midnight to finish," George said, remembering Ambrose's request.

Jessica gasped. "Oh my, so it's true. He is a master of the dark arts.

He told me I would never be able to escape him, even in death. He found a way to bring me back. And now, it's going to happen all over again." She started sobbing once more.

George took her by the elbow and led her to the sofa.

"Please don't let him," she pleaded as they sat down. "Please, you have to help me."

"How?" he asked. "What can I do? Shouldn't you go to the police?"

Jessica looked at the artist as if he was crazy. "The police? And tell them what? That I've been dead for—what year is it?"

"Twenty-twenty-two," George replied.

"Thirteen years?" she uttered in disbelief. "They'll think I'm crazy. They'll lock me up. And then he'll find me and take me. He'll never let me go." She dabbed at her tears again with the tissue. "Oh, if only Marcus was here. He would know what to do."

"Marcus?" George asked. "Who's that?"

"Marcus Fairchild, the man I was with before Ambrose."

"Well, let's call him,"

Jessica shook her head, and her face wrinkled up as she started crying even harder. "We can't. Marcus died before I did, in a horrible accident. I always believed Ambrose was responsible." She reached for the locket hanging around her neck and opened it.

Inside was a two inch tall photograph of a man wearing a white suit. The type of outfit a groom might wear at a wedding. Although the photo was tiny, George recognized the background to be the same as the one Jessica was pictured with.

"Oh, Marcus, I miss you so much."

George struggled to think. Maybe he could get her to a woman's shelter or something.

Before he could speak, Jessica's distraught visage lit up with hope. She smiled at George. "You," she said to George. "You can save me."

"Me? I'm just a guy who draws comics on the web. You need a lawyer, or a private detective, somebody like that."

"You brought me back," she reminded him.

"That wasn't me. It was the paints, the brushes."

She held up the locket so the picture of Marcus was facing George. "You can bring him back, too."

"What?" George asked? "No, no way. I'm not doing that again."

"Oh, please," she said, those green eyes beckoning. "You're my only hope. If I can come back, then Marcus can come back and we can have the life we were supposed to."

George looked at the photo. It was so tiny. "I don't think I can," he said. "That's such a small picture. I mean, when I painted you, I had something with some detail in it. I can't even tell what color his eyes are."

"They're gray," she said. "Such beautiful gray eyes."

Then an idea occurred to George. "Wait a second. Let me try something." He grabbed a digital camera from his desk. It had a super hi-res sensor. Maybe he could blow it up enough… "Can I have that for a second?" he asked Jessica.

She took the locket from around her neck and handed it to him.

George placed it on his desk and zoomed in on the man within, hoping the camera would be able to compensate for his shaking hands. He checked the result on the small screen on the back of the camera, then fished out the memory card and slid it into a reader attached to his computer. A few clicks of his mouse later, he had the image blown up on the monitor. He could clearly tell the man's eyes were gray, his hair was jet black, his skin deeply tanned yet youthful.

Jessica clapped her hands in delight. "I knew you could do it. You're so clever!" she said, grabbing George into a hug and planting a kiss on his cheek.

He blushed.

"You must hurry. It has to be done by midnight," she urged.

"Midnight? Why?"

"Isn't that when you said Ambrose is coming back?"

"Yes, but it took me nearly nine hours to do yours."

The smile on Jessica's face turned into a disappointed frown. "You have to. You have to at least try."

George got lost in those green eyes again. The brushes seemed to call out to him. He loaded the palette with the colors he needed to get started and grabbed the largest brush. It seemed to charge him up with an energy he'd never felt before.

His hand moved in large, broad strokes. Tiny gestures introduced subtle details and the shape of a man quickly appeared on the canvas, a man wearing a white wedding suit, with hair as dark as the night, and eyes as gray as an oncoming storm.

George lost track of the time. He was a man possessed with a level of skill he'd only ever dreamed of having. When he was almost done, he took a step back and was surprised to find himself soaked in sweat. He glanced at the clock.

Ten minutes till midnight.

Had it only been less than three hours? It felt like he'd been painting all night.

"Oh, George, it's perfect," Jessica told him. "Finish it. We're almost out of time."

George dipped the very tip of his brush into the black paint and dabbed two identical circles of it in the center of each of Marcus's gray eyes.

Portals to his very soul.

George felt a light kiss on his cheek.

"You did it," Jessica said. "I knew you could."

He looked over at Jessica, expecting to see her smiling, happy face. But instead, she had a fierce expression, primal and lustful. She was staring directly at the portrait of her long lost lover.

George looked back at the painting and dropped the brush he was holding when it began to move.

Marcus blinked his eyes, then turned his head from side to side. He lifted his hands in front of his face in wonderment. He mouthed something, but the sound didn't make it out of the painting.

Then the imposing figure stepped forward, crossing the Persian rug and stepped out onto the dirty carpet of George's apartment.

"Jessica," he said aloud. His voice was deep and full of promises yet to keep.

"Marcus," she answered, throwing her arms around him and giving him a long, passionate kiss.

There was a knock at the door.

The couple parted.

"It's Ambrose," Jessica said, as if it was a warning.

"Ambrose," Marcus repeated. Then he noticed George standing a few steps away. "Who's this?"

"That's George. He's the artist."

Marcus smiled. "Indeed he is. Ambrose chose well."

"Wait, what?" George asked. Something about what he said didn't make sense. How did Marcus know Ambrose would choose an artist to bring Jessica back to life?

"Answer the door," Marcus commanded.

George nodded, then crossed to the door and opened it, forgetting all the warnings Jessica had given him about how vile the tall man was.

"Is it ready?" Ambrose asked, a hopeful smile on his face. "How does she look?"

George stepped aside, and Ambrose's expression shifted from joy to fear.

"Jessica! Marcus?" he asked. "How?"

Marcus laughed.

That was not at all what George had expected.

"What have you done?" Ambrose asked the artist. "I told you to wait."

"I'm sorry," George replied. "I didn't do it on purpose. I just got caught up in it."

Ambrose turned to Jessica. "But you told me you wanted to be with me. That if I was able to bring you back on this night, we would have the rest of our lives together. And you're here. You're healthy. Why?"

"Oh, you poor man," Jessica said, dripping with pity. "You played your part, but did you really think I would ever want to spend one more second with you than I absolutely needed to get what I wanted?"

"I don't understand," George said. "I thought you were afraid of him."

"Afraid of Ambrose? Is that what you told him, my dear?" Marcus asked Jessica.

"It did persuade my new friend George to paint your portrait before midnight."

George looked at Ambrose, who seemed shocked and surprised. "She told me you were a warlock or something, and you kept her prisoner and wanted to possess her forever."

Ambrose shook his head. "She told me the same thing about Marcus. She begged me on her deathbed to get that chest and that canvas and then hire an artist to paint her portrait on it, on this day before midnight. And we'd be together. Forever."

"Yes, well, slight change in plans," Jessica said, clutching Marcus as he placed his arm around her.

Ambrose looked at George. "Why didn't you wait for me?"

"He didn't have any choice on that account. He wasn't exactly painting alone," Marcus explained, casting a glance down at the artist's chest.

George looked at it as well and saw something he hadn't noticed before. A monogram in the bottom left corner. The initials M.F.

Marcus Fairchild.

George wondered if he actually had been possessed.

"You'll never get away with this," Ambrose promised.

"Ah, but we already have," Marcus gloated. "The first time around we discovered Jessica's illness too late, and I unfortunately met my untimely end trying to cure her. But there was always Plan B. You should always have a Plan B. Things never go the way you expect them to. And you, Ambrose, always had a fondness for Jessica. We knew we could count on you to carry out our plans—albeit unwittingly.

"The tricky part was the timing. Would you follow through on her request to paint her portrait on this particular date, so far into the future? The Canvas only works in this manner only once every hundred years or so, and then only for a day. Jessica promised me you were so infatuated with her that you would be a dependable custodian of the means of our reunion."

Ambrose roared in anger. He charged the couple, but Marcus deftly drew a pistol from a holster hidden under his jacket and fired twice.

The tall man clutched at his chest, then started to fall, right toward the painting of the once again now empty room.

Marcus waved his hand at the painting, mumbling a few unrecognizable syllables and instead of crashing through the canvas, Ambrose fell *into* the room.

George looked closely. His neighbor's lifeless body, splayed out on the Persian rug, was now part of the painting. He looked over at Marcus, lifting his hands into the air in surrender, praying he wouldn't meet the same fate.

"Oh, put your hands down," Marcus commanded. "I'm not going to hurt you."

George put his hands down. His eyes wandered toward a poster on his wall of a young Marylin Monroe.

"Sorry," Marcus said. "It won't work again. But keep painting." He looked Jessica up and down and spun her around, smiling. "You've got a real talent."

The couple walked out of the apartment, closing the door behind them.

George collapsed into his desk chair and brought up the project he was working on before Ambrose had pounded on his door earlier that day. He eyed the stack of money that was sitting next to the monitor.

In all the excitement, he forgot that Ambrose still owed him six thousand dollars.

He looked over at the painting of his dead neighbor and saw that spilling out of one of his coat pockets was a stack of new one hundred dollar bills.

Reset

"My life sucks," I said, lying on my back on the somewhat uncomfortable couch of my therapist's office.

"Have you tried turning it off and back on again?" Dr. Pototo replied while scribbling furiously on the small pad she held in her lap.

"Excuse me?"

"You know, just reboot."

"I'm not a computer," I said dismissively, wondering where my stodgy therapist had suddenly found a sense of humor.

She paused her writing and peered at me over the tortoiseshell frames of her reading glasses. "You do realize all of this is a simulation," she said plainly.

I stared back at her, waiting for her middle-aged features to break into a mischievous smile.

Such an expression of humor was not forthcoming.

"Do you mean to claim that you haven't heard of simulation theory?" she remarked, returning her gaze to her notepad and resuming her scribbling.

I actually was familiar with the concept she was talking about. The theory goes that just as we can create simulations like those in computer games or scientific models of biological processes or the earth's climate, it stands to reason that eventually we will be able to create one that matches the complexity of what we know as "real life." And if that simulation is advanced enough, it could create another simulation and so on. So, mathematically, it is almost a certainty that our existence is merely a simulation being run by either an extremely advanced race of beings, or a byproduct of a simulation creating a simulation perhaps several layers deep. It was enough to make your head spin.

"That's just pure speculation," I said, dismissively.

"Really?" she asked. "Then how do you explain Tik Tock millionaires? Honestly, social media influencer as a job? And what about octopi and platypi? The fact that the moon always shows the same side to the Earth. The Big Bang. Nicolas Cage, a sex symbol? In fact, look no further than my name, Pototo. It sounds like someone's discarded typo for the word potato. The signs are all around you."

I thought about what she said. I had to admit, the Nicolas Cage thing had perplexed me since my youth, but the fact that the moon completed exactly one rotation per revolution around the earth so that it constantly presented the same face all the time was merely physics, wasn't it? Or was it just a lazy programmer not wanting to design the back side?

The therapist finally noticed that I had stopped talking, or perhaps merely ran out of things to write about me on her pad, and sat back and stared at me with a pitying expression. "Surely I'm not the first one to tell you that you're not really real."

"Yes, as a matter of fact, you are," I replied, a note of anxiety creeping into my voice.

She looked at me as if trying to remember something, then returned her attention to her notepad and started flipping back the pages scanning for something. "Oh, right, my mistake. You're an NPC. You're supposed to be oblivious to all of those details. Sorry.

So…" she flipped back to the page she had been previously writing on. "Your life sucks. Tell me more about that."

"An NPC?" I asked. "You think I'm a Non-Playing Character?"

"Yes, but don't let that bother you. Most people are."

"But you're not?"

"No, of course not," she said with a laugh. "Don't be ridiculous. Now, please focus. Your life sucks…"

"Is this a joke? Is there some equivalent to April Fool's Day in September that I'm not aware of? What kind of therapist are you? Aren't you supposed to try to make me feel better? Now, in addition to dealing with my depression, I have to worry that my life is just a series of bits and bytes that mean nothing because I'm just a pre-programmed sprite bouncing around some random simulation."

"Actually, you're probably made of qubits. Quantum computing is much more likely to be the foundation of a massive simulation like this."

"Whatever!" I shouted, as I sat up and glared at Dr. Pototo. "How can you expect me to talk about my problems after telling me that it all just doesn't matter?"

She shrugged. "As I said, my mistake, but please do try to put it out of your mind."

"I can't!" I insisted, raising my voice to just under a shout. "It's all I can think about now. Why did you have to say that?"

"Say what?"

"'Have you tried turning it off and back on again.'"

"Well, that usually does the trick, doesn't it?"

"You want me to kill myself and come back to life?"

"No, no," Dr. Pototo said, shaking her head. "Don't do that. I didn't mean it literally. I was thinking you could do a reset, return to a previous save point and clear out some of the complications you've accumulated. I would do it for you, but I do enjoy the challenge of trying to help with talk therapy. It's very challenging."

"Save point? I don't have a reset button!" I said, wondering why I was still sitting in this office, allowing this woman to mess with my head.

Dr. Pototo sighed. "All right, since this is partially my fault—"

"Partially?" I asked.

She ignored my question. "—I'll tell you where to find your control panel so you can reset and forget all about this."

"Really, it's that simple. Then why am I paying you a hundred bucks an hour?"

"Do you want my help or not?" she asked, folding her notebook closed and resting it and her hands in her lap.

"Okay, sure," I said, humoring her, wondering if I would be able to cancel the automatic withdrawals she was making on my credit card.

"When you get home, open your bedroom closet and look for a spot about the size of a paperback book on the back wall that feels like it doesn't belong."

"What do you mean 'feels like' it doesn't belong?"

"Have you ever done one of those Magic Eye posters, where it looks like a random pattern of some sort, but if you cross your eyes slightly, you see a three dimensional picture?"

"Sure," I said. I actually was quite good at viewing them—much to the frustration of my girlfriend, who never could make them work for her.

"Stare at the back wall of your closet and try to do that."

"Then what?"

"Then when you find the spot, trace its outline with your finger and you'll have access to your control panel. Find the button that says 'Revert to Previous Save Point' and then pick a time and place before you were burdened with your current problems."

"My control panel," I repeated.

"Exactly."

"Revert to previous…"

"Save point," she finished for me.

"Gotcha," I said.

She looked at me and smiled, giving me the clear indication that our session was over.

I spent a good half hour slowly meandering my way back to my apartment, spending half the time furious with Dr. Pototo at wasting my time—or worse, mocking me—and the other half wondering if it was true. Obviously it wasn't, but how did Nicholas Cage score that role opposite Cher in Moonstruck?

No, no, that was crazy. I remember hearing that his uncle was some famous director, Scorcese or Copolla—one of those gangster movie guys. I resolved that as soon as I got home, I was going to look up whatever agency or department regulated psychologists in this state and file a formal complaint.

When I did return to my apartment, however, instead of heading straight for my computer, I found myself standing in front of my bedroom closet.

A part of me was starting to push aside the crazy notion that I was just a secondary character in a simulation, and I suspected that by morning, the daily chaos that was my life would erase the notion from my consciousness altogether.

But another part of me was wondering, *what if…?*

I opened the closet door, grabbed the shirts and jackets hanging off the rod, and tossed them onto my bed. Once I had a clear view of the back wall of my closet, I stared at it, trying to stare past it as if I was deciphering an optical illusion.

And then I saw it.

A faint rectangle in the upper left corner.

Without thinking, I reached out and traced its outline with the finger of my right hand.

And a screen appeared.

I nearly fell as I stepped back in surprise.

There it was. My control panel.

It was all true.

I could feel my heart racing, my breathing becoming shallower, my vision constricting as if I was going to pass out.

I leaned over, allowing the blood to rush back to my brain, then immediately thought, *what blood? What brain?* I was just qubits. But apparently, my qubits followed specific physiological rules that affected me just as if I was real—whatever reality was. Maybe I was dreaming? Only this didn't feel like a dream. It was too coherent.

Once I got myself back under control, I stood up and inspected the panel. My name was prominent at the top and next to it was the button labeled "Revert to Previous Save Point." But my attention was drawn to a series of... properties, I guess, is the best word to describe them. There were dozens visible, but I could see that they were part of a scrolling list. I reached out and touched the screen, wondering if it worked in the same manner as my phone.

It did. I was able to scroll through the list and see the settings for hundreds of aspects of my life. There near the top was "Anxiety," and its value was 92. Between the property name and the value was a slider control, positioned almost all the way to the right. I reached out and moved it to the left. As I did so, the number changed from 92 to 31.

Suddenly, I felt as if a great burden had been lifted from me. All the thoughts that constantly filled my mind with uncertainty and fear—would I lose my job, could I pay my rent, did I have cancer—were gone, or at least greatly diminished.

I scrolled down and spotted confidence and raised it from 27 to 85.

Then I continued searching for more settings with a determination and purpose I had never felt before.

Perseverance, 35 to 90.

Fear, 75 to 15.

I noticed that there was a tab at the top of the list that had different categories. In addition to the psychological settings, there was one for physical and one for environmental.

In the physical settings, I adjusted my height from five-foot-four to an even six foot. Fortunately, my clothes changed along with my body. I changed my hair from balding to luxurious. And my musculature from "Dad Bod" to "Athletic."

Under the environmental settings, I increased my wealth from $4,342 to $1,000,076—I didn't want to be too greedy, but I also upgraded my Honda Civic to a Porsche Spyder.

I felt amazing.

Okay, I had to admit, it was a little disconcerting to discover that the world was indeed just a simulation, but at the same time, I now had a level of control over my life that people would kill for. Now my life was suddenly... good. I no longer had to worry about making ends meet, wondering why other people won life's lottery, and I always seemed to get the short end of the stick. Now *I* had the Golden Ticket.

And I was going to use it.

I picked out a shirt I had bought years earlier and never wore because I didn't think it looked good on me. Now, when I slipped it on and buttoned it across my sculpted abs and pecs, it looked amazing.

I went into the bathroom and picked up my comb to make sure my hair was strategically covering the balding spots, only to find I had a coif that would make Patrick Dempsey jealous. I looked at my teeth, then rushed back into my bedroom to up them from "slightly askew" and "yellow" to "perfectly straight" and "gleaming white."

Then I noticed that the fob for my Porsche was on the corner of the kitchen counter where I normally threw the keys to my Civic.

I rushed outside, clicked the unlock button and found my yellow 918 Spyder parked across the street. I got in and drove to Emily's house.

I wondered if she would recognize me? Would my girlfriend of two years would be surprised at the changes I had assigned myself, or would she would even notice?

I rang the bell and got my answer.

"Jeremy!" she shouted as she threw her arms around my neck and pulled herself up for a passionate kiss. That was new, but I wasn't complaining. "What a nice surprise. I didn't think I was going to see you until Saturday."

"I couldn't wait that long," I told her, smiling. My relationship with Emily had always been one of the things I worried about. In my mind, she was a solid six, bordering on seven, while I was at best a high four or low five, and considered myself lucky that she didn't realize she was out of my league.

But now I was a nine, nine-and-a-half. And my paranoia that she was constantly looking to trade up was gone.

But I wondered…

"Let's go to the bedroom," I suggested.

"Jeremy!" she admonished playfully. "I'm a mess."

"You're always beautiful to me," I assured her.

She blushed, then placed her hand in mine and bashfully led me to her bedroom. "Just give me a minute in the bathroom, okay?"

"Sure," I replied.

Emily smiled and disappeared behind the bathroom door.

I went to her closet.

It was jammed with blouses and dresses and pants and shorts. I tore them all down from the rack and dumped them on the closet floor.

Then I stood back and let my focus drift, searching for her control panel.

There it was. Right in the center. I traced its outline, and the screen appeared.

I scrolled through her psychological menu, noting that her libido was already set pretty high, but nudged her self-confidence up a few points.

Under the physical menu, I increased her cup size from A to C and took her weight down a few pounds. She had always complained about both, and I figured it wouldn't do any harm. But that's all I changed—except under her environmental settings I did tweak her bed size from "Full" to "California King" to accommodate my increased stature.

I closed the closet door just as Emily emerged from the bathroom. She was wearing the silk kimono I had given her a couple Christmases before. She always looked great in it, but now she was absolutely stunning.

"Are you ready?" she asked.

I nodded eagerly, and we spent the rest of the afternoon in bed until we were both exhausted and completely satisfied.

The next morning, I left before Emily awoke. I knew she had to get to work, and if I stayed, I risked making her late. Besides, I had my own job to get to.

I hated my job, but did I have to?

I rushed home and opened my closet door. The control panel was gone, so I stared past the back wall once again, traced the outline, and brought it back to life. I scrolled through the environmental settings until I found the Job option and slid it from "worker" to "CEO." Then I thought better of it and backed it off to "VP of Marketing." Actually, I didn't need a job any more considering my hefty bank balance, but there were a couple of scores I wanted to settle before I retired.

I drove to the office and pulled my Porsche into my reserved parking space.

I took the private elevator up to the executive suite, strode confidently to my glass-walled office exchanging pleasantries with my assistant and sat down behind the wide wooden desk. My photo of Emily smiled at me. I smiled back, enjoying the peace and quiet of my own space, no longer stuck in those cramped, open-plan workstations I used to work at.

"Johnson? What are you doing in that office?" A voice asked.

I looked over at my office door to see my old manager, Eric, standing there, a perplexed look on his face.

Why did it bother him that I was here? Everyone else took it in stride, as if it had always been this way.

"I thought you were an NPC!" he stated condescendingly.

"A what?" I replied, trying to play ignorant.

He pulled out his phone and started tapping furiously at the screen. "Ah ha!" he said. "I was right. You are an NPC. Who bumped you up to VP? Was it Killian? Or Farnsworth?"

"I don't know what you're talking about," I said. "Maybe you should get back to work. I have a lot on my plate and I don't have time for your jokes."

He laughed. "Wow, someone really messed with your settings." He continued tapping away at his phone. Then his eyes widened. "I knew it." He smiled and looked at me, shaking his head. "Back to the sales department for you." He swiped at this screen, gently at first, then more purposefully. "Damn. I'm locked out." He stared at me for a moment, then appeared to have an idea. "Moorehead should have high enough access. I'll just revert you to a previous save point and you'll be back to your miserable self."

Eric slipped his phone in his pocket and started walking toward the corner office where the CEO, Michelle Moorehead ruled the roost.

I stepped out of my office and checked my Rolex.

It changed into a Timex.

Dammit! I wasn't going down without a fight.

"Hold all my calls," I said to my assistant, then raced for the elevator then out of the building.

My Porsche was gone, but I spotted my Civic parked at the far end of the lot. As I ran toward it, I could feel my strides shortening as my height and subsequently my inseam shrunk back to their previous settings.

I drove like a madman, racing to my apartment, leaving my car double-parked and bounded up the stairs of my building. I fumbled with keys and doors until I was finally back at my bedroom closet, staring at the back wall.

Only I couldn't see it. That faint rectangle was beyond my ability to discern it.

I stopped, took a deep breath, stepped back a little, then tried again.

My focus loosened as I stared past the wall.

Suddenly, there it was. It was no longer in the upper left corner, but near the floor. I reached down and traced the outline, and my control panel appeared.

I breathed a sigh of relief.

Then I noticed that the "Revert to Previous Save Point" button was flashing, and instead of the words it previously displayed, there was a countdown message, "Reverting to Save Point in..." and a robotic voice started counting down. "10... 9..."

How could I stop it? If it reverted as it promised, then I would forget everything, even how to access my settings. Everything I had changed would go away. Emily would leave me.

There was no obvious cancel button, but I noticed a small icon near the bottom that looked like a warning sign, a yellow triangle with an exclamation point inside of it. I tapped it.

A new screen appeared, but the Save Point button continued counting down.

"7... 6..."

There was a menu of advanced settings.

One of them was labeled, "Upgrade NPC to Autonomous mode."

"5... 4..."

I smashed it.

A new dialog box appeared with a seemingly endless list of Autonomous Mode Preferences.

"3... 2..."

I didn't have time for this. There was a button near the top that was marked, "Randomize Preferences."

"1..."

I tapped it.

I sat in a comfortable leather chair while a woman lay reclined on an oddly familiar couch. There was a notepad in my lap and a pen in my hand and I wore wire rim reading glasses.

"My life sucks," the woman said with a tone of despair and hopelessness.

I smiled.
"Have you tried turning it off and back on again?"

The Snow Bully

The snowball hit Ralph's head at just the right angle and in just the perfect spot to knock his glasses from his face and send him tumbling into the snowbank next to the sidewalk outside of the school.

Cory Binger laughed, joined by a chorus of his lackeys.

Ralph pulled his face out of the snow and got to his knees. He looked at the small crowd of students who had gathered just behind Cory and his crew, but couldn't make out anything but the colorful shapes of their winter coats without his glasses.

"Have a nice trip?" Cory asked. A classic zinger that the bully never seemed to tire of.

His entourage provided the obligatory laugh track.

The warning bell rang out from the school, signaling that it was getting close to first period.

Cory led his gang toward the building and the other students who had been watching Ralph's humiliation filed past him as he looked about in vain for his missing glasses.

Sarah Firestone approached, reached into the snowbank and

pulled out the missing eye wear. She handed them to Ralph.

"Thanks," Ralph said. He put his glasses on and got to his feet, smiling gratefully.

Sarah rolled her eyes. "You're such a loser, Ralphy," she said, then turned her back on him and followed the last of the students into the school.

Ralph brushed the snow off his pants, grabbed his backpack, and ran to catch up.

It was the last week before Christmas vacation, and today there was a special assembly he didn't want to miss. A ventriloquist was coming to put on a show. Ralph had never seen a real ventriloquist in person. He'd seen them on TV, and his grandpa said there used to be one on the radio—but that seemed like it would be cheating if you couldn't see him.

The assembly wasn't until seventh period, and the day seemed to drag on in slow motion as Ralph sat through all his classes, doodling in his notebook.

Finally, the bell rang, signaling it was time to head to the auditorium. Teachers led small herds of students down the hall and filed them into pre-assigned rows.

Ralph was lucky. Ms. Hamilton's class was in the third and fourth rows. He was unlucky, however, that the class Cory Binger was in was seated right behind him.

Fortunately, the teacher knew how to handle the bully and, after his first few attempts to annoy Ralph, Cory was kept at bay.

The lights dimmed.

The murmur of the students fell to a low whisper as Mr. Weatherton, the principal, walked out onto the stage to address the class.

"Welcome to the winter assembly," he began, "I want you all to give a warm Thomas Alva Edison School welcome to Mr. Smith and Grumpy!"

The curtain opened as Mr. Weatherton departed.

A spotlight shined on an empty spot on the left side of the stage.

"Hey, what are you doing? We're over here!" a high-pitched voice shouted from the dark.

The spotlight moved to a stool in the middle of the stage where a tall, thin man wearing one of those flat caps Ralph's grandfather sometimes wore sat. Sitting on his lap was a small clown, dressed in a dingy white clown suit with droopy pom-poms and a frilly collar. He wore bright blue shoes and white gloves. His hair was bright red, his face was white, and he had an outline of a frown painted around his mouth.

Grumpy was certainly the perfect name for the ventriloquist's dummy.

"Why did you bring me to the zoo?" Grumpy asked Mr. Smith.

"We're not at the zoo," Mr. Smith replied. "We're at a school."

Grumpy peered out at the audience. "Are you sure we're not at the monkey house?" he asked.

The kids laughed.

"It smells like we're at the monkey house," Grumpy said. Then he turned to Mr. Smith and sniffed his shirt. "No, wait, that's you."

The kids laughed again.

Ralph was impressed. Mr. Smith's lips barely moved whenever Grumpy spoke, and the puppet had a wide range of expressions. Even his eyes moved.

The show went on for more than half an hour. Mr. Smith kept on promising that Grumpy would sing a Christmas carol, but he never seemed to get around to it until the very end. Then he sang a version of "Frosty the Snowman," in which he mangled all the verses to the amusement of the kids.

When the show was over, Mr. Weatherton returned to the stage and thanked Mr. Smith and Grumpy. "Do you like being a zookeeper?" Grumpy asked the principal, and the kids laughed again.

"Sorry," Mr. Smith said to Mr. Weatherton. Then he turned to his dummy. "Say goodbye, Grumpy."

Grumpy turned to the students and said, "Goodbye, Grumpy!"

Everyone clapped as the curtains closed and the lights came back on.

The final bell rang, and the auditorium became a free-for-all. The teachers lost all authority over the kids as they ran toward their lockers and freedom.

Ralph waited for the main rush to leave before making his own exit. He got his backpack and coat from his locker, then spied Cory and his gang waiting at the main entrance to the school. So, instead of going out that way, he made his way to the back door that led out to the teachers' parking lot.

The teachers' cars were all still there—they usually hung around for a half hour or so after school ended. At the end of the parking lot was a van, with "Mr. Smith and Grumpy" painted in big circus letters across its side.

Ralph saw Mr. Smith carrying Grumpy out to the van. The tall man opened the side door and set Grumpy inside, then climbed in himself. As he did so, the top of the door frame caught the brim of his flat cap and it fell from Mr. Smith's head onto the pavement of the parking lot. The side door of the van slid shut on a motorized track, then the vehicle pulled away.

Ralph ran over, shouting and waving. "Wait, wait! Mr. Smith! You dropped your hat!"

But Mr. Smith didn't hear him, and the van turned onto the street and drove away.

Ralph picked up the flat cap and turned it over in his hands. It seemed old and was a lot softer than he expected. There weren't any tags or labels on the inside, no phone number Ralph could call to return it to Mr. Smith, so he stuffed it in his backpack and shuffled off toward his house.

The snow in Ralph's front yard from the previous night's storm was perfect for building a snowman. But he didn't build a snowman the same way most kids did. It wasn't just a series of giant snowballs stacked on top of each other, he used smaller pieces to make the snowman's feet, then his legs, the body and eventually the head. He had gotten pretty good at it. And with the help of a small stepladder, he was able to craft a pretty decent looking statue of a man out of snow.

Of course, the thing he was most proud of was the pumpkin he had saved from Halloween. It had a scary face painted on it, and Ralph had taken care not to carve it or damage the skin. It was getting soft in parts, but it made for the perfect head for his creation.

"That's a stupid-looking snowman," Cory Binger shouted from across the street.

Ralph turned just in time to get hit square in the chest by a snowball. He fell onto his butt, then a whole barrage of snowballs, some of them as hard as ice, came his way as Cory and his gang threw a few dozen they had obviously had stacked up while Ralph was busy making his snowman. He raised his arms in front of his face and just sat there and allowed the snowballs to hit him as the bullies exhausted their ammo.

When they were done, Cory shouted, "Your snow-blob sucks!" His friends provided their obligatory laughter and the group of them thankfully continued on their way.

Ralph sighed as he brushed the snow off his pants and scooped out the pieces that had fallen down the back of his neck. He got to his feet and looked up at his snowman.

A particularly hard piece of ice had hit the pumpkin, creating a crooked gash right where its mouth had been painted on. At first, Ralph was mad, but then he realized it made his creation kind of scary. The late evening sun was shining in a way that made the gooey pumpkin guts inside look like a zombie's rotting flesh.

"I think I'll call you Abraham," Ralph told the snowman. "After Abraham Van Brunt, the headless horsemen. Abe for short."

The snowman said nothing.

Ralph thought back to the ventriloquist show, and the finale where Grumpy the clown sang his twisted version of "Frosty the Snowman." How cool would it be if Abe could come to life like Frosty had?

It there really was such a thing as a magic hat.

Then he remembered the flat cap the ventriloquist had dropped in the teacher's parking lot. He ran over to where he had left his backpack and pulled the old woolen cap from the pocket he had stuffed it in and looked at it.

A ventriloquist was kind of a magician, wasn't he? Could it be there was some magic in his cap? That Abe could come to life, play with Ralph… maybe help him get back at those bullies?

"What do you say, Abe?" Ralph asked the lifeless pumpkin-headed snowman. "Do you want to help me build a fort? I bet you'd be amazing in a snowball fight. Maybe we could get even with Cory and his gang."

Abe just stared straight ahead, his twisted grin snarling at the setting sun.

Ralph considered climbing the stepladder to place the cap atop Abe, but it had gotten knocked down in the barrage, so he just tossed it up like Frisbee, hoping for the best.

The flat cap landed perfectly on the pumpkin head, its brim pointed straight ahead.

"Ralph! Time for dinner!" Ralph's mom shouted from the front door.

"Coming, mom!" Ralph shouted back.

He waited a few seconds, searching for some sign of life in the snowy statue, but he remained frozen in place. "Oh, well," Ralph said. "You're still a pretty cool snowman even if you're not alive." He picked up his backpack and ran into the house.

A strong breeze knocked the last dry brown leaves from a nearby tree.

And Abe's head turned ever so slowly toward the house.

The next morning, Ralph ran from the house like a streak. He was going to be late for school if he didn't hurry. He barely had time to notice that there was something different about Abe. Was he in a different spot? Had someone tried to move him?

No time to think about it now. Ralph had perfect attendance and no tardies so far this school year, and was determined to keep his streak unblemished.

He made it just as the warning bell rang. Standing outside the main door, looking for something, was Cory Binger's posse. Were they waiting for Ralph? Where was Cory? Sneaking up behind him, ready to shove a handful of ice-cold snow down the back of his pants?

Ralph turned around, but Cory was nowhere to be seen. He was the last one funneling into the school, and Cory's lackeys paid him no mind.

Rumors about Cory spread quickly throughout the day. Someone had heard that he was in the hospital. Another student had information that he was suffering from frostbite and they were going to have to amputate all his fingers and toes. By lunchtime, the story had filled in somewhat.

Someone had thrown a large chunk of ice through Cory's bedroom window in the middle of the night, then had apparently heaped buckets of snow inside as well, burying the boy under an indoor avalanche.

What made the story all the more incredible, was that Cory's bedroom was on the second story of his family's house.

"We know it was you who did it, Ralphy" Jeff, Cory's second in command accused as Ralph was poised to take a bite out of his sandwich.

One of the other boys knocked the peanut butter and jelly out of Ralph's hands.

"Did what?" Ralph asked, confused.

"You tried to kill Cory," Jeff answered.

"What?"

"Don't play dumb."

"How?"

"I don't know exactly, but we know it was you!"

"Didn't someone break his second story window and cover him with snow?" Ralph asked.

"You had that ladder," Jeff reminded him.

"It's like three feet tall," Ralph countered.

"We're getting even with you, Ralphy. I'd sleep with one eye open if I was you."

"How do you sleep with one eye open?" Ralph asked.

Jeff struggled to find an answer to the question in his tiny little mind and instead, pointed a menacing finger at Ralph and said, "You're dead!"

Some of the students within earshot gasped.

Ralph shrugged it off. He knew Cory's gang wasn't going to actually kill him. They might knock him to the ground, roll him around in the snow and kick his legs, but his life wasn't in any real danger. They were more annoying than anything.

Still, did they actually believe Ralph had anything to do with whatever happened to Cory the night before? The notion was ridiculous.

Then he remembered what he had noticed as he had raced out of the house that morning.

Abe had been moved.

Or had moved.

Did that ventriloquist's cap work? Was it actually magic?

The rest of the day dragged on, and when the last bell rang, Ralph ran to his locker, not bothering to even put his coat on as he sped out the back door of the school, through the teachers' parking lot and down the street toward his house.

When he arrived, he was panting so hard he thought he was going to pass out. Even with his coat tucked under his arm, he was feeling hot, and his breath formed great plumes of steam with every exhalation.

He stood in front of Abe and studied him.

It was more than him just having moved. His arms and legs were in different poses than he had sculpted. And his head, instead of looking straight across the street, was looking down at Ralph, its painted eyes studying him.

"Is it true?" Ralph asked. "Are you alive?"

"Yesss," Abe replied in a deep, gravelly voice. Pumpkin seeds sprayed out of his mouth as he hissed the last part of his answer.

"Holy cow!" Ralph exclaimed. "It worked. I can't believe it."

Abe stared at him. He seemed to be breathing, his icy chest heaving at regular intervals.

Then Ralph asked, "Are you the one who tried to kill Cory Binger?"

"You wanted me to get even with him."

"I meant for you to hit him in the face with a snowball or something. Not break his window and bury him in snow."

"Sorry," Abe said, bowing his head.

Ralph felt bad. He was the one who had wanted Abe to help him strike back at the bully. It wasn't his fault he overdid it. He was only a day old. "That's okay, you didn't know any better," Ralph said.

"I didn't know..." Abe echoed.

"Right, but now you do. I don't want you to really hurt anyone. Okay?"

"Okay."

A snowball smacked Ralph on the back of his head.

He turned to see Jeff and the rest of Cory's gang along with additional reinforcements heading in his direction, scooping up snow to compact and hurl Ralph's way.

Ralph ducked behind Abe. "Don't just stand there, do something!" he urged.

"Do what? I don't want to hurt anyone," Abe growled.

"Snow balls. Can you throw snowballs back at them?"

"Yes. Can throw snowballs."

Abe bent over and scooped up a large chunk of snow. Then he reached into it with one of his arms, pulling out a perfectly round snowball, and fired it at the closest boy.

It hit him square in the face.

Another snowball flew, taking out the next boy, then another and another.

The oncoming formation started to break up. Some of the boys decided to flee before getting a face full of snow, but Jeff pushed on. He had a half dozen chunks of road ice cradled in his arm, hurling them at Ralph with all the fury he could muster.

Abe blocked the projectiles. Each time he was hit by snow or ice he absorbed it into his body, making himself bigger and apparently stronger.

The other boys shouted at Jeff to back off, but Jeff didn't appear to hear them. Rage ruled him. There was no way he was going to let Ralph get the better of him.

Abe threw a snowball that hit Jeff right in the forehead.

The bully stopped in his tracks, dazed.

Another snowball—a huge one, the size of a cantaloupe—struck him in the chest and knocked him to the ground.

Some of the other boys ran over to help him.

Jeff regained his senses. He saw Ralph standing next to Abe.

The bombardment of ice and snow ceased.

Jeff slowly got to his feet. He turned around and saw the boys who had started to flee standing at a point they thought was out of range. "Get back here, you cowards!" he shouted.

The other boys shared a look, then decided it was in their best interest to comply with the revenge-minded bully.

Jeff glared at Ralph and Abe as his army, twenty strong at least, lined up on either side of him. There was an expression of rage on Jeff's face, made all the more intimidating by the growing and reddening lump in the middle of his forehead from Abe's snowball.

"Get him!" Jeff ordered.

He took a step forward, but before anyone else could move, Abe unleashed a volley of snowballs that was bigger and faster than Ralph thought possible. It was like he was a snowball machine gun.

Most of the boys hit the deck. Some of the ones who started to flee earlier tried to escape again.

Only Jeff continued pushing forward as snowballs smashed into him.

Suddenly, a van pulled up on the street separating Ralph from Jeff and his now reluctant army.

It was Mr. Smith's van, with the colorful circus lettering on the side.

The driver's side window rolled down and a red-haired head poked out. "Get in!" he shouted as the side door slid open.

It was Grumpy.

Mr. Smith's ventriloquist's dummy was driving the van!

"Hurry up!" the clown urged.

"Abe, too?" Ralph asked.

"Yes, especially Abe!"

Years of training from teachers and parents about getting into cars with strangers froze him in his tracks. But Grumpy wasn't technically a stranger, was he?

Snowballs started banging into the other side of the van.

"Get in!" Grumpy repeated.

Ralph climbed into the dark, windowless van. "Come on," he said to Abe.

Abe dropped his pile of snow and adroitly joined Ralph inside the van.

Grumpy hit a control that caused the side door to start closing, but drove off before it had a chance to shut completely.

Ralph grabbed onto a strap attached to the wall of the van and held on as the clown drove them away from Ralph's house. One last snowball—probably thrown by Jeff—smacked into the side of the van as they raced away.

"Where are we going?" Ralph asked, suddenly afraid that maybe putting his trust into a talking dummy was not the best choice he had ever made in his short life.

"We're just getting away from those crazy kids," Grumpy assured him.

Curious, Ralph peaked into the front seat to see how Grumpy was managing to drive the van. His feet didn't reach the floor, but there was a set of levers that connected to the vehicle's pedals, and a knob attached to the steering wheel that made it easier for Grumpy to turn it.

They drove for about a mile and then pulled into the parking lot of the local grocery store.

Grumpy turned off the engine. He jumped down off the booster on the driver's seat and looked at his passengers. "So, you found Mr. Smith's cap," he said.

Ralph suddenly realized that Mr. Smith wasn't sitting up front with Grumpy. He noticed the small clown staring past Ralph and Abe at something propped up in the back of the van. It was a mannequin. And it looked oddly like Mr. Smith.

Then Ralph put it together.

It wasn't Mr. Smith's hat.

It was Grumpy's

"Figured it out, huh?" Grumpy asked.

"He's the dummy," Ralph said.

"In a manner of speaking."

"How?" Ralph asked.

"That's a big question," Grumpy replied. "The truth is, I don't really know."

The clown grabbed an upside down milk crate and sat down. "It all started when I was in high school. As you can tell, if being a redhead wasn't enough of a reason for the other kids to tease me, I'm a little challenged in the height department, too.

"I decided early on that I wasn't going to let it stop me from being successful. I wanted to be a comedian—but ironically, no one took me seriously. I was about to give up when one day, I was walking through the park when a big gust of wind blew this cap," he pointed at the flat cap perched atop Abe's pumpkin head, "off the head of a man sitting on a park bench. I ran over to catch it and carried it back to him, but when I got there, it wasn't a man, it was a statue that was posed on the bench. I'd been through that park many times and had never noticed it before, but it didn't look new. I didn't see anyone else around, so I shoved it in my pocket and didn't think about it until later, when I was walking through a department store.

"Someone called out to me that I had dropped my hat. I turned around and saw the cap on the ground. I don't know why, but I had the urge to just toss it at the nearest mannequin. When I did so, it landed perfectly atop his plastic head like it was drawn there by magnets."

"That's like what happened to me," Ralph said.

Grumpy nodded, admiring the way the flap cap perched atop the snowman's pumpkin head. "I decided to just leave it there and walked out of the store. A little while later, I had the feeling someone was following me. I turned around, and there was Mr. Smith.

"I didn't realize that he was the mannequin right away. But once I put it all together, I had my great idea."

"Mr. Smith and Grumpy," Ralph said.

Grumpy smiled. "Mr. Smith and Grumpy. I started getting booked in comedy clubs, and I've been doing parties and things like school assemblies. I sent a tape in to *America's Got Talent*. Keep your fingers crossed for me!"

Ralph nodded and showed that he had the fingers of both hands crossed.

"I'm guessing just as the hat found me when I needed it, it found you when you did. When I heard on the news that that boy had been attacked by some mysterious invader, it reminded me of some of Mr. Smith's early efforts to defend me. I was driving back to the school when I saw the cap on your—whatever that is."

"His name is Abe."

"After Abraham Van Brunt?" Grumpy asked.

"Exactly! The headless horsemen. Most people think it was—"

"—Ichabod Crane."

"Right! But I actually read the story."

"Me, too!"

The boy and the clown smiled at each other.

"Listen, I know you made a new friend," Grumpy said, nodding at Abe, "but do you think now that every kid in town thinks you have a killer snowman, Mr. Smith might have his cap back?"

Ralph's smile fell away. He looked over at Abe. He barely had a chance to know him, and now Grumpy was asking him to essentially say goodbye. Forever.

Abe looked at Ralph and smiled. "It's okay," he said in his deep, rumbling voice. "Did I help? Was I a good friend?"

"Yes," Ralph replied. "You were the best." He threw his arms around Abe's icy chest and hugged him, pressing his cheek against the snow until it started to hurt from the cold.

Abe patted him gently on the back.

"Say goodbye, Abe," Grumpy said.

Abe turned to Ralph. "Goodbye, Abe."

Ralph smiled.

Grumpy walked over to the pumpkin-headed snowman and carefully lifted the flat cap off his head.

It came away easily, and the life drained away from Abe as he collapsed into a pile of snow, with the pumpkin resting atop it, askew. Then the cap flew out of Grumpy's hands and atop the mannequin.

Mr. Smith blinked his eyes and looked at Grumpy and Ralph with a smile. "Hello, Grumpy. Hello, Ralph."

"Hey, how come he knows my name?" Ralph asked.

Grumpy shrugged.

Mr. Smith glanced over at the pile of snow that had once been Abe. "Whatever he was is now part of me," he explained. Then he looked at Ralph and asked, "We can still be friends, can't we?"

Ralph nodded, then gave Mr. Smith a hug, one that was considerably warmer than the one he had shared with Abe.

"Sorry to cut this short," Grumpy said, "but we're gonna be late for our next gig if we don't hit the road now. Do you mind walking home from here?"

"Sure, that's fine," Ralph said.

Grumpy reached over and hit the button that caused the van door to slide open.

Ralph jumped out.

"Wait," Grumpy said. "I have something for you."

The clown climbed back up into the front seat, opened the glove compartment, and pulled something out and wrote on it with a stinky marker. He turned around and presented Ralph with an autographed photo of the mannequin and himself.

The message read, "For our friend Ralph, all the very best, Mr. Smith and Grumpy."

And below that, he drew a snowman with a pumpkin for a head.

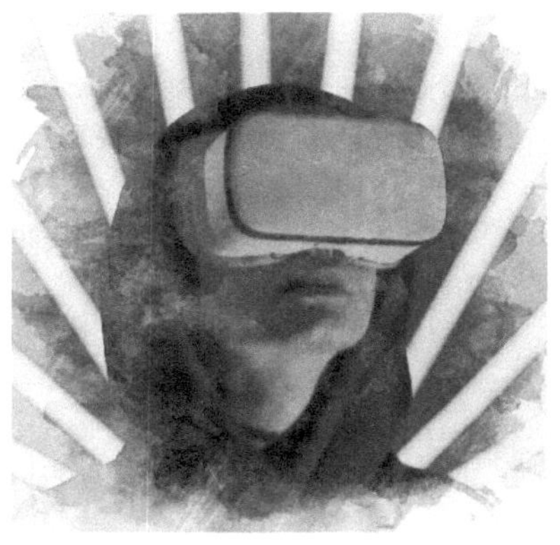

Virtual Reality for Dummies

"The reason for the return?" Dean asked the woman standing on the other side of the customer service counter.

She hesitated for a moment before replying. "They don't work the way they're supposed to."

"In what way?"

"There are… extra things in there."

Dean inspected the virtual reality headset the woman had brought in. It was in the original box, but as was typical for returned electronics, it didn't quite fit back inside the packaging as it had originally.

The device looked like a pair of high-tech ski goggles, only instead of tinted glass, the wearer's eyes were covered by a combination of lenses and tiny video screens that projected a virtual 3-D image in front of them. There were also cameras built into the device's frame so that the user could experience an augmented reality where information and avatars of other users could be viewed by the user, superimposed over the real world. He looked at the inside of the device, checking to make sure the lenses were free of any dirt or dust that might be causing the problem.

"I don't mean inside the headset—well, not physically, anyway."

Dean set the goggles down. "I'm not quite sure I know what you mean?"

"Put them on," the woman suggested. "You'll see."

Grabbing a disinfecting wipe from the dispenser on the counter, Dean wiped down the soft padding around the rim of the goggles where they made a light-proof seal around the user's face. He used a can of compressed air to spray the interior, clearing it of anything that he might not be able to see. Then he turned the device on and lifted it to his face.

It started in augmented reality mode. Dean saw the electronics shop and the customer who had brought the goggles in as if there weren't over a thousand dollars of electronics blocking his view. He looked at the woman, then turned his head until the device's menu appeared, floating in mid-air in front of him. He reached out with his free hand and made a tapping motion at the "Demo" option. A new menu appeared, and he selected the shopping app.

The device began scanning various items within view, and when it recognized them, a virtual label appeared floating above it, showing customer reviews and sale price information.

"Looks okay to me," Dean said. He turned to look at the woman. "Was it a specific app that was giving you problems?"

"Try looking behind you," the woman suggested.

Dean continued looking at the customer.

She made a circling motion with her finger, urging him to turn around.

He spun about to face the rack of returned items waiting to be repackaged and either returned to the vendor or reshelved.

Standing in front of him was a beast, nearly eight feet tall, with glowing yellow eyes and several pairs of horns protruding from the top and sides of its head, covered top to bottom in red fur. It opened its mouth, revealing multiple rows of glistening teeth like those of a shark. A deafening roar issued forth, its effects reaching deep into

Dean's head and stomach, sending shivers down his spine.

He tore the goggles away from his face, expecting to see the creature still standing in front of him, but there was nothing.

"You see what I mean?" the woman asked.

Dean realized that he was breathing heavily, his pulse was racing. He spun back around to face the customer. He was familiar with this VR headset, he had a pair himself at home. As far as he knew, the augmented reality shopping app did not have any demonic beasts in it.

"Did you upload any new software?" Dean asked.

"No," the woman replied. "I didn't add anything. It just started acting that way a couple of days ago. It's not supposed to do that, is it?"

"No, it's not supposed to do that," Dean assured her. "Did you connect to any public Wi-Fi networks?"

"No—well, just here in the store. But when I was at home, I used my own internet connection."

"VPN?" Dean asked.

"What's that?" the woman asked back.

"Never mind. If you don't know, you probably don't have one."

"Can you fix it? Or maybe give me an exchange?"

Dean inspected the receipt that the woman had presented with the goggles and checked the date. "Looks like you're past the thirty days return date, but if there is a defect, we can exchange it for a refurbished model."

"Refurbished?" she asked. "That doesn't seem right. It's brand new. I only used it a couple of times. It was sitting in the box for four weeks before I had a chance to try it out."

Dean was suspicious of the woman's claim. No one would drop that much money on a luxury item like this and not want to try it out right away. "Is it just in the shopping app?"

"Shopping app?" the woman inquired. "I haven't tried that one yet. I was doing the virtual tour of the Louvre, and a couple of the games."

"And the giant furry demon shows up in all of them?"

"What giant furry demon?"

Dean was confused. He put the goggles back on, then turned around to verify that the virtual beast was still there. Drool glistened on its white teeth, dripping down its pointy chin and forming moist trails in the dark red fur that covered its muscular chest. The creature took a step toward Dean, swiping at him with a large, meaty hand, the fingers of which ended in razor sharp claws.

He stepped back, then took the goggles away from his eyes.

He looked at the woman. "Big, red, covered in fur, multiple sets of horns, big pointy teeth."

"Doesn't ring a bell," the woman replied.

"Then what were you talking about?"

She thought for a moment, as if searching her mind for the appropriate words to use. "I guess I would call them bat-crows."

"Bat-crows?"

"Bat-crows. Kind of a cross between a bat and a crow."

"I figured," Dean said. "I didn't see anything like that. Just the big furry demon."

"Well, I didn't see anything but the bat-crows," the woman insisted.

Dean bit his lower lip, consulting his memory of the customer service training he had received for what to do in a situation like this.

He came up empty.

He turned his stare to the headset, inspecting it as if he could tell what was wrong just by looking at it.

"Maybe we should talk to your manager?" the woman asked timidly.

Dean involuntarily inhaled sharply through clenched teeth, making a hissing sound.

His manager, the head of customer service, was ironically not a people person. The only thing he hated more than customers asking questions was employees interrupting his seemingly endless paperwork tasks to escalate an issue.

He looked to see if either Eric or Mandy, his coworkers, were around. But both were out of sight.

The woman was getting impatient, switching between glaring at Dean and the door on the wall behind him nestled between the shelves of returned purchases with a metallic nameplate reading "Manager."

Dean sighed. "I'll see if he's available." He turned and walked the short distance to the door and lightly knocked.

"Come," said a high-pitched, nasally voice on the other side.

Dean turned the knob and leaned into the office without actually stepping inside. "Sorry to bother you, Kevin," he said, "but I have a customer who's having an unusual problem with her VRX-50 and she's past the thirty days return limit."

"Offer her a refurbished unit."

"She doesn't want a refurb. It's practically new."

Kevin spun around in his office chair and glared at Dean over the lenses of his half moon reading glasses. "What's wrong with it?"

Dean took a moment to moisten his suddenly dry mouth before answering. "It has... extra things in it."

"What does that mean, 'extra things'?" Kevin asked.

"It appears that there are random NPCs in the augmented reality field."

"The VRX-50 doesn't do that."

"I know. But I checked it myself. There is something there. And it is rather disturbing."

Kevin raised an eyebrow. "Disturbing?"

Dean nodded.

Kevin lifted himself out of his chair with an exaggerated effort.

Dean stepped back as the manager emerged from the cluttered office, his face transforming from his usual resting grimace to an artificial smile that instantly turned to unadulterated ire when he saw who was standing on the other side of the counter. "You," he said, his voice dripping with animosity.

"I'm sure I'm just as unhappy about needing to be here as you are to have to address my problem," she said.

Kevin scoffed. "Oh, I imagine I'm several orders of magnitude more unhappy than you are." He turned to Dean. "I assume this is your first interaction with Ms. Underbranch."

"I think we've known each other long enough that you can call me Olivia," the woman replied.

"Nice to meet you, Olivia," Dean replied reflexively.

"You, too, Dean," Olivia replied, reading his name from his badge.

Kevin maintained his disgruntled demeanor. "Ms. Underbranch," he said, "is a frequent customer of customer service. It seems she's the unluckiest person in the world, as everything she purchases from this establishment turns out to have a problem."

"Not everything. The snacks I buy in the checkout lane are always quite tasty."

"I'm so glad to hear that," Kevin intoned sarcastically. He turned his attention to the headset resting on the counter. "This is the offending device?" he asked in a way that discouraged an answer.

Olivia answered anyway. "Yes. It's got extra things in it."

"So my subordinate told me."

"Put it on," Olivia suggested.

"No, thank you. I am of the percentage of the population who find virtual and augmented reality, 3D movies and most amusement park rides extremely nauseating." He turned to Dean. "Go get the HDHD."

"The HDHD?" Dean asked.

Kevin almost imperceptibly rolled his eyes and shook his head as he explained what was perfectly obvious to himself. "The high-definition holographic display."

"Oh, right," Dean replied. He stepped around the counter to fetch the specialized monitor that was on a portable display in the computer section of the store.

Kevin, meanwhile, fished through a box of cables until he found the one he was looking for. He plugged one end into a small socket on the side of the headset, then held the other in his hand while he waited for Dean to return.

"You know, I haven't had any problems with that robot vacuum I bought last year," Olivia mentioned casually.

"That's nice," Kevin replied.

Dean returned with the monitor. He handed the power cord to Kevin and Kevin handed Dean the other end of the cable attached to the headset and both men set their respective plugs into the appropriate sockets.

The HDHD came to life, showing what the headset was seeing in a rather impressive glasses-free 3D. It showed the part of the store that the goggles were pointing at with the shopping app's augmented reality tags seemingly floating in mid-air.

"Those are supposed to be there," Kevin said.

"Not those," Dean replied. He picked up the headset and pointed it behind the counter to the spot where he had seen the vicious creature moments before.

The monitor reproduced the back wall of the customer service counter perfectly... without the presence of any roaring, horned beasts.

"What am I supposed to be seeing?" Kevin asked.

"Try pointing it up to the ceiling," Olivia suggested.

Dean tilted the headset up toward the spider web of beams that supported the roof.

Something appeared to have flown out of one corner of the display.

"There, did you see it?" Olivia asked.

Dean shook his head.

Kevin simply glared.

"I'm telling you, there are things in there. Maybe they're only visible if you're wearing it," she postulated.

Kevin took in a deep breath. "How would that make any difference? It doesn't know if it's strapped to your head or not."

"Actually," Dean offered timidly, "there is a sensor to track eye-movement, so it technically does know if you're wearing it."

"You know what I mean," Kevin insisted. "It's not going to show you something different based on if you're wearing it or not. Certainly not for the shopping app. It's a pretty straightforward Augmented Reality application." He turned to Olivia. "Looks like you're the proud owner of a perfectly working electronic device. Thank you for shopping with us." He picked up the headset and handed it to the woman.

As he did so, the screen showed a 3D image of Olivia standing at the counter with the rest of the store behind her.

Then a sort of purple goblin with compound eyes like a fly and suction cup fingers like a tree frog climbed up on her shoulder and peered directly at Dean.

"Look, look," he shouted as he pointed at the display.

But as Kevin turned his attention to the monitor, he inadvertently changed the orientation of the headset and the scene shifted to a view of a display of mobile phone cases.

"What?" Kevin asked, annoyed.

"Point it at Oliv—I mean, Ms. Underbranch," Dean said urgently.

Kevin kept his eyes on the monitor while he directed the cameras of the headset toward Olivia. She smiled meekly.

The purple, bug-eyed goblin-frog grinned as well, showing rows of hundreds of needle-like teeth.

"Ah!" Kevin shouted.

"Ah!" Dean shouted as well.

Olivia turned her head toward the monitor and shrieked as well. "Ah!" She brushed at the creature perched on her shoulder and it scampered away.

"What was that?" Kevin asked.

"That's what we were trying to tell you," Dean answered.

"That's not supposed to be there!" the customer service manager said adamantly.

"I didn't think so," Olivia stated. "That's why I brought it in. Though that's not what I was seeing."

"Yeah, I saw a big, red, furry horny thing," Dead added.

Kevin pointed the headset in a slow arc around the store. Sitting in a nearby massage chair was the goblin-frog, happily enjoying the rumble of the vibrating recliner. "Hold this," he instructed Dean. "Keep it pointed at that chair."

Dean took the headset and held it steady while Kevin emerged from behind the counter and walked slowly toward the creature. He cast glances back at the monitor to make sure it was still there. When he passed between the headset and the chair, his body blocked the view of the goblin-frog. As he got closer, the creature appeared to be watching him.

Keeping his eyes on the monitor, Kevin reached out toward the bug-eyed imp.

It opened its mouth and snapped at his hand.

Kevin jerked it back, then walked up to the holographic display to take a closer look.

The creature's multi-faceted eyes seemed to reflect tiny images of Kevin's narrow, bespectacled face.

"That's impossible," he stated authoritatively. "How can I see myself in its eyes? The camera isn't pointed at me."

"Maybe we should turn it off," Dean suggested.

Kevin ignored him. He reached into the image projected by the display, poking the goblin-frog in its round belly.

His finger made a dent in the creature's flesh.

And it giggled. "Hee hee hee."

"Maybe you shouldn't do that," Dean warned.

"Incredible," Kevin said, ignoring his employee. "How do they do that? And why aren't they marketing this feature? It's simply amazing!"

The manager poked the goblin-frog again, then a few more times in rapid succession, trying to discern if there was any latency in the interaction.

The goblin-frog was not amused. Its expression changed from that of pleasant amusement to vicious annoyance, and it bared its needle-teeth again, this time snapping out at Kevin's outstretched finger before he could retreat.

"Yow!" Kevin exclaimed.

He held his hand in front of his face.

The index finger was missing.

There were no spurts of blood, or torn, ragged bits of flesh. It simply ended in a well-defined cross section below the second knuckle.

"What the hell?" Kevin exclaimed with a note of panic.

"Maybe that's why they're not marketing this 'feature,'" Olivia offered.

"Should I call an ambulance?" Dean asked.

"Should I call an ambulance?" Kevin mocked back. "Of course you should call an ambulance. Then get over here and see if you can find the rest of my finger!"

"I don't think that's going to happen," Olivia said, nodding toward the creature in the monitor.

It was chewing Kevin's finger, crunching the bones into splinters, and devouring the flesh. When it was done, it spit out the fingernail, which fluttered heavily to the floor.

Kevin leaned over and picked it up with his other hand. There was still a bit of bloody tissue attached. Revolted, he dropped it.

The creature burped, then peered directly at Kevin with its multifaceted eyes. It leaned forward, then grabbed a hold of the edge of the holographic display and pulled itself out of the three dimensional image.

Kevin backed up.

Olivia and Dean watched, transfixed.

A few other customers took notice as well, as if it was some kind of tech demo.

"This is impossible," Kevin said, completely oblivious to the evidence that his statement was objectively false.

Suddenly, something flew out of the display. It had the head of a hook-beaked raven, but instead of being covered with feathers, its wings were black, leathery skin stretched over a twisted skeletal structure that resembled that of a bat.

"That's it," Olivia said, pointing at the demonic raptor as it soared around the store. "That's one of the things I saw when I wore those goggles!"

"You're right. It does look like a bat-crow," Dean said.

The goblin-frog had Kevin backed up against the counter. There was fear in his eyes. "Get it away!" he shrieked. "Get that thing away from me!"

Dean spotted an empty box on the far end of the counter. He grabbed it, then carefully snuck up behind the purple creature and slammed the box over it. He leaned on the container to apply his full weight, keeping the little monster trapped.

"Thank you, Dean," Kevin said with uncharacteristic appreciation.

"What should I do with it?" Dean asked.

Before he could answer, the bat-crow swooped down and bit off Kevin's right ear. Just took it clean off, leaving an open—but seemingly somehow instantly cauterized—wound on the side of his head. His glasses fell askew, losing one of their anchor points.

"What was that?" Kevin screamed, putting his hand to the side of his head and screaming even louder. "Don't just stand there, catch that thing!"

Dean lifted his weight off the box to search for something he could use to capture the bat-crow, but when he did so, the goblin-frog beneath the box immediately tried to escape.

"Look!" Olivia said, pointing at the display.

Now the giant, red, horned, furry demon Dean had seen when wearing the goggles appeared in the display. It poked its head through the holographic image and looked around curiously.

"Don't worry, it's too big to fit through," Dean assessed.

Then, as if it had heard Dean and wanted to prove him wrong, the furry demon took a few steps back, then ran at the opening of the display and dove through.

It landed with a store-shaking thud, a little dazed, but it quickly recovered and raised itself to its full eight-foot plus height.

The furry demon opened its mouth and roared that same bone-chilling, gut-squishing howl Dean had heard when he was wearing the goggles.

Then it reached for Kevin, picked him up in one massive, clawed hand by the waist, and bit off his head.

Kevin's body went limp.

Dean backed up and the goblin-frog immediately threw the box aside, leaped onto Kevin's lifeless body, and started eating the rest of his fingers.

A bat-crow alighted at the furry demon's feet and pecked at the scraps of flesh that fell to the floor as the giant horned monster chewed messily.

More bat-crows flew out of the monitor and fought each other for the scraps like seagulls battling over a discarded French fry.

"Turn it off!" Olivia said.

Dean didn't hear her at first. He watched as the furry demon consumed Kevin's body in increasingly larger bites while the goblin-frog tore off pieces to satisfy its own hunger.

"Turn it off!" Olivia repeated.

Dean looked at her, the words finally registering, and he reached for the headset and flipped the power toggle on the side.

The monitor went blank.

The creatures disappeared.

As did the last morsels of Kevin.

Applause broke out.

While Kevin was being consumed, a crowd of customers had gathered around the Customer Service desk, and apparently had thought the whole thing was a show. An impromptu demo of some new holographic projection tech.

Most of the shoppers quickly lost interest. Some turned to the nearest sales reps and asked how much that cool monitor cost.

Dean was amazed at the alacrity of the associates who quickly converted the customer's questions into potential sales of one of their biggest ticket items. He stepped back around to the other side of the counter.

Olivia Underbranch stepped closer, and they stared into each other's eyes for a moment.

"So, perhaps a full refund rather than an exchange?" Dean asked, pointing at the VR goggles, afraid to touch them.

"Yes, I think that would be best," Olivia answered.

"Store credit?"

"Not on your life."

The New Guy

I was running late for my first official day on the job and didn't see the woman pushing the baby carriage out into the crosswalk until it was too late. The wheeled bassinet went flying through the air, and my SUV tilted slightly as the woman fell under my vehicle and I rolled over her before screeching to a stop.

Only, that's not what actually happened.

I slowed down as I approached the intersection—even though the light was green. The woman was distracted and didn't realize she was walking into traffic. I gave a polite honk on my horn and she pulled back in plenty of time to avoid a certain tragedy. The woman gave me a grateful nod, and I smiled back as other less patient commuters leaned on their horns and raced around me.

But that alternate moment, that bifurcation of reality that I experienced, had felt so real. The sounds, the heart-stopping shock of seeing the baby carriage tossed into oncoming traffic, the way my SUV pitched and jerked to a halt.

Had I just daydreamed the whole thing in that fraction of a second before I took action to avoid the accident?

Or did I just experience a premonition?

I didn't have time to ponder the matter further. I was going to be late if I didn't keep going. So I drove on, putting the experience and the feelings it had engendered aside, focusing on getting across the train tracks ahead of me before the lights started flashing and the crossing arms descended.

The bells started dinging just as I rolled over the tracks.

How did I know that was going to happen? You couldn't see the trains coming from where I was on the road until you were right on the tracks, but I knew for a certainty that if I hadn't sped up, I would be caught behind a hundred car freighter.

Coincidence, I assured myself. I had driven down this road a thousand times and knew that there were usually a few diesel engines dragging an endless caravan of intermodal containers behind them at this time of day.

The job I didn't want to be late for was my first day on the security detail of the CEO of Quantum Pharmaceuticals. Franklin Forrest was one of the richest men in America and possibly the world. I had been recommended for the job by a friend of mine who worked general security at the company's headquarters, a lavish campus of buildings and curated parks about thirty miles outside the city.

That's where I was headed now.

I pulled into the employee parking lot and hopped aboard one of the waiting shuttles just in time to be dropped off in front of the executive office building with a few minutes to spare.

Mac Eisengard met me at the front door and guided me through the security station. I had identified him by the badge clipped to his jacket. He was my immediate supervisor, the team leader, and I could tell by his demeanor that he wasn't pleased to have a new guy on his squad.

"Follow me," he said, leading me away from the reception desk and toward an unmarked door off in one corner. There was a scanner for a badge. Mac paused when we reached it, so I pressed my own ID against the featureless pad. The door clicked, and I pushed it open and entered, holding it open for Mac.

He shook his head. "Never hold a door open for someone you don't know. You may think you know who I am, but until just a few seconds ago, we had never met. I could be anyone."

Mac was right. I knew that. It was in the orientation materials I had reviewed the previous night. "Sorry," I said meekly.

"Sorry will get you killed in this job," h warned. "That's the last one you get."

"Yes, sir."

Mac pointed at a locker. "That's yours. Your communications gear and your weapons are inside. Press your thumb against the lock."

I did so, and the light flashed from red to yellow, and then green. The door to the locker sprung open.

"It's now keyed to you and you alone." He pressed his thumb against the biometric sensor of his own locker and pulled out his gun. He removed the magazine, inspected it, then slammed it back into the grip and made sure a round was chambered before sliding it into his shoulder holster.

I did the same.

On the top shelf was a bulky device that resembled a thick phone. From the orientation materials I had reviewed, I knew it was the muti-band communicator, which worked on radio, cellular, Wi-Fi and Bluetooth data connections, so that no matter where you were on the sprawling campus of Quantum Pharmaceuticals, you would be connected to everyone else on the security team. I turned it on and slid the device into an inside pocket of my jacket, then placed the earpiece in my right ear.

"Comm test one," I said quietly.

The device replied, "Communications status active."

Mac seemed unimpressed. He led me into a break room where three other men, also dressed in black suits with crisp white shirts, sat around a table sipping at cups of coffee. Two of them wore dark glasses.

"New Guy, this is the team. Team, this is New Guy," Mac said.

They regarded me suspiciously.

"He doesn't look familiar," one of them said.

"He's from outside. Used to be a cop," Mac explained.

"Shit, chief, how are we expected to work with a total newbie?"

"This comes from the top. So no complaints and make it work."

That seemed to silence the others.

I had expected some resistance. It seemed to me being on the CEO's security detail was a plum assignment, and there was likely a long list of other people who worked in security at the company who coveted the very job I had walked into.

I wasn't completely sure why I had been selected. It was a very unusual interview process. There was the usual: a questionnaire and a physical exam complete with blood tests and DNA swabs.

After clearing those hurdles, I was called in for another test. I sat in a room while a series of images flashed on a screen in front of me.

Then I was asked a series of questions.

Then more images cycled by even faster.

Then more questions.

I wasn't quite sure what they were testing. The examination didn't seem to have anything to do with what I had seen. But however they scored it, I managed to pass.

Finally, I was brought into a room with a well-dressed woman and a man in a lab coat sitting at a metal table. The woman motioned for me to sit as well. From her body language and her manner of speaking, I guessed she was a lawyer.

"Quantum Pharmaceuticals would like to make you an offer of employment," she said. "Your starting salary will be two hundred thousand dollars, with a signing bonus of twenty-five thousand."

She placed a document in front of me.

"Please review this and sign and initial where indicated."

The papers had various flags stuck to them on different pages. I read through the first one that spelled out my compensation, then skimmed through the sections about non-disclosure and confidentiality and expectations of maintaining certain fitness and weapons proficiency standards. There was also a section on benefits and time off rules.

I initialed at all the indicated spaces, then when I reached the final page, I signed my name and dated it.

The woman picked it up and leafed through each page, making sure I hadn't missed anything. Then she nodded at the man in the lab coat.

He rose and pulled what looked like some kind of inoculation gun from the pocket of his lab coat with a small vial of purple liquid attached.

"What's that?" I asked.

Before I could get an answer, the man pressed the end of the device against my arm and pressed the trigger. It made a hissing sound as the fluid rapidly disappeared into my arm.

"What the hell?" I protested, standing up and rubbing the spot on my arm that was now intensely sore. "What did you just do?"

"That was a collection of vaccines. Your position requires frequent travel to many places that expect you to be protected against various diseases. It's all right here in the contract you signed," she added, offering the papers to me to inspect for myself.

"You could have given me a little warning," I said, kneading the ache out of my triceps.

The woman ignored my complaint and handed me a thick binder filled with pages and various dividers. "Here is your employee manual. It includes all the security protocols you're expected to know. You will report for duty to Mac Eisengard at the Executive Office Building at 8:00 am tomorrow."

"I'm supposed to read all that by tomorrow?" I asked.

"Again, this was clearly laid out in your contract, which you initialed and signed," the woman reminded me.

I sighed, then took the binder and went home.

I managed to make my way through all the material—much of which was familiar because of my police background—before I reported for my first day and failed my first test of security policy when I held the door for Mac.

Now three more faces judged me, a tight-knit group that probably had worked together for years, and now were being forced to add another member to their team.

"Don't get us killed," one of them, a man with a clean-shaven head and thick mustache, warned.

"I thought it was Forrest we were supposed to keep alive," I replied.

The one of the group not wearing dark glasses, who had a buzzcut of red hair, and a scar across one cheek, laughed. "I like this kid," he said. "Don't let them get to you, New Guy. Follow orders, keep your head on a swivel, and you'll do fine. By the way, I'm Vince. That guy over there with the cue ball head is Mikey and the lump of muscle over there is Meat."

Mac raised his hand to silence us as he received a message through his communicator. "All right, enough jabbering," he said. "Let's get to work."

Mac led us out a back door to a service elevator and up to the penthouse. We waited in a corridor in silence for nearly half an hour. Mac and the others seemed to be watching everything around them at once. I tried to do the same, employing the threat assessment techniques I had learned at the police academy.

An ornate double-door opened, and Franklin Forrest appeared, followed by an entourage of assistants, including the lawyer I had met the previous day.

Mac issued hand signals, indicating that he and Vince would take the lead and the rest of us would follow in the rear.

We went down the spacious private elevator reserved for the CEO, exited the building through the lobby, and approached a caravan of waiting cars. Forrest and most of his lackeys, along with Mac and Vince, got into a stretch limo, while Mikey, Meat and I piled into an SUV parked ahead of it.

We took off and drove about five miles until we reached a hospital. There appeared to be a ceremony taking place, and a banner thanking Quantum Pharmaceuticals for their generous donation to a new children's wing was hung prominently.

There were television cameras present to record the brief speeches, and the presentation of a plaque to Forrest. Then, one of the administrators asked the CEO if he wouldn't mind taking a few minutes to visit with the children. They had their own thank you planned.

Forrest was clearly not interested in the notion of spending any amount of time with sick kids, but he forced a smile and said graciously, "Of course! That sounds wonderful."

Meat snickered. He leaned over to Mikey and whispered, "Fifty bucks says he's out of there in less than a minute."

Mikey thought about it for a sec, then nodded. "You're on. There are cameras."

Apparently Forrest's obvious dislike for kids, or sick people, or both, was an ongoing source of amusement for the security detail.

We followed a small group of hospital staff down a wide corridor. At the end of it in gleaming gold letters on the wall, were the words, "The Franklin Forrest Children's Wing."

On the other side of the doors was a lobby area. A small group of kids, some standing, some in wheelchairs, all wearing hospital gowns, were arranged in two rows. Most of them had chemo induced bald heads, and some were accompanied by IV stands.

Once the group settled into place, the children began singing "We Are the World."

Forrest smiled uncomfortably throughout the performance.

When it was done, a young girl approached carrying a large, handmade thank you card, scribbled with various drawings and printed signatures. "Thank you, Mr. Forrest," she said.

Forrest kneeled down to her level and accepted the gift. "Thank you, darling," he said, sweetly. "What's your name?"

The girl smiled meekly, then took on an ashen pallor. She stepped forward and vomited all over Forrest.

"Look what you've done! This is a ten thousand dollar suit!" Forrest exclaimed. The CEO roughly pushed the girl back.

She fell down, smacking her head against the tile floor, and began crying.

A nurse rushed over to pick her up and carry her away.

Mac approached the camera man that had come to record the presentation. He snatched the video rig off the man's shoulder.

"Hey, you can't do that," the man protested.

Vince stepped between the cameraman and Mac as the team leader removed the memory card from the camera.

Mikey and Meat went into action, snatching phones out of the hands of a few nurses who had been recording the performance. They made sure the devices were clear of any evidence of Forrest's incident, and returned them.

I watched in shock and surprise. I had heard that Franklin Forrest had a reputation for having a temper, but I never imagined it would be exposed in a setting like this.

Once Mac and the others were convinced they had cleaned up any evidence of the affair, Mac issued a command to leave into his communicator, which I heard through my earpiece.

Since I was closest to the door we had come in through, I stepped forward to make sure the way was clear.

A man burst into the room. He held a large, glass beaker in his hands and shouted at Forrest, "This is for all the millions you have experimented on to make your blood money!"

He hurled the contents of the beaker at the CEO. It hit him and those closest to him, and where it splashed, it burned, dissolving skin and the muscle beneath. Forrest's eyes sizzled as the acid seared his cornea, and the fluids behind them leaked out.

The CEO screamed in agony, raising his hands too late to protect himself from the attack.

Mac and Vince drew their guns and emptied them into the attacker.

I stared at the door.

No one had come through. Mac and Vince were escorting Forrest out of the room back toward the corridor.

"Wait, stop!" I shouted.

Mac looked at me impatiently. "Out of the way, New Guy."

I turned to Vince. "Keep him back." Then I approached the door so I could see through the small slit of a window down the corridor beyond. There was someone rapidly approaching.

I got closer to the door, and just as it started to open, I kicked at it, knocking whoever was behind it onto the ground.

Screams of agony issued forth from the other side.

The nurses scrambled to get the rest of the children out of the lobby.

"What the hell was that?" Mikey asked. He pushed past me to open the door.

Lying on the floor was a man dressed as a hospital maintenance worker. To one side was a broken beaker, the contents of which must have been a highly corrosive liquid since there was a steaming hole where his chest had once been, and his face and hands and clothing were pitted with burn marks.

"Back door," Mac said immediately.

We formed a phalanx around the CEO, who surprisingly didn't seem shocked by the thwarted attack. By the time we got outside, the limo and SUV had been moved to the rear of the hospital and we all got into our respective vehicles and drove away.

Mikey turned to me once we had gone about a mile. "How did you know that guy was there?"

"I saw him through the window," I said.

"Naw," Mikey protested. "You didn't have an angle to see down the hall when you warned us."

"I guess I saw something."

"What's the big deal?" Meat asked. "He saved the boss. Sounds like a good day's work to me."

When we got back to the executive office building, I was summoned up to Forrest's office. Alone.

He gestured for me to sit on a couch while he perched himself on an armchair next to it.

"They tell me you're known as New Guy," he said.

"Yes, sir."

"Drop the sir, you saved my life, you can call me Frank."

"Okay, Frank."

The CEO chuckled at the way I said it. "Tell me what you saw, New Guy."

"I saw what everyone else saw," I replied.

"Before that," he said.

I could see in his eyes that he somehow knew about my premonition.

I shrugged. "I just had a feeling something bad was going to happen."

"Hmm," he said, disbelievingly. "How much of a warning did you have? Approximately how many seconds was it before you knew what was going to happen, and what actually happened?" he asked.

I didn't answer. I didn't know how to.

Forrest leaned toward me. "You're very special, New Guy. We've spent a long time and a lot of money searching for you. You hold the key to a whole new class of drugs that will take humanity to the next level."

"What do you mean?" I asked.

"You have a certain combination of genes that have expressed themselves in just the right way to make you receptive to a new product we've been developing."

I thought back to the purple liquid in the inoculation gun. "You're experimenting on me?"

Forrest leaned back in his chair. "You agreed to it when you signed your employment contract. And from what I've seen, it's worked beyond my wildest dreams."

I was starting to get worried. "What did you give me?"

"I gave you the ability to see the future. I believe with time, you'll be able to see further, and have more control over what you see. Right now, your mind is adjusting to its new abilities, abilities connected through quantum affinity to the future."

"What are you talking about?" I asked.

"Oh, I'm not quite sure how it all works myself. But I have a building full of scientists who assure me they can induce a mutation in human beings that will amplify a dormant precognitive sense. And you are the first one to successfully realize that power."

I shook my head. "It was just a lucky guess."

He smiled, a knowing grin that dismissed my denial as if I had never uttered it.

"I have quite a future planned for you, New Guy. And there's a lot of money to be made in that future."

Someone entered the room. I looked over and saw a woman standing nervously in the doorway.

Forrest turned toward the door, but it was still closed. There was no one there. "Was it a man or a woman you just saw?" he asked.

"Woman," I replied without thinking.

"Come in, Ms. Hawley," he shouted.

The knob on the door opened, and the woman I thought I saw there a moment earlier stepped inside. "I didn't know you were busy, Mr. Forrest," she said timidly.

"That's all right. Please, I wanted to speak with you."

She nervously approached, wringing her hands. "I'm sorry about the hospital," she said.

Forrest grinned menacingly. "You told me it was going to be a simple ceremony. Then there were kids. Sick kids. And someone tried to kill me."

"I had no way of knowing. They were just so grateful to you—"

"No need to explain, Ms. Hawley. You're fired. Security will see you out."

"But Mr. Forrest, it wasn't my fault, I—"

"Get out!" the CEO shouted. He stood, towering over the shocked woman. "Get your feeble little mind out of my office."

She was frozen with fear.

Forrest slapped her.

She put a hand to the cheek that was struck and began crying.

"Oh, stop it. I didn't hurt you. But I will if you spend one more second in my presence."

The woman turned and fled. The heel of one shoe broke off, but she left it behind as she disappeared behind the door.

Forrest turned to me with an exasperated expression. "Good help is so hard to find," he said. Then he added, "That will be all, New Guy. I'll see you tomorrow."

That night, I reviewed the non-disclosure and confidentiality clauses of my employment contract. I wasn't a lawyer, but it was clear that becoming a whistle-blower to either Forrest's treatment of sick kids and employees, or the experimentation I had been subjected to would not be a smart move on my part—legally or fiscally. Quitting also triggered a severe penalty.

I was trapped.

When I reported for duty the next morning, the other guys were even more standoffish than they had been on my first day—except for Vince. He approached me while I was getting coffee.

"So, what did the big guy have to say?"

I cast him a suspicious look. "You know I can't discuss anything that happens in that office. I assume you signed the same contract I did."

He laughed. "Oh, come on. You can tell us. We're not going to spill the beans."

"Nice try," I said, looking over at Mac.

The team leader met my stare, then shrugged. My suspicion that the question was another test was vindicated.

"Big day today," Mac announced. "Public event, big announcement, a lot of people and press. We're going to be backed up by the B and C teams, as well as some of the general security guards."

"What's going on?" I asked.

"Haven't you been paying attention to the news?" Vince answered. "The boss is going to announce he's running for president today."

"He'll probably win, too," Meat said. "Guys like him always come out on top."

I had heard speculation, but in the TV interviews Forrest had done, he had vehemently denied he had any political aspirations. Obviously, he had reconsidered.

"It's going to be here, on the steps in front of this building. Security teams have been sweeping the grounds and all the other structures for the past day. We'll have snipers posted on every rooftop, and no one gets near who hasn't been vetted and cleared—including employees."

"Right, like at the hospital," Mikey said.

"The hospital was a cluster fuck," Mac agreed. "Today is not going to be anything like that. It's A-game all around. Got it?"

Everyone nodded.

Mac passed out schedules printed on thin cards we could slip into our jackets. He approached Vince. "Listen, you're going to be on the perimeter today. The boss wants New Guy as his body man."

Vince looked over at me. Mac had clearly said it so I could hear. "No worries, chief, I'd want him by my side, too."

There were hundreds of people in the crowd, signs proclaiming "Forrest for President," "Women for Forrest," "Blacks for Forrest," and "Latinos for Forrest" had been passed out and were being waved eagerly by the attendees.

There was red, white and blue bunting on the building's façade, and a podium had been erected in front of the main entrance.

The news cameras had been relegated to a platform behind the crowd, and the signs were conveniently double-sided, so they were sure to see them.

Meat and Mikey were positioned just off the podium to the sides, with Vince taking up the center front spot.

Mac and I flanked Franklin as we waited just inside the headquarters building. I scanned the crowd from behind my sunglasses in my best impersonation of a Secret Service agent.

The music changed from generic, patriotic themed songs to a rousing fanfare.

We escorted Franklin Forrest out onto the stage. Several other men and women in suits filled in seats behind the podium.

The crowd erupted into cheers as Forrest came into view.

The CEO waved at the crowd as he took up his position behind the lectern, with me off to his left and Mac on the other side. He smiled broadly and gestured for the excited supporters to settle down. "My fellow Americans," he began, causing the crowd to erupt in mindless cheering once more.

There was a distant crack, which I recognized as the report of a sniper rifle. Had one of the rooftop teams spotted a threat and taken it out?

Instinctively, I turned to Forrest to get him to safety, but the action pained me. I looked at my shoulder where there was a through-and-through bullet wound that was now seeping blood.

Then I looked at the man I was supposed to protect and saw that I was too late. The bullet that had gone through me had hit him square in the chest. Right through the heart.

Forrest smiled broadly and gestured for the excited supporters to settle down.

It hadn't happened yet.

From my vision, I could tell the shot had come from a clump of trees off to my left. The assassin must've been planted there for more than a day, waiting for his opportunity. I peered at the leaves, trying to make out where the gunman was concealed.

The man who had volunteered to risk his life to end the prospective tyranny of a Franklin Forrest presidency looked through the scope of the high-powered rifle. He was surprised to see Forrest's body man looking straight at him, as if he knew exactly where he was.

Had his cover been blown? Was he about to be taken out before he could complete his mission?

Then something strange happened.

The bodyguard lowered his sunglasses… and winked. Then the dark suited man took a slight step to the side, giving the assassin a clear shot.

He pulled the trigger, and Franklin Forrest died almost instantly from a bullet to the heart.

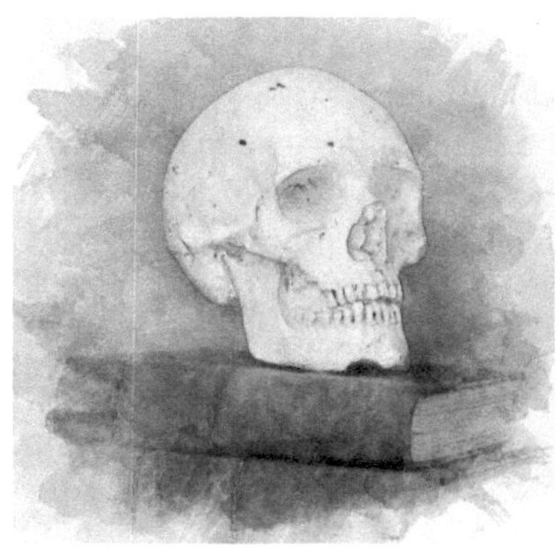

Death and Taxes

The bell tinkled.

Felix looked up from the book he was reading to the front door of the small storefront office to see who had opened it and caused the small silver bell attached to the lintel to ring.

This time of the year, the office was usually quiet. The big tax day rush had passed and Felix wouldn't see many more customers until the deadline for those who had filed extensions was looming.

The man who entered seemed cautious and confused. He was carrying a large cardboard box presumably filled with W-2's, 1099's and assorted receipts. He looked at Felix, then cast his gaze over the array of empty desks surrounding him.

As the door swung shut, it caused the bell to tinkle again.

The man looked up at the small, silver dome hanging above the door approvingly. He coughed into his elbow as he scanned the parking lot in front of the office, as if checking to make sure no one had followed him.

The stranger looked to be about thirty. His clothes were rumpled, his hair was messy, but his eyes were keen, sharp and alert, constantly on the lookout for danger.

He turned back toward Felix. "Are you open?" he asked.

"Yes, sir. We most definitely are. How can I help you?" Felix closed his book and slid it into a drawer.

"Do you do taxes?"

"We do. Have you filed an extension?"

"I haven't. I've had a lot of personal stuff going on lately."

"I'm sorry to hear that, sir," Felix replied.

"I wasn't sure this was a tax place," he said.

"Why is that?"

"Well, the name. 'Death and Taxes.' I thought it was some clever marketing gimmick for a restaurant or a gift shop."

"I'm not sure I'd want to eat at a restaurant called 'Death and Taxes,'" Felix said.

"Nor would I," the man agreed.

"Then it's a good thing we help people do their taxes, and that you seem to have tax obligations you need assistance with," Felix replied, nodding at the box tucked under one of the man's arms.

"Yes, I suppose it is."

"Though if you did have any death related matters, we could certainly help with that as well."

"You mean like probate or inheritance?" the man asked.

"Something like that," Felix replied.

The man stepped toward Felix's desk and placed the box on one corner. "So, how do we get started?" the man asked.

"Please, have a seat," Felix offered.

The man sat, clearly uncomfortable. He looked around, casting furtive glances over his shoulder.

"Is there something wrong?" Felix asked.

"No," the man answered. "I just need to get out of town and was hoping to get through this quickly."

"Well, that all depends on how complicated your return is." Felix said, eyeing the box on the corner of his desk. "Let's get started with the basics." He turned toward his computer screen and poised his hands over his keyboard. "Name?"

"Harold Potter."

Felix raised an eyebrow, but didn't make any "Harry Potter" remarks, much to Harold's obvious relief. "Address?"

The accountant's hands flew over the keyboard as his newest client dictated his personal information.

"Do you have any W-2's?" Felix asked.

Harold grabbed the box and set it on his lap. He dug through the loose collection of documents, invoices and cash register receipts and handed over several loose sheets.

"Thank you," Felix said. He laid the forms out on his desk, then his right hand danced upon the numeric keypad, transferring the printed numbers on the paper form into the corresponding boxes on the computer screen. "1099's?" Felix asked.

Harold fished out several more forms from the box.

"Investments?" Felix inquired.

"Not per se," Harold replied.

Felix knew better than to press clients who were vague with their answers. His name would be on the form alongside the taxpayer, and potentially the IRS could call him in, but if he didn't knowingly do anything wrong, he wasn't criminally liable himself. So, the less he knew about what the client didn't want anyone else to know, the better.

The accountant guided Harold through the a long series of forms—some answers to his questions engendering the need to add even more forms to the return—but the computer kept track of it all and made sure all the requirements were being satisfied. It was a much better system than the old days, when you had to leaf through hundreds of pages of instructions printed on flimsy newsprint. Now everything was cross checked and up to date and the company provided the very best software for Felix—and during the busy season—the other accountants.

It took almost four hours for the diligent tax agent to make his way through the stack of papers Harold had brought in. Most of the time was spent categorizing expenses. Although Felix didn't pry into things that his clients wanted to keep private, anything that they placed in front of him received his full and proper scrutiny. That said, he didn't mind getting creative at times, but always within the letter of the IRS regulations.

The whole time, Harold would occasionally cast a glance toward the door. A few times, he got up to get a better view of the activity in the parking lot outside.

Finally, Felix arrived at the final number. "7,454 dollars," he announced.

Harold seemed surprised. "Wow, I've never gotten a refund that big before. I should come here every year."

Felix grimaced. He had made this mistake in the past, assuming that his client knew the general direction in which their tax liability lie. But obviously Harold was oblivious to the fact that his earnings far exceeded his withholding and deductions. "I'm sorry, that's 7,454 dollars that you owe."

"What?"

"You owe the IRS 7,454 dollars."

Harold's eyes widened at the news. He tried to speak, but started coughing instead. After a fit that lasted more than a few seconds, Harold cleared his throat and stared at Felix, incredulous.

"That can't be. I got a three hundred dollar refund last year."

"Yes, well, it appears that most of your income this past year was from your Schedule C activities—which, as you know, is money earned from self-employment. Unfortunately, that means you're responsible for both portions of the Social Security withholding as well as the Medicare and state and federal taxes. And your W-2 income was withheld at a rate assuming more exemptions than you qualify for, so you were a little light on that end as well. Plus penalties for being late."

"Seven thousand dollars," Harold said, reclining in his seat.

"7,454," Felix reminded him.

"But no cents."

"The IRS rounds everything to the nearest dollar."

"That's nice of them."

"Yes, it is," Felix agreed.

"I'll be honest with you. I don't have that kind of money in cash. I've been a little strapped lately. I was hoping I was going to walk out of here with a check."

"I'm sorry, Mr. Potter, but the figures don't lie."

"No, no, I'm not saying they do. I know you did your best. It's my fault for not staying on top of things. So, what's the bottom line? What happens if I don't pay?"

"There will be interest and more penalties that accrue. It can add up quite rapidly."

"I can imagine."

Felix sat back and folded his hands in his lap while he allowed Harold to soak in the bad news. He didn't think it was the right time to explain that the total did not include the fee for his time and services.

"So," Harold began, "any suggestions?"

Felix paused.

The question was inevitable. They all asked it—the ones who owed more than they expected or could afford.

He did have a "suggestion" but after the recent tax day rush, he was hoping he could have a break from engaging in the other side of the business.

"Well, sir, as you noted, the name of our establishment is 'Death and Taxes.'"

"Yes, almost too clever," Harold replied.

"It's not so much clever as a simple description that is inclusive of another service we offer—in addition to helping you fill out your tax forms."

Harold appeared curious. "What service would that be?"

"Death," Felix replied.

"Death?" Harold asked, punctuating his question with another cough.

"Yes, death," Felix confirmed.

Harold looked at the accountant for a moment, then smiled and started laughing. "You got me. That's very good. Death. Of course. No, seriously, do you have some sort of payment plan or personal loan service?"

"No, we don't, sir. Just the death thing."

"Oh, now it's a death *thing*."

"In a manner of speaking."

Harold noticed that Felix was not laughing or even smiling. That cool, calm, emotionless number cruncher's exterior had not been breached. He leaned toward Felix. "I'm afraid I'm not following you. What exactly do you mean by 'death thing'?"

"Well, to put it simply, in exchange for the funds you require, we get a portion of your life."

"My what?"

"Your life. We effectively shorten it, bringing you that much closer to death, hence the 'death thing.'"

"I can't tell if you're joking," Harold replied.

"Oh, I don't joke. In fact, I've been told I have no sense of humor at all," Felix insisted.

"I believe you," Harold said. "So, what is this? One of those hidden camera TV shows? Is Howie Mandel going to pop out from behind that door and shout, 'Gotcha!'?"

"No. Howie Mandel does not work here."

"Boy, you weren't kidding about not having a sense of humor," Harold observed.

"We do have a Margaret Mandelbaum at the home office—"

"Forget Howie Mandel. How does this 'taking' part of my life work?—assuming I actually believe you can do it."

"Oh, I assure you we can. We do it all the time. You simply sign a contract stating that the last however many days, months or years which are required to settle your debt will be subtracted from the end of your life."

"What's the catch?"

"Catch, sir?"

"Am I selling my soul to the Devil, or something like that?"

"Oh, no. We have no fiduciary relationship with the Devil. Your soul remains yours, and that matter will be settled in whatever manner suits the life you've led. We just take a little bit off the end of your life."

"And what do you do with it?" Harold asked.

"Do with it?"

"Yes, these days, months or years that you claim. What do you do with them?"

"I'm sure I don't know, sir. I just arrange the paperwork."

"You must have some idea," Harold pressed.

"Not in the least. Not my department," Felix asserted. "Would you like to know how much of your life would be required to satisfy your tax debt—along with our firm's fees for services?"

Harold sat back again. "Sure, why not? How many years would I have to give up?"

Felix spun around and removed a cover from an odd looking adding machine resting on the credenza behind him. He lifted the machine and placed it in the center of his blotter, nudging the computer keyboard aside as he did so.

He started entering numbers, after which he pulled a lever attached to the side of the machine, which caused a roll of paper to advance revealing a long list of digits. After a few minutes of tapping and pulling, Felix ripped the paper off from the back of the machine and inspected the final number.

"Five months, seven days," he announced.

Harold seemed surprised again, only this time pleasantly so.

"That's it? No hours, minutes or seconds?"

"Like the IRS, we like to round off our calculations."

"That does simplify things."

"Yes, sir."

"So, let me get this straight," Harold said, placing his hands on the desk and sitting upright. "I agree to give up the last few months of my life, when I'm likely incontinent, impotent and senile, and you take care of my tax bill."

"And the fees for our services, yes, Mr. Potter."

Harold considered. "Okay. Where do I sign?"

"You seem very eager. I urge you to take some time to consider the implications of this deal," Felix cautioned.

"Well, the truth is, I've got nothing to lose. I walked in here hoping to get my taxes done so I could get some quick cash. You see, my Schedule C income, which you so artfully classified as 'consulting services,' is more of an independent contractor situation."

"I don't need to know this, sir."

Harold ignored Felix's protestation. "I'm what's called in the common parlance a hit man. And my boss has a unique way of maintaining a certain level of quality in his contractors. Every couple of years, he hires a whole new staff, and gives each of us veterans a contract on one of the new guys, and the new guys—or gals—get a contract on one of us. Whomever survives gets the job."

"He must save a lot of money on retirement plans."

Harold smiled. "Indeed. The thing is, you never know when he's going to spring these surprise 'evaluations' on us, so, at this very moment, there is a young, hungry hit man looking to take my life and my job. My current financial situation put me at a disadvantage, I was hoping to make a few purchases to aid in my counter-assassination efforts, but your deal provides me with an alternate way to resolve my current situation."

"How so?" Felix asked.

"If I am to be felled by this rookie, then when I sign your contract, I should just drop dead—since he's likely to kill me in the next five days rather than months. But if I'm ultimately to succeed and survive, I won't."

"That's quite an interesting notion," the accountant said.

"Exactly. So, even though I didn't get what I expected, you may be able to provide me with something I need. Where do I sign?"

Felix pulled the appropriate form from a desk drawer and filled in the necessary fields. He marked the signature line with an X and spun the document around for Harold to sign, offering a pen.

"I don't have to sign in blood or anything?" Harold asked.

"No, sir. Black ink will do."

Harold took the pen and scribbled his name at the bottom of the document.

He put the pen down, then stared at Felix, part of him expecting to simply expire.

But he didn't.

There was no heart attack, or stroke, or assassin's bullet piercing his brain. He simply coughed once again. "There you go," Harold said, satisfied.

The bell over the front door tinkled.

Harold hit the ground.

A gun fired, and a bullet zipped through the air where he had been sitting a fraction of a second earlier and slammed into a desk lamp, shattering its glass frame and bulb.

Felix sat perfectly still, watching as the man with a contract on Harold Potter's life entered the office. He fired several more shots at the floor in front of Felix's desk—but the hit man was gone.

A look of fear crossed the younger man's face, soon thereafter replaced by an expression of surprise as a bullet found a way into his neck, and then a second one pierced his forehead.

The man dropped to the ground.

Harold arose from his hiding place, holding his gun on the fallen assassin. He walked up to the body and put three more bullets into the corpse's chest, then slid his weapon into his concealed holster. He crossed back to Felix's desk and picked up the box of receipts and tax forms. "Sorry about the mess."

"Not at all, sir. We have people for just such an occasion," Felix replied. He peered at the dead man laying in the middle of the office, his blood soaking into the carpet.

"Well, pleasure doing business with you."

Harold turned toward the front door.

"Mr. Potter," Felix said.

Harold turned around. "Yes?"

"I couldn't help but notice that several of your receipts were of a medical nature and somewhat recent."

As if to answer, Harold coughed. "Just a persistent cough I've been battling. Probably allergies."

"I also couldn't help but notice that your clothes are a little loose. Have you been losing weight?"

"A little," Harold confessed. "What are you getting at?"

"Well, one of my coworkers had similar symptoms a couple of years ago. It turned out he had stage four lung cancer."

"I'm sure it's nothing serious," the hit man said confidently as he headed for the door.

"Of course, sir. Have a nice day," Felix said. Then he added, "It's just, at the time he was finally diagnosed, the doctors told him he had only five months to live."

Harold turned back and looked at Felix and smiled. "I'm fine," he said confidently. "Thanks again for your help."

He coughed into his elbow, but noticed a few dark red specks on his sleeve.

"We're here to serve," Felix replied, as he typed out a quick requisition on his computer for a crew to come and collect two bodies.

Harold took three more steps toward the front door, then dropped to his knees, and died.

The Taking Tree

For all her young life, Grandpa taught Daphne about the trees on their land, the different species, where they grew, which of them bore fruit and nuts, and what the various woods were useful for. When one fell in a storm or had just reached the end of its time, if it was the right kind, he lovingly milled it into lumber which he used to make the furniture he sold for a living. The rest they used as fuel for their stove and fireplace.

At every opportunity, he passed on his reverence for the trees to Daphne, instilling in her his devotion to the majestic forest that surrounded them. It seemed from Daphne's point of view that they went on forever. They would often walk along faint, shaded trails through the trees for hours.

In truth, though at one time he laid claim to thousands of acres, over the years he had been forced to sell off various parcels to pay his taxes and other expenses when he didn't have enough wood to make tables and chairs to sell in town. At present, he owned fewer than a hundred acres, including the hill that his home and workshop were built upon.

At the crest of that hill stood an ancient oak, its gnarled trunk so big it took Daphne twelve steps to walk completely around it. Its branches spread out so far that even on a sunny day it felt like dusk was looming when you sat beneath it.

Eating lunch under its boughs with Grandpa was one of Daphne's favorite things to do. Even when it rained, they would enjoy the sandwiches and lemonade Grandpa would pack for them, the foliage shielding them just as well from a cool autumn shower as the hot summer sun.

As the years passed, it was Daphne who took over the task of making the lunch, replacing the packaged cookies Grandpa would sometimes buy with ones she baked herself, and adding a little less sugar to the lemonade than he did.

She took one of the wooden rocking chairs from their front porch and placed it under the tree, as it was getting harder for Grandpa to get up and down off the gingham blanket she spread on the mossy ground beneath the old oak. She would fix him a plate with a sandwich and a pair of cookies. These days the sandwich was often left untouched, but he always finished off the cookies, drinking the lemonade to quiet the coughing fits he seemed beset by more frequently each day.

Grandpa insisted he was fine, but Daphne knew better. The cough he blamed on allergies and dust was getting harsher and wetter, and when she washed his clothes, she saw specks of blood on the crooks of his shirt sleeves.

Then one day, Grandpa found himself unable to get out of bed. Daphne wanted to bring a doctor to their home, but he convinced her to just sit with him instead. A doctor would make him go to a hospital, and those places were noisy and stunk of medicine. He wanted to stay in his own bed, where the afternoon breeze carried in the scent of the woods and the flowers currently in bloom, and he could see the stately oak atop the hill through his window.

Daphne brought his usual lunch in to the bedroom on a tray and set it on the table next to the bed.

Grandpa didn't even look at it, not even the oatmeal raisin cookies that were his favorite.

She sat in the rocking chair, facing grandpa. His gaze was fixed on the tree framed by the curtains of his bedroom window, dancing in the breeze.

"When was the last time I told you a story?" he asked in a hoarse voice.

Daphne smiled. It had been years since she had grown out of that bedtime ritual, preferring to do her own reading of the books she regularly checked out of the modest library in town. "I don't know," she replied. "It's been a long time."

Grandpa nodded, the movement of his head barely perceptible. "Did I ever tell you the story of the dryads?" he asked.

Daphne certainly knew what dryads and hamadryads were. Nymphs from Greek mythology that inhabited the woods and protected the trees. She had read about them in countless books and stories, but couldn't remember Grandpa ever telling her about them.

"I don't think so," she replied.

Grandpa closed his eyes for a moment, then turned to face Daphne, forcing his mouth into a smile. "You never needed to know," he said.

"Know what?"

"How they can be summoned. People think they are just a myth, but they are real. And there are times when they are needed. And I fear that time may be near."

"What are you talking about, Grandpa?"

"I thought I would have more time... more time to prepare you before I passed."

Daphne fought back a tear. "Don't talk like that. You're going to live forever, Grandpa," she said.

He smiled again. "I must pass on what I know. It cannot die with me as I fear I am the last person on this Earth to know how to summon the spirit of the tree."

"You should rest, Grandpa. Don't try to talk. Save your strength." She reached out and placed her hand on his. His skin felt cold and papery.

He grabbed her wrist with a force that frightened Daphne. The scars earned from decades of woodworking that formed a lattice along his forearm seemed to whiten with the strain. His eyes were wide open, and a sense of urgency shone from their dark pupils. "Listen to me. You must know how the dryad is called," he insisted.

Daphne nodded. "Okay," she replied.

The iron grip on her wrist relaxed, and his hand slackened and fell back onto the bed. He looked over at the glass of lemonade on the night table, and Daphne leaned over and guided its straw to his lips. He sipped slowly and carefully for a moment, then turned away and Daphne returned the glass to the table.

Grandpa took a deep breath. It seemed like he was going to start another coughing fit, but instead he turned his gaze back out toward the old oak. "You must take an acorn from the tree, before it has a chance to fall to the ground," he recited, as if he was passing on something that was told to him generations past. "Then dig a hole under the branches of the tree, but where it can see the light of the full moon when it rises."

Daphne couldn't make sense of what he was saying, but listened intently anyway.

"Do not wet it with water. You must use blood." He turned to face Daphne, a desperate look deepening his wrinkles. "You must use blood," he repeated, "enough to soak the ground."

He swallowed dryly.

Daphne reached for the glass of lemonade, but he waved her off. She sat back, contemplating whether she should fetch a doctor despite Grandpa's wishes.

He continued speaking, as if talking in his sleep. "From an acorn sown in this manner will come the spirit of the tree… the dryad… and she will protect it and all the trees of the forest." His voice trailed off.

Daphne had a sudden fear that he was dead. But then she saw his chest rise slightly, then fall again, and when she placed her fingers on his fragile wrist, she could discern a pulse.

She sat there, just watching him sleep, rocking back and forth in the chair hewn from the wood of a tree from his own forest.

* * *

It rained that night. A storm that lasted from the last light of dusk until the sun finally broke through the clouds again at dawn.

Daphne went into the kitchen to put on a kettle for tea. It wasn't until she had lit a fire in the old wood stove and sat down at the kitchen table that she noticed the back door was open.

The threshold was still damp—it must've been open all night. Had someone broken in?

Or had someone gone out?

Daphne rushed to Grandpa's bedroom. The bed was empty. She ran back to the kitchen and out the back door.

In the rain-soaked ground was a muddy trail, as if something had been dragged through it, bending the sparse blades of grass, leaving a rut that lead up the hill toward the old oak tree.

Daphne followed the trail. "Grandpa?" she shouted. "Are you out here?"

The tracks grew fainter as the grass got thicker, but the direction they were headed was unmistakable.

At the base of the oak's trunk was a damp, dirty lump.

She picked it up and discovered it was Grandpa's pajamas, soaked in mud.

But where was he?

Daphne stood at the base of the tree, glancing around the clearing that surrounded the hill for Grandpa or any sign of where he had gone.

But there was nothing.

How far could a sick, naked old man get? she wondered.

"Grandpa!" she called into the stillness of the morning. "Grandpa, where are you?"

An acorn fell from a high branch and hit her on the head. She looked up, expecting to see him nestled up in the branches, grinning at her, ready to jump down and laugh at the grand joke he had played.

But all she saw was the twisted, ancient branches, older than the United States, Grandpa had told her, with their shiny, pointed leaves and acorns dangling.

Then she saw something else. Something she'd never noticed before. A large burl, at least six feet across, set into the trunk about ten feet off the ground. It must've been there for decades to have grown so large, but for some reason this was the first time she had seen it. Maybe she had never looked up at that spot before, or maybe there had been branches covering it that had fallen away.

Then she looked down at the pile of dirty pajamas and underwear, wondering just where Grandpa had gone?

It was about a month after Grandpa disappeared when the man showed up.

Daphne saw him out the kitchen window. He emerged from the woods, pausing to inspect the trees. When he entered the clearing and saw the grand oak perched at atop the hill, he cinched the straps of his backpack and strode directly toward it.

Daphne went to the hall closet and took out the shotgun Grandpa kept tucked behind the winter coats and boots.

She settled the weapon into the crook of her arm, then headed for the back door and set herself on a course for the tree. Her distance was shorter, and the man didn't seem to notice her approach, as his eyes were fixed on the towering trestle of foliage.

Once he was close, she racked the shotgun.

Its distinctive sound caught his attention. Daphne wasn't aiming it at him, but he raised his hands regardless, attempting to show he meant no harm.

"Hold on there," he said in a surprisingly disarming voice. "No need to shoot. I surrender."

"You're trespassing," Daphne told him. "Turn around and go back where you came from."

The man locked eyes with Daphne, assessing whether her intent matched the tone in her voice. He nodded, then moved one hand slowly toward a pocket in his vest. "Now, that's not quite true," he said with a grin that charmed Daphne much more than she wanted to admit. "It ain't trespassing if it's my land."

"It's not your land." She swung the barrel of the shotgun in his direction. "I'm not going to tell you again. Leave."

A pained expression erased his grin as he pulled a folded sheet of paper out of the pocket. He held it out to her. "This deed says otherwise."

Daphne reached out for the paper, then took a step back as she unfolded and inspected it.

"You see," the man continued, "the previous owner was in arrears on his taxes. The county put this land up for auction, and now it belongs to me."

"That's wrong. It's belongs to Grandpa," she said.

"Okay," the man said in a calm, reasonable voice, "then maybe we should go talk to him."

"He's gone," Daphne responded.

"When will he be back?"

Daphne didn't answer.

The man drew the obvious conclusion. "My apologies and condolences. You're his granddaughter then. I'm guessing you thought this land passed on to you. But the fact is he was more than a year behind on his taxes. Surely you must've gotten a letter or a phone call."

He looked toward the small house and the nearby barn that had served as Grandpa's workshop. There were no power or telephone lines leading toward it, and no driveway wound its way through the surrounding forest toward the nearest road.

"You live here all by yourself? No electricity? What do you do for food?"

"I have food. If I need to, I go into town."

"It's quite a walk," the man replied.

"I don't mind it."

He nodded in understanding.

"Well, listen, I'm sorry about your grandfather, and I'm sorry that he didn't keep up with the taxes and put you in this position, but these woods," he said, waving his arm around in a sweeping gesture, "that house," he added with a look in the direction of Daphne's home, "and this tree," he said with a tone of awe in his voice, "all belong to me, now."

Daphne knew about such things as taxes and forfeitures and auctions. She had read about them among the thousands of books she had checked out from the library over the years. But for her, the world was this land, the house, and the town three miles away. She'd never had need of anything else. Grandpa always took care of her.

But Grandpa was gone.

She lowered the gun, and a tear ran down her cheek.

"Listen, why don't we go to your house and talk this over? Maybe we can come to some sort of accommodation," the man suggested.

She nodded, then started trudging back toward the house.

Daphne poured some lemonade, prepared a plate of cookies, then joined the man at the kitchen table.

He was admiring its carefully crafted surface and the chair he was sitting on. "Did your grandfather make these?" he asked.

"Yes, he had a workshop out in the barn."

The man whistled his admiration. "And with no power tools, that is old school." He took a sip of the lemonade, seemingly equally impressed with its flavor, as he was the quality of the table it rested upon. "I'm a furniture maker myself. I picked up this land because it's one of the last tracts of old growth left around here. I'm lucky someone at one of the lumber mills didn't snatch it up."

Daphne didn't say anything.

"I saw a burl on that oak on top of the hill. Do you have any idea what a knot of wood that size is worth?" he asked.

She didn't answer.

"Thousands. If you were to make it into a dining room table, maybe a desk. Heck, a burl that size I could do both with matching chairs."

"You want to cut down my tree?" Daphne asked, horrified.

The man laughed. "Well, isn't that what they're for?" he asked, patting the table they were sitting at.

"Grandpa never cut them down. He only took the ones that fell, or were struck by lightning."

He nodded. "Probably why he couldn't pay his taxes."

Daphne folded her hands in her lap and looked down.

"Look, I'm not a bad guy. There's no reason why you can't stay here. I won't even charge you rent."

She looked up, hopeful. "And you'll leave the trees alone?"

"Well, then I'd be in the same spot as your grandfather, and the next guy to pick this place up would probably clearcut the lot. There's a lot of valuable timber out there, no need to cut down the whole forest."

"And Grandpa's oak?" she asked hopefully.

He shrugged apologetically. "You see now, that's the one that's going to allow me to be so generous." The man rose from the table, hefted his pack onto his back, and looked at Daphne.

"That's the deal. You can stay here as long as you like, but the trees belong to me now," he said. "Take it or leave it."

Daphne was silent.

"You think it over," he said, then grabbed a cookie and headed out of the house.

Daphne searched through the old rolltop desk where Grandpa kept track of his furniture business. In one drawer, she found a stack of letters from the county, overdue notices and warnings. She tore them up in frustration, pounded the solid wood surface of the desk until her hands ached and then leaned forward and rested her head on it and cried.

What could she do? She was all alone.

Then she remembered Grandpa's last conversation with her the night before he disappeared.

She recalled the ritual he had described to bring forth the dryad, the protector of the trees.

It was crazy, but maybe there was something to it. Something had happened to Grandpa under that old oak. Could it have been a dryad that had taken him to his reward? To become a part of the trees he had loved so much? Had that burl been there all along, or was it...

She struggled to remember what he had said. She knew it required a full moon, and fortunately one would be rising that very night. Also, an unfallen acorn—the tree was ripe with them at present.

And blood.

She would have to soak the acorn in her own blood without somehow killing herself in the process. She found the large Bowie knife in its sheath Grandpa always had attached to his belt, grabbed a washcloth and an old pillowcase from the linen closet, then climbed back to the top of the hill.

The man was gone, and the sun was just starting to set.

The moon would be rising over the eastern horizon, so she used the knife to carve a small ditch out of the densely packed soil under the tree, careful to remain under the protection of its boughs, but in a spot where the moonlight would find it.

Then she searched the branches for the perfect acorn, one that wasn't still green, but instead plump with promise. She carefully plucked one from its branch and nestled it into the rent earth.

Kneeling, Daphne positioned her arm over the hole, then ran the razor-sharp blade of the Bowie across her flesh. The cut welled with blood, but little more than drips fell upon the acorn.

Daphne pressed the point of the knife into a spot halfway between her wrist and elbow and pushed it into her flesh. She ignored the pain and sliced toward her elbow—just an inch or so—then withdrew the blade.

Blood quickly pooled on her arm. She positioned the wound directly over the acorn, then let the blood spill onto the ground.

There was so much. Within seconds, the acorn was submerged in the thick red liquid. She grabbed the washcloth and pressed it against the wound. It was instantly soaked, transforming the white terry cloth fabric into crimson. She grabbed the strips of the pillowcase she had cut earlier and wound them tightly around her arm to the point of being painful. The bleeding seemed to have slowed if not stopped completely. She tied the remaining strips around her arm, then covered the acorn in its ensanguined furrow with dirt.

She felt light-headed and laid back, staring up at the gnarled bark covering the burl on the great oak's trunk as darkness enveloped her.

* * *

The sound of a loud diesel engine woke her.

It was morning.

She looked around, but couldn't see its source.

Then, a great yellow machine crashed through the woods, heading straight for the hill.

Daphne pushed herself up to a sitting position, causing a wave of pain in her left forearm. She gazed at the makeshift bandage, then looked at the spot where she had planted the acorn and watered it with her own blood.

It was just a patch of ground.

What did she expect? A magic seedling? That a wood nymph would grow from it?

Grandpa was just a crazy old man after all.

The sound of the excavator climbing the hill grew closer, then stopped altogether.

Daphne got to her feet and looked over at it. Its folded arm with a toothed bucket at the end of it was nearly ten feet tall.

The man, who was now the land's owner, cut the engine and stepped down out of the cab, then unstrapped an enormous chain saw from the back of the machine. Its blade was nearly as long as Daphne was tall.

"Step away, little girl," the man said condescendingly. The friendly overtures were gone. He was single-minded in his purpose. "I checked in town. The old man who owned this place didn't have any children—let alone a granddaughter. I don't know what kind of sick relationship you two had, and I don't care. But you don't want to get in my way."

With a practiced motion, he grabbed the pull handle, and let the momentum of the saw falling away from him combined with an upward yank bring the mighty machine to life with a gasoline-powered roar.

Daphne shook her head, helpless. She rushed toward the tree and set herself between it and the man.

"You think I won't do it? This is my land. That is my tree. And you are the one trespassing. I have every right to cut right through you," he swore.

Daphne felt a well of emotion rise up in her, starting at her feet, then up through her gut all the way to her head, a level of anger she had never experienced before. It felt like… power. As if her feet were rooted to the ground and she was as immovable as the oak behind her.

Strength coursed through her veins, and determination hooded her eyes in a way that gave the man pause.

An acorn hit him on top of the head, surprising him.

Then another dropped, landing on his shoulder.

He looked up and a half dozen more showered down on him, causing him to almost lose his balance. He raised the long blade of the chainsaw and cut through the nearest bough as if it was a hot knife slicing through butter.

The branch crashed to the ground.

Daphne felt a pain in her arm, as if it had been cut from her body.

But when she looked at it, it was still there. She curled her hand into a fist, and a torrent of acorns released from branches above the man, pelting him with a hundred hard nuts.

He backed away and tripped over the branch, losing his footing and his grip on the chainsaw. He landed on the hard ground heavily, his face inches from the sharp teeth of the saw. He scrambled to his feet, picked up his tool, and opened the throttle until its roar was deafening.

Daphne held her ground. Both her fists were now tight balls, her feet anchored tightly in place, waiting for him to strike.

The man advanced with the chainsaw, its whirring chain so close to Daphne that she could feel it a throwing off small drops of oil toward her cheek. If he wanted this tree, he was going to have to go through her.

Then, suddenly, he snapped back as if something had yanked him. He dropped the chainsaw, and this time its blade ground to a halt in the dirt, causing the motor to sputter and die.

One of the branches of the old oak was somehow wrapped around the man's waist.

It lifted him off the ground.

More branches got hold of his arms and legs as he struggled wildly against them.

Then Daphne realized it wasn't the tree that was retaliating against its attacker.

It was her.

She was orchestrating the movement of the oak's limbs, passing him from branch to branch until he was pressed against the trunk of the tree, right above where she was standing.

"Who are you?" the man asked as the bark of the old oak started to engulf him.

"I am the dryad of this tree and this forest," she answered.

And she instantly knew it was true.

The reason her ritual hadn't called forth the wood nymph was because the dryad was her.

Grandpa hadn't told her what she needed to do. He was recounting what he had done. It was Grandpa who had summoned her from the tree, then raised her as his granddaughter so that she might protect the forest when this day came.

The man howled as bark grew over his neck and ears and eyes until he was silenced when wood filled his mouth.

Daphne felt the power drain out of her, flowing down from her head and hands, through her body and out the soles of her feet, back into the roots of the tree.

She looked up.

There were now two burls bulging from the trunk of the old oak.

She turned to the first one and said, "Thank you, Grandpa."

Then she gazed out at the forest, and the trees seemed to bow toward her as a strong wind blew through their branches.

Alien Me

The voices woke me. They were oddly familiar, but also different in some way that bothered my senses.

"Telemetry recording is on," one of the voices said. It was a woman's voice, someone I knew. But my mind was cloudy. The connections between what I was hearing and my memories weren't working properly. The name of the person I was listening to was on the edge of my recall, but frustratingly out of reach.

I tried to open my eyes, but my lids failed to move.

I tried to move my head, but again, something was blocking my attempt. Was I paralyzed? Had I been in some sort of accident?

I listened more intently. My hearing seemed to be the only sense that was working. There was some machine in the distance that was beeping at regular intervals.

And I could hear other sounds. Something moved across the floor on wheels. I think there was a fan blowing somewhere as well, and some sort of electric hum that I couldn't identify.

It could be a hospital room. Or perhaps an operating room.

Was that why the voices sounded odd to me? They were being muffled by surgical masks? Was I one of those rare cases where someone woke up under anesthesia and broke through the drugs that rendered me unconscious so that I would be aware of what was happening while the surgeons cut me open?

Could I feel pain? Would I experience the excruciating agony that accompanied a scalpel slicing through my skin, and sutures repairing whatever damage had delivered me into this situation?

But there was no pain. Whatever was paralyzing me was thankfully sparing me that unimaginable torture.

"Okay, let's deactivate the visual sensory blocks," a male voice said.

Deactivate visual sensory blocks? They were intentionally blinding me? What had happened? Were my eyes damaged? My brain?

Suddenly, I was able to see.

A bright white light filled my vision. Gradually it dimmed, and shapes started to form. I tried to blink, but although it seemed I could now open my eyes, I couldn't close them. I could see a light in front of me. Or was it above me? I felt like I was lying on my back, but I couldn't be certain. The more I focused on what I could see, the more my newly restored sight confirmed that I was peering upward. There were lights and apparatus visible above me.

But they didn't look like the kind of things you might find in an operating room. For one thing, the ceiling was not as high as I expected it would be. And the light was too bright to make out any details, but it was not like what you'd expect to find in a surgical theater and appeared to be poised on the end of an articulated arm.

Beyond it, the ceiling was plain white, as far as I could tell. Sterile and seamless.

Why couldn't I move my head? Why couldn't I move my eyes, or look around?

I was starting to panic. What was happening to me? Who were these people? Where was I?

I tried to recall the last thing I could remember. I was in my lab with Jenna, my wife. We were finishing a takeout dinner—Thai food, Jenna's favorite. We were talking about something. But like the nebulous connection between the voices in the room where I was trapped—unable to move—and my memories, the topic of that conversation eluded me. I must have told a joke, however, because I could recall at one point she nearly sprayed a mouthful of Pad Thai all over the table, trying not to laugh too hard.

Jenna and I had been together since college. I could remember that much. And once I recalled that, more details about our relationship fell into place. We had gotten married on the beach on a terribly windy day. We had two children, both girls, and she was constantly trying to get me to agree to try again for a boy. We lived in a house we had built on a piece of land Jenna had inherited.

We worked for a tech startup, one that a friend of ours from college had funded with the proceeds from a previous startup that had left him a billionaire. Oddly, I couldn't remember either the name of the company or what we did.

Maybe I did have brain damage. Had I been in an accident? Did I break my neck in addition to injuring my head? Is that why I couldn't move and wasn't feeling any pain?

But why wasn't I in a hospital?

It was becoming more and more apparent to me that wherever I was, it was not a medical facility that I could recognize.

What else could I remember? Had we gone home? I struggled to recall the events after our office dinner, but all I could remember was blackness. A blackness dotted with small, distant twinkling lights. I knew what this was. Why was my brain denying me the ability to put a name to it?

The sky! It was the night sky, filled with stars and a few wisps of clouds floating by on an evening breeze.

We were outside. Standing on a balcony just outside my office. We were on the top floor of a three story building, our arms wrapped around each other, waiting for something to happen.

Then I remembered what we were waiting for. There was a meteor shower that night, and Jenna had wanted to see it and make a wish. I suspected she was wishing I would give in and go along with her plan for another kid.

We didn't have to wait long. Meteorites streaked across the sky, some of them close enough and bright enough to light up the woods around us. Jenna clutched me tight as it seemed the metallic rocks from space seemed to be getting nearer.

Then one of them actually landed. It smashed into the woods not far from us, throwing up a flare of light, followed a few seconds later by a loud boom.

"Oh, I hope it doesn't start a forest fire," Jenna said. "Maybe we should go out and make sure."

"It's got to be four or five miles away. And who knows if it landed near the road," I replied.

"Shouldn't we call someone?"

"We're not the only ones who saw or heard it. If it started a fire, someone closer will call."

Jenna wrapped her arms around me, but I could tell she wasn't going to be satisfied unless she knew for herself that the meteorite hadn't created a conflagration that had somehow escaped the attention of everyone else in the county.

To be honest, I was kind of curious to see what had landed.

"Okay," I said. "Let's go check it out."

But I couldn't remember anything beyond that point.

Had we tried to find it? Did my ten-year-old Prius make it to the crash site? Or did we run into a fallen tree, or have a blowout that sent us careening into a ravine?

Jenna.

Was Jenna okay? Had she been hurt?

The voices pulled me back from my reverie.

"Is he responding?" the male voice asked.

Why was it so familiar?

"I think so, but I can't tell for sure," the female voice replied.

Then my mind finally made the connection. The woman who was

just out of view… was Jenna.

As if she could hear my thoughts, she leaned over into my field of vision, staring straight into my eyes.

Jenna.

What was going on? She didn't seem harmed herself—which was a relief—but what was she doing? Who was she talking to?

Then, the owner of the other voice leaned in as well.

If I could have screamed, I would have.

It was me.

The face of the man looking down at me was the same one I had seen in the mirror for the last thirty-seven years.

What the hell was going on?

He shook his head—*my* head.

"I don't know," he said. "Maybe there was a problem with the integration process…"

Integration process? What was he talking about?

Panic welled up in me, but the usual sensations that accompanied those rare moments when I felt out of control were missing. I couldn't feel my pulse racing, or my breathing growing faster and shallower. Maybe I was attached to some sort of heart-lung machine.

But that didn't explain the man who was my exact—and I mean down to the nick on my chin from shaving that morning—replica.

Who was he? Why did he look like me? Sound like me? And why was Jenna helping him do whatever it was they were doing to me?

Then it hit me. Why did I assume it was Jenna—or at least my Jenna? If there was a dopplegänger of me, why did I assume the woman who looked like my wife was actually her?

Why did I assume either of them… was human?

What if that meteorite wasn't a random piece of rock that had had the misfortune to intersect Earth's orbit?

What if it had been something with a purpose?

Something alien.

Something capable of making perfect replicas of myself and Jenna.

Had they had intercepted us on the way to the crash site—or rather, landing site—or had we actually made it there and stepped right into their trap?

In either case, the aliens had disabled us, rendered us immobile and unconscious through some advanced technological means, or perhaps using some alien biological process to subvert our ability to fight back, to resist.

And then they had duplicated us. It looked like they had taken the clothes from our bodies to wear themselves, and then what? Beamed us back aboard a mothership? Or maybe simply put us in the back of the Prius and drove us some place where they could conduct their experiments.

Is that why my memory seemed so full of holes? Had part of the duplication process included copying my mind as well? Was that the *integration process* he—or rather it—had mentioned earlier?

If you thought about it, it was the perfect way to invade Earth. Take over the population, replace us until they had enough of them to overpower and control us.

How long had they been at it? Had they been doing it for years? Or were Jenna and I their first victims?

I still wondered, though, why had they kept me alive? Was there still something they needed from me? If I was alive, was it possible that Jenna was as well?

What if our abduction and duplication weren't random? What if they had come specifically for us?

I still couldn't remember what I did, what my research was about. Had they extracted that information from me during the *integration process*? Did they miss something? Is that why they were keeping me alive? To dig those remaining memories out of my mind? Was what Jenna and I did crucial to their plan?

Or did we hold the key to stopping them?

Think, Alan, think! What do they want from you?

It was no use. I couldn't remember. Other memories came flooding back, memories of Janey and Kira, our daughters. The first moments I held them in my arms, their first steps, birthday parties with their friends, reading them stories in bed, teasing them while we watched scary movies in the dark.

There had to be something. Some reason I was special, some purpose they hoped to achieve by subjecting me to their alien experimentation and mental dissection.

What was it I did? What work did Jenna and I share?

If I could hold on to that knowledge, somehow thwart the efforts of these alien impersonators and keep them from getting whatever it was they needed from my mind, maybe I could stop them.

I needed to be able to move. If I could escape somehow, maybe I could raise the alarm and prevent whatever nefarious plans they had from coming to be.

But whatever they had done, whatever devices or drugs had immobilized me and put me at their utter mercy, it was beyond my ability to overcome. Nothing I tried worked. I still couldn't even move my eyes or blink, let alone wiggle a finger or toe or stand.

"Something's going on," the Jenna clone reported. "We're getting activity."

"Anything you can identify?"

She shook her head. "No, I haven't seen this before."

Then another thought occurred to me. How long had I been their prisoner? How long did it take for whatever alien process they used to duplicate a human to complete? It felt to me like it had been mere hours, but I had no way of confirming that. They could have been keeping me in a coma for days, or even months.

But would that fit into their plans? Had they already insinuated themselves into our lives? Into our children's lives?

Oh, God. Had they duplicated Janey and Kira, too?"

The thought was too much for me to bear.

I had to get out.

I had to escape.

I had to stop them!

"Could it be attempts at motor activity?" alien me asked.

The Jenna clone pondered the idea. "Perhaps. But why? Does it think it can move?"

The face that had once been my sole property cocked an eyebrow as he stared into my eyes. "I don't know."

Yes, yes, I'm trying to move, I tried to shout. *Whatever you did to leave me like this, just turn it off. Let me speak and maybe I'll tell you what you want to know. Or maybe I'll find a way to kill you, you alien bastards!*

"Whoa, something just happened," Jenna clone said.

"Yeah, but not what we wanted to happen," alien me said, disappointed.

Good, I thought to myself. *You'll never get what you want from me. As long as I have an iota of life left, I will fight you!* I promised. *I'll see you in hell, you vile, despicable—*

"Shut him down," alien me said.

And everything went dark.

Alan and Jenna stared at their handiwork on the table. Jenna switched off machines while Alan disconnected various leads.

"What do you think went wrong?" Jenna asked.

"I don't know. I was sure for a moment there that we would get confirmation this time."

Jenna placed a comforting hand on Alan's shoulder and drew him into a warm embrace. She pulled back and gave him a quick kiss, a promise that they would succeed someday. "We'll crack it."

"Yeah, hopefully before Dillon's money runs out."

"Dillon's money will never run out. He believes in us."

Alan shook his head, his mind returning to the problem. He sat on a stool and stared at the large crystalline sphere sitting on the workbench. He couldn't see them with the naked eye, but embedded in its structure were nearly a hundred billion artificial neurons, designed to mimic the human brain.

It was his and Jenna's dream to be able to duplicate a human consciousness inside of their NuMind. Jenna and Alan didn't care for the moniker. It had been Dillon's idea. And since he wrote the checks, he got to name it. However, the process they used to map those billions of neurons from a human brain still obviously needed some work. The several dozen attempts they had made to imprint Alan's mind using the high-resolution EEG scanner Jenna had invented, had so far failed—though this last attempt had yielded at least something.

The NuMind was showing activity, and some of it was close to what you would expect from a human brain. But were they kidding themselves that they could duplicate such a complicated biological computer inside something inanimate?

It had been Jenna's idea to add some sensory input, both auditory and visual, but had that helped? Or was it too much for the NuMind to handle?

Well, that was a problem they could tackle another day.

"Come on," Jenna urged. "Let's get home. We promised the girls they could watch the rest of the meteor shower tonight."

"Do you think they'll still be awake?" Alan asked.

"Of course, I haven't been able to get them to sleep since you made them watch *Invasion of the Body Snatchers.*"

"I didn't *make* them watch it. They love watching those old science fiction movies with me," Alan said.

"Yes, that is certainly something they got from you."

"We're going to watch *The Blob* next," Alan promised, walking with Jenna out of the office.

Jenna shook her head and sighed as she switched off the lights. "Someday," she warned, "you're going to wake up thinking you're in one of those movies."

The Incarnadine Teacup

"You say you have the murderer in custody?" Isaac Black asked.

"That's correct," Detective Brown replied.

"You have the motive, the weapon, physical evidence, even a confession," Isaac said, questioningly.

"Yes, the case is all wrapped up, and the killer is in custody," the detective confirmed.

"Then why the hell are we here?" Jeremy White asked.

Detective Brown looked at Isaac, who grinned curiously as he adjusted the dark glasses that hid his sightless eyes. "Aren't you going to tell me why I brought you in on this case?" he asked the blind man.

"Yes, since the detective is being so mysterious, please do enlighten us," Jeremy goaded his companion.

"All right," Isaac said. He turned unerringly in Detective Brown's direction. "We're here because you don't know *how* you solved the case."

"What?" Jeremy asked. "How could he not know how he solved

it? It's solved. I'm sure there were clues and such."

Isaac cocked an inquisitive eyebrow at the police detective.

"He's right," Brown confirmed. "We only knew where to find the evidence and that there had been a murder at all because one of the residents here detailed the whole crime before anyone knew that one had even been committed."

Jeremy looked around. They were in the common area of a retirement home. A host of septuagenarians, octogenarians and likely a few nonagenarians, sat in various couches, armchairs, and wheelchairs. Some were watching a game show on television, others were playing cards, and at one table a quartet of old ladies were drinking tea around a mosaic of mahjong tiles. In his previous career as a nurse, Jeremy White had worked in a facility like this one, assisting the elderly, caring for their needs, both mental and physical.

That was until he accepted a unique assignment through the Amaranth Foundation for the Deaf and Blind, helping with the rehabilitation of a policeman who had been blinded after being shot in the head. The detective, Isaac Black, hadn't considered his miraculous survival a blessing, though. At least not in the beginning.

When Jeremy met first met him, he was depressed and seemed determined to thwart anyone's attempts to help him. So Jeremy acceded to Isaac's wishes. Whenever Isaac would say that he was hungry, or needed to go to the bathroom, or made some other demand, Jeremy would calmly and clearly describe the steps Isaac would need to accomplish the task himself. Eventually Jeremy broke through Isaac's stubbornness, and despite the loss of his sight, he became amazingly adept at navigating his apartment and the subsequently world around him.

But it was when the president of the foundation, Lydia Rosenblum, started bringing "her little puzzles" to Isaac that he found his renewed purpose. At first it was simple things, like helping find lost items, solving small mysteries, challenges that engaged his mind in the same way that had made him one of the most successful detectives in the Chicago Police Department.

Then one day his old partner, Brown, had reached out to get Isaac's opinion on a seemingly uncrackable case. Isaac solved it in the course of an afternoon, and ever since then he—with Jeremy's assistance—had been helping the police with their toughest unsolved crimes.

However, at present they were being called in on a case that required Isaac's innate deductive reasoning for a completely different purpose.

"Which woman was it that related the details of the crime?" Isaac asked.

Brown shook his head, partially in amazement, but mostly in frustration at being unable to stymie Isaac's uncanny ability to fill in the blanks without, it seemed sometimes, any supporting information at all. "Come on now, that was a guess," he accused. "I never said it was a woman."

Isaac smiled. "That's precisely how I knew," he explained. "You purposefully left out the sex of the witness hoping to lead me to believe it was a woman, so that I would assume you were trying to mislead me into thinking it was the opposite and conclude it was a man, ergo it was a woman."

"He guessed," Jeremy confirmed.

"Yes, well, I assume you want to speak with her."

"In a moment. First, I want to go to the crime scene."

"This way," Detective Brown said, pointing them in the direction of a hallway where a uniformed policeman was stationed.

They walked through the common area to a wide corridor, where the residents' private rooms were located. Jeremy described every detail in a low voice to Isaac as they continued toward one of the doors where another policeman was stationed. Whenever Isaac was in a new place, his assistant would relate the salient aspects of their surroundings, allowing Isaac to build a mental map to the point of enabling him navigate the area without assistance.

When they arrived at the guarded room, the officer opened the door for them and the police detective and his guests entered.

"Wow," Jeremy exclaimed upon seeing the contents of the room.

"I can't work with 'wow,'" Isaac reminded him.

"Sorry, where to begin? The room is about twelve by sixteen. The door to the bathroom is to our right, the bed is opposite—it's unmade. There's a lamp and a cell phone on the night table on this side of the bed. At the far end of the room is a pair of chairs with a low coffee table and a large screen television mounted to the wall opposite them. The curtains are mostly drawn, but I can see a lawn through an opening in the drapes. Magazines on the coffee table—investing and current events. In the space past the bathroom there is a small kitchenette, small fridge, sink, toaster oven and a table with two chairs."

When he finished, Isaac turned to Jeremy, as if waiting for him to say something else.

"That's about it," Jeremy concluded.

"You said 'wow' when we walked in. I didn't hear anything that would justify that exclamation."

"Oh, that was regarding his apparent complete lack of style. The bedspread is red, the chairs in front of the television are turquoise, and the coffee table looks like gray Formica. The kitchen table and chairs are an avocado green, the walls are a dingy yellow, his lamp shade is orange, the phone case is pink and there's a throw rug next to the bed that is a pattern of earth tones. Trust me, you're lucky you're blind. This room hurts my eyes."

Detective Brown chuckled.

"Thank you," Isaac said. "I assume the victim was found dead in his bed?"

"Yes, that's right," Brown confirmed. "Aren't you going to tell us what his favorite food was and how many times a week he shaved?"

Isaac smiled. "Toast with butter and jam. And he shaved every day."

Jeremy scoffed. "Okay, the food part was easy, there's a toaster and a fridge, and the residents aren't like to be allowed to have beer in their rooms, so obviously he used it to keep the butter and jam chilled, but we didn't look in the bathroom."

"He's obviously a bachelor," Isaac remarked. "What makes you think he wouldn't want to look nice for the ladies?"

Jeremy looked at Detective Brown for confirmation.

"The victim was clean-shaven," the policeman said with a sigh.

"I'm ready to talk to your witness, now," Isaac proclaimed, then spun around and walked out of the room and back down the hallway toward the common area.

Jeremy and Detective Brown rushed to catch up with him.

Isaac wound his way through the maze of chairs and tables until he arrived at the large round table where a group of women were playing mahjong. "Good afternoon ladies," he said. "Which one of you is the psychic?"

Three of the ladies looked up at Isaac, then glanced at the fourth woman who was arranging her tiles in an ever-changing order.

Jeremy stepped close to Isaac. In situations like this, Isaac preferred him to incorporate his description into the conversation. "Hello, my name is Jeremy, and this is Isaac," he began. "That's a lovely dress you have on. Is pink your favorite color?" he asked the woman who was playing with her tiles.

She ignored the question, and instead said, "I like toast, too."

"Okay," Jeremy said. He surveyed the rest of the woman and noticed that they all had cell phones set in front of them. A sign of the times, he assumed. He gestured at the devices, all individualized with cases of varying colors and designs. "Have I seen you ladies on Tik Tok?" He asked, then snapped his fingers as if recalling something. "You're the ones who do those sexy dance moves. I recognize your fancy phone cases."

The women giggled demurely.

"Where's my tea?" the other one asked.

"It's right there, Gladys," the woman to her right said, sliding the pink tea cup at her elbow in front of her.

Gladys reacted as if the incarnadine vessel had appeared out of thin air. Then lifted it to her lips and took a small sip. She looked up and noticed Isaac, Jeremy and Detective Brown standing across from her. "I like pink," she said, holding up the cup.

"You should get a pink case for your phone instead of that gray one," Jeremy suggested.

She looked at him, unresponsive.

Jeremy leaned forward and pointed at her phone. "You should get that in pink," he repeated.

Gladys looked at her phone as if it was the first time she had seen it. "That's not mine," she insisted and pushed it aside.

"That's your witness?" Jeremy asked Detective Brown.

He nodded. "Yes, according to the Mahjong Club here, she just started jabbering about someone demanding to know where the money was, and that he would never find it. She started shouting for Leonard to leave him alone."

"Leonard is the killer," Isaac interjected.

"Yes, obviously," Brown said. "Then she went on about how Leonard was choking poor Mr. Wilson—the victim," he added before Isaac could jump in. "Then the orderly, Leonard Cook, came running down the hallway from Mr. Wilson's room. Gladys here stood up and pointed at him, shouting, 'He killed him! He killed Mr. Wilson!'"

"How in the world did she know that?" Jeremy asked.

"That's why you guys are here. I'm a little hesitant to put in my report that a psychic old lady fingered him," the detective replied.

"She's not psychic. She's just off her meds," one of Gladys's companions said. "She's been acting weird all day."

"In what way?" Isaac asked.

"Oh, off in her own little world. Ignoring us. Talking to people who aren't there."

"And how long have she and Mr. Wilson been boyfriend and girlfriend?" Isaac asked.

"Shh," another woman of the group warned, glancing around to make sure none of the other residents had overheard. "That's a secret," she said. "Ruth Hamilton thinks she's his girlfriend, but he only had eyes for Gladys."

"How did you know that?" the third woman asked Isaac. "Who told you?"

"No one," Isaac assured them. "She mentioned that she likes toast. I imagine he would make her some in his room from time to time."

"Every morning," the woman confirmed. "Then he would bring her out here to play mahjong and go back to his room to watch his news shows. But I think she really liked him more than the toast. She always complained that the crumbs got in her dentures."

"Maybe Ruth Hamilton put Leonard up to it," Jeremy suggested.

Isaac and Brown shook their heads dismissively.

"Just a theory," Jeremy added defensively. "Maybe the medications she's on have been suppressing a latent psychic ability, and when she didn't take them this morning, it woke up that part of her brain and she—"

"Stop talking, Jeremy," Isaac said.

"Well, I don't hear you coming up with any theories."

"I don't need a theory. I know exactly what happened," he declared.

"Thank goodness," Brown said quietly. "Let's wrap this up. I don't like being around this many old people."

"I'll be right back," Isaac said, then left Jeremy's side and walked down the center of the hallway to the murder victim's room, entered briefly, then returned. He looked over at Gladys. "I'm sorry for your loss," he said to her.

"Thank you, dear," she replied. "But when you get to be my age, it happens all the time."

"How did you do that?" Brown asked. "I've been questioning her all day, and I couldn't get her to respond to a single question."

"Did you slip her meds into her tea earlier?" Jeremy asked.

"Seriously, White?" Detective Brown remarked. "Do you think I wouldn't have checked that out already? I spoke with the nurse who gave Gladys her morning pills. She said she took them without complaint."

"I like Nurse Judy," Gladys said. "She's nice. She gives me applesauce with my pills. Makes it easier to swallow them."

"She's not under-medicated," Isaac told his assistant. "She's just a little deaf."

"Deaf?" Brown asked. "She seems to be hearing us just fine right now."

"Of course," Isaac replied. From his pocket, he pulled out the phone with the pink case that had been on the victim's night table and placed it in front of Gladys.

"You found my phone!" the old woman exclaimed.

Jeremy's face lit up with revelation. "Of course. Damn it, Isaac, how do you always make it seem so obvious? I feel like an idiot that I didn't see it earlier."

"I still feel like an idiot," Brown confessed. "What am I missing here?"

"Hearing aids," Jeremy explained. "The new ones are Bluetooth enabled. You can connect them to your phone and use its microphone instead of the one on the aid."

"It's so much clearer," one of the ladies at the table said. She pulled back her carefully coiffed gray hair, showing the device nestled in her ear. "We all have them."

Then the police detective finally put it all together. "Aha, so when Gladys had toast with Mr. Wilson this morning, she left her phone behind and heard everything that was going on in the room as it happened. But how did she confuse her phone with his?"

"She didn't," Isaac said. "It was Mr. Wilson who mixed them up when he walked her back. Certainly it's obvious to you both that only a color-blind man would have picked out the clashing decor Jeremy described to me. To him, a pink case would look like a gray one and vice versa."

"He always had mismatched socks on," of the Mahjong players chimed in.

"That explains why Gladys was acting so weird all day. She wasn't hearing anything going on around her, just whatever Mr.

Wilson was watching on TV," Jeremy realized.

"Precisely," Isaac confirmed.

"Well, thank you again," Detective Brown said. "I almost feel like that was so obvious I shouldn't have to pay you for solving this one."

"You're not paying me for solving it," Isaac said. "You're paying me to not tell anyone you didn't figure it out on your own."

Detective Brown smiled. "Pleasure doing business with you, Mr. Black." He turned and scurried out of the retirement home as quickly as he could.

"Are you boys single?" one of the women asked.

"Or are you two together?" another inquired.

"Yes, and no," Jeremy answered quickly, then checked his watch and turned to Isaac. "We really should be going. We've got that thing."

"Ah, yes, the thing," Isaac said, with a grin that Jeremy knew meant Isaac would hold his cooperation in beating a hasty retreat from the matchmaking mahjongers over him at some point in the future.

Isaac placed a hand on Jeremy's shoulder and allowed him to guide him out of the facility into the afternoon sun.

"You know, if you keep turning down offers from old ladies to set you up with their granddaughters and nieces, you'll end up spending your golden years with me," Isaac cautioned his assistant.

"Maybe by then they'll have invented seeing aids, and you won't need me anymore."

Isaac stopped in his tracks.

Jeremy spun around to face him, seeing that his employer and friend had a serious look on his face.

"I hope you know that if that did happen, it wouldn't change things between us. I wouldn't mind growing old with you. You're my best friend."

Jeremy squeezed Isaac's arm affectionately. "Thanks, Isaac, that means a lot."

They continued walking toward a waiting taxi.

"Besides," Isaac added, "you're finally making the eggs the way I like them."

The Gargoyle's Bread

Hank Newsom raced down the lonely two-lane highway in the car he had stolen shortly after breaking out of the state penitentiary.

The escape had been simple. Underpaid guards were easy to bribe and Hank had enough cash stashed from the robbery that had landed him in prison to make it worth their while. The ethically challenged lawyer who had tried to defend his hopeless case was at least reliable enough to manage his ill-begotten gains and arrange the payoffs.

Now he had to make it out of the state and eventually out of the country to a non-extradition jurisdiction—preferably one with lots of beaches. He was on his own at this point, but he was confident he could elude the state police and the U.S. Marshals as long as he didn't take too many chances.

Stealing this car had been one that was necessary. He needed to get as far away as fast as possible. The car had been parked behind a bar. Judging by the supply of makeup products in the glove compartment, he assumed it had belonged to one of the waitresses.

Hopefully she wouldn't notice it was missing until the bar closed, which gave him a good six or eight hours to make tracks.

The sun was starting to set on the cold, windy autumn day. He had a full tank of gas and planned on driving through the night along the lightly traveled roads that criss-crossed the rural landscape. He was starting to wish he had stopped inside the bar to get something to eat as his stomach was growling, reminding him that he hadn't had anything since the previous day's dinner.

The speed limit was laughably posted at fifty-five miles per hour, a legacy from a decades old effort to save gas, but Hank kept the speedometer on the high side of ninety most of the way, kicking up a cloud of dust in his wake.

When the tire blew, Hank had no chance to get the vehicle under control. The car pulled toward the gravel shoulder, where a pothole caught the front wheel and set the old Dodge tumbling bumper over fender down the road like a sky blue, sheet metal tumbleweed.

When he awoke, Hank was no longer in the car. He was lying in a dead bush, its thorny branches poking and scratching him with every movement.

He tested his limbs. His knees felt like someone had taken a baseball bat to the joints, but he was able to bend them. There was a gash on his right arm that was bleeding profusely. He tried to reach over and put pressure on the wound with his left hand, but when he tried to bend that arm, there was piercing pain between his wrist and elbow.

Bone protruded from the flesh. Any movement was agony.

Hank lifted his head until he could see around him. He was in a gully. About twenty feet away was the car, resting upside down. He couldn't see the road from where he was, so it was likely any vehicles passing by couldn't see him, either. On the horizon, he could see storm clouds approaching.

He tried to sit up.

Thorns pressed into the underside of his legs. He used his right arm to push himself up, then rolled over onto his battered knees, keeping his left arm tucked against his body to minimize the motion. He lifted himself to a three-point crouch, then stood up.

A wave of vertigo nearly caused him to topple over. He lowered himself to one knee. Blood was still pouring from the cut in his arm. When he looked closer, he could see a sliver of metal in the wound. With his left hand useless, he bent his mouth down to his forearm and clenched the strip of steel between his teeth.

He started to pull it out slowly, but each fraction of an inch felt like fire. He made sure he had a tight grip on the metal with his teeth, then pulled his head back and ripped it out.

It turned out the sliver was more like a shard.

A fresh gout of blood pulsed from the enlarged cut. Hank nearly passed out again. He bent his arm as tightly as he could, grabbing his shoulder with that hand to keep pressure on the wound. He wouldn't be able to keep that up for long, though.

Hank slowly got back to his feet. He could see over the edge of the gully now. The road was empty, but flagging someone down was a risky proposition. He'd likely end up in a hospital, which would be one step away from going back to prison.

He turned around to see what else was around him.

In the distance, rising from the gently undulating prairie, was a great black tower, like something that had once been surrounded by a medieval castle. It was the only structure in sight, and hopefully there was someone who could help him staunch his wound. Setting his broken arm would be tricky, but if he could make it to the next state, he knew a doctor who would do the job without the usual paperwork.

He took a few wobbly steps and managed to climb his way out of the gully and start limping toward the tower.

It was getting colder as the approaching storm darkened the evening sky. At any moment, it would start to rain.

The tower turned out to be further away than he thought. As he approached, he could discern a battlement surrounding the top that extended past the rough stone walls. He thought he could see a light flickering somewhere behind the crenelated parapet. Hopefully, that meant there was someone there. He would have to risk that someone calling the police. But at this point, getting caught wouldn't be worse than dying.

Fat raindrops began pelting him as he drew closer, then the heavens opened up and a torrent of rain soaked him to the bone instantly. By the time he reached what he hoped was the entrance to the tower, there was nearly an inch of water washing over the hard ground, and a growing wind sent the icy droplets straight at his face.

The door was set back into the wall, offering Hank a slight respite from the tempest howling around him. It was out of place in the rough-hewn blocks of the tower, gleaming, windowless steel set on hinges on the outside of the building. Hank knew enough about doors to recognize that this was a big security mistake. An enterprising thief such as himself could cut the hinges off and remove the door if so motivated. He knocked, then pounded on the thick steel. Its bulk absorbed his efforts as if he was stomping on solid rock.

He reached for the door handle. It was a lever-type latch, one that you pressed down on with your thumb, then pulled open. To his surprise, it opened freely. He quickly folded his arm back against his chest to stop the fresh flow of blood.

Hank stepped inside. The hallway within was dimly lit with candles in sconces along the wall. "Hello!" he shouted.

There was no reply.

He took a few steps inside as the door started to swing shut behind him. "Is there anyone here? I need help!"

The hallway seemed to grow dimmer as Hank felt light-headed and dropped to his knees.

A figure appeared in the hallway before him. A man in a plain brown robe, cinched around the waist with a white rope. His face bore an expression of panic as he seemed to stare past Hank toward the door behind him.

The man ran toward the door, but it clicked shut before he could reach it.

Hank lowered himself to the ground, the pressure he had been putting on the gash on his arm lessened, and he could feel the warm blood pool on his chest as the world faded to black.

When he awoke, he was lying on a cot, the type with canvas stretched across a wooden frame. He immediately felt hungry, then remembered the accident and the injuries he had suffered.

Hank lifted his arms. The broken one had been set and splinted and rested in a sling. The one that had been pierced by a shard of metal was bandaged. There was a little bit of blood soaking the coarse, woolen fabric wrapped tightly about his forearm, but not a lot and he suspected someone had crudely stitched up the wound before dressing it.

Slowly, he sat up. He wore a plain brown robe, identical to the one worn by the man he had seen before passing out. All of his other clothing and shoes and socks had been removed, but there was a pair of leather sandals strapped to his feet. He looked around the room and spotted a bundle of clothing sitting on a stool near the open door, his shoes beneath it.

How long had he been out? Had his car been discovered? Had the man who helped him called the police? He wasn't in a hospital, or jail, so there still was a chance he could make good his escape.

The man from earlier appeared in the doorway carrying a tray laden with a wooden pitcher and cup. He saw Hank trying to lift himself off the flimsy cot and ran to the injured man's side, setting the tray down on a small wooden table. He grabbed Hank as he started to collapse back onto the cot.

Hank could see clearly now that the man was a monk. In addition to the robe, he wore a wooden cross on a loop of rawhide around his neck. He eased Hank back down.

"Thank you," Hank said coarsely. He looked up at his benefactor, who smiled and nodded, then poured some water into the wooden cup and offered it to Hank.

Hank accepted the cup and poured the cool water over his parched tongue. It was difficult to swallow at first, but once he got the first sip down, it became easier. He handed the cup back to the monk. "Where am I?" he asked.

The monk looked around the room as if the answer was obvious.

"Yes, I know I'm in a room, but where? What is this place?"

Hank's host seemed at a loss on how to explain it further.

"Listen, I'm guessing you're one of those 'vow of silence' monks, but there's no one else around. If you want to just tell me, that might save a lot of time."

The monk shook his head vigorously.

Hank sighed, then realized that might work to his advantage.

"So, that means you haven't called for help?"

The monk sadly indicated that he hadn't.

"No email? No texts?"

Again, the monk dismissed Hank's questions with a shake of his head.

"You did this?" Hank asked, raising his bandaged arm.

The monk nodded enthusiastically, miming a sewing motion, confirming Hank's assessment.

"Thank you. You probably saved my life. I was in an accident out on the highway. You wouldn't happen to have a car I could borrow, do you?"

The monk slowly shook his head.

"Yeah, I didn't think so. How long was I out?"

The monk held up five fingers on one hand, and four on the other.

"Nine hours?"

Another affirming nod.

"Shit—pardon my French—I appreciate your help, but I really need to get going." Hank tried to lift himself up again, more slowly this time, and managed to stand unsteadily.

The monk placed his hands together, held them up to the side of his head, and closed his eyes.

"I've already slept nine hours," Hank countered. "I really need to be on my way. If you can just point me in the direction of the nearest town, I'll get out of your hair." It wasn't ideal, but he needed to keep moving. Eventually, someone would find the stolen car, connect it with the breakout from prison, and refocus the search for Hank to this area.

The monk expressed his reluctance.

Hank took a tentative step. His left knee threatened to buckle under him, but he managed to reach out and put a hand on the monk's shoulder to steady himself. He limped carefully toward the stool by the door where his now dry clothes sat, his strength growing with each step, but he quickly realized the effort of getting dressed was more than he was ready for at the moment.

"Food?" Hank asked, his hunger reawakening. "I need something to eat. Need to get my strength back."

The monk again mimed that Hank should sleep.

He ignored his host and walked out of the room, bracing himself against the cold stone walls.

The monk ran ahead of Hank, directing him to take a right turn out the door to the small room. To the left was a stairway that led upwards. Hank looked in that direction, but the monk urged him to keep moving away from it.

At the end of the hall was a sparse kitchen. There was a loaf of bread on the plain wooden table in the center of the room.

"Can you spare some of that bread, brother?" Hank asked as he limped toward the table and reached for the loaf.

The monk moved with surprising speed to cut Hank off. He snatched the bread off the table and cradled it against his chest.

"I just want a little bit. I can pay you," he said, reaching into his pocket for the wad of cash he had for gas and food before realizing he wasn't wearing his own clothes.

The berobed friar turned away, holding the loaf close.

"What's wrong with you?" Hank asked. "I just want something to eat."

The monk shook his head vigorously.

Hank found himself getting angry. What reason could this misguided Samaritan have to tend to his wounds, but then deny him the most basic sustenance? He limped toward his reluctant host. "Give me that bread," he insisted.

The monk tried to escape the close confines of the kitchen, but Hank grabbed the coarse fabric of his robe and pulled the man toward him. He grabbed at the bread, and the two of them struggled over the loaf until Hank tore away a heel, much to the horror of the monk.

"What is your problem?" the escaped convict asked. He glared at the monk while he lifted the hunk of bread to his mouth.

The monk's eyes widened and his mouth gaped in horror.

Hank paused, then looked down at the bread.

Inside the crust, the crumb was soaked with a crimson liquid.

Hank dropped the heel and stumbled back away from it. "Is that blood?" he asked, as the liquid spilled onto the stone floor.

The monk bowed his head.

"Why?" Hank asked. "What's wrong with you?"

The monk's posture sank in an expression of shame. He put the remainder of the ensanguined loaf in the sink, then picked up a candle from the table and walked back out into the hallway.

Hank paused as his eyes were drawn to a long knife on the counter. He picked it up, slid it into the sling holding his broken arm, then followed as the brother exited the kitchen.

He led Hank toward an alcove, where there appeared to be a mural of some sort painted on the stone wall. There was a row of candles in front of it. The monk lit them with the flame from the taper he held.

The flickering light revealed a sequence of scenes that told a disturbing story of a demon terrorizing worshipers at a church. Then the same creature being battled by cross-bearing monks. Finally, the beast imprisoned in a tall, square tower.

A second sequence revealed the creature in chains, drinking blood from the body of a beheaded monk. Then another monk teaching his brothers to put blood in a loaf of bread. And last, a quiescent demon satisfied with the offering.

"You're trying to tell me you that you've got some sort of demon trapped in this tower? And you have to make that blood bread to what? Keep him from escaping?"

The monk nodded enthusiastically.

"You are completely Looney Tunes, mad as a hatter crazy," Hank said. "Look, I really don't care what you're doing here. But I have to go. So, if you do have any food that's not soaked in blood, I would really appreciate it."

Hank's host shook his head.

"Nothing else? What do you use to make the bread?"

The monk tried to think of a way to explain the answer to the question.

Hank grunted in frustration, then turned around and headed back toward the kitchen.

He threw open cabinets and drawers, tossing their sparse contents onto the floor. He found wooden bowls, spoons and cups, a few other knives. There were all the accouterments to make bread, but none of the ingredients.

He howled in frustration. The exertion weakened him. He felt light-headed and started to collapse to the floor, but suddenly the monk was at his side, holding him up and guiding him to a chair.

"You must have something. Anything," Hank pleaded.

The monk shrugged apologetically.

"I have to go. I can't stay here any longer. I need to find something to eat. Do you have anything I can use? A bicycle? A skateboard?"

The monk shook his head.

"Of course not. Fine, I'll walk. Just give me some water. I know you have that."

His host nodded and picked up one of the wooden cups Hank had scattered on the floor, and carried it to the stone sink that had a hand pump next to it, filled the cup and brought it to Hank.

He drank it eagerly. It was cold and satisfying, and he could feel some of his vertigo fading.

"Thank you. More, please."

The monk took the cup, refilled it, and Hank emptied it again.

He raised himself to his feet and paused to make sure he wasn't going to pass out. Then he walked slowly out of the kitchen, navigating the dim hallways until he saw the giant steel door he had come in by.

There was an electronic keypad where the door handle should have been. Hank poked at the keys and digits lit up on a display, glowing red. After he had entered eight numbers, the device issued a dissatisfied series of tones and the glowing display went blank.

Hank turned around and found the monk had followed him. "What's the code?" he demanded.

The monk shrugged, a somber look on his face.

"You don't know the code to get out of here?" Hank laughed. "Did I escape one prison just to get trapped in another?"

The monk shrugged, pointing down the hallway in the direction they had gone to view the murals.

"Oh, right, I forgot. You can't let the demon out. How do you get what you need to make the bread? Where does the blood come from?"

The monk remained motionless, either unwilling or unable to respond.

"There has to be a way out of here," Hank insisted. "If I can break out of a maximum security prison, I can certainly get out of a little stone monastery."

He walked back down the hallway, finding the passage that led to the stairway he had seen earlier. The steps were dark. Hank grabbed a candle from one of the nearby sconces and started climbing the stairs.

They seemed to ascend around the interior perimeter of the tower, seven full flights until he reached a door. A wooden door, one without any locks, just a crude latch. He opened it and stepped out onto the roof of the structure.

In the center was a large brazier in which a fire was burning, defying the wind and rain. Apparently, the storm was still raging, but the fire seemed immune to it.

Beyond the flames was a statue, a grand gargoyle resembling the demon in the murals, sculpted from the same dark rock that made up the walls of the tower.

Hank stepped over to one of the gaps in the parapet and looked down. He was at least ten stories up. And there didn't seem to be any means to get down.

A cold rain started to fall.

Again, the monk appeared at Hank's side. Like the fire, he, too, seemed immune to the forceful gale.

"Do you have any rope?" Hank asked. He tugged at the one that cinched his robe and held it before the monk. "You must have more of this somewhere."

The monk indicated his own simple belt.

Hank looked at the statue.

The fire seemed to bring it to life, but that was just a trick of the light. It was just stone. "It's just a statue," Hank said to the monk. "I don't get it."

The monk pulled out the two pieces of the loaf Hank had torn apart from inside his robe and set them before the gargoyle. He seemed disappointed.

"Just tell me," Hank pleaded. "What the hell is going on here? Why am I able to just walk in here, but you need a code to get out? Why is the only food you have blood-soaked bread?"

The monk walked up to the brazier and pulled a stick from the flames. He used the charred end to sketch a crude outline of the beast on the stone at their feet, then a small oval representing the loaf of bread.

Then he drew an X over the bread and added a stick figure of a man.

"What does that mean?" Hank asked.

The monk just tapped at the stick figure emphatically.

Hank's patience was at an end. He grabbed the monk's robe and pulled him close. "I don't care about whatever vow of silence you took. Make an exception. Tell me how to get out of here or I swear to God, I will kill you." Hank let go of the monk, then withdrew the knife he had hidden earlier in his sling.

The monk seemed unpersuaded by the threat. He pointed at the drawing.

"It's not real!" Hank shouted. He advanced on the monk until the simple man was standing at the edge of the brazier. Hank pressed the edge of the knife against the silent man's neck.

The monk never even flinched.

Hank unleashed his building fury. He drew the blade against the spot where the carotid artery was. The sharp blade cut deeply, slicing into the monk's neck. The action should have nearly severed the man's head.

But there was no blood.

Then the wound healed before Hank's eyes.

The monk looked… disappointed. Almost sorry that he didn't die.

Hank backed away. "What are you?" he asked. He continued walking backwards until he bumped into the statue of the demon. He turned and stared at the giant stone sculpture.

It glared down at him, the fire bringing its eyes to life.

Then there was a low growl, followed by an unnerving roar.

Hank turned around.

Where the monk had stood was now a glistening, ichor-colored creature.

A demon.

The stone gargoyle's twin—but very much alive.

It reached for Hank with a giant taloned hand.

The knife fell from Hank's grasp and clattered against the stone. "No, stop, you don't have to do this!"

But his pleas were swallowed by the roar of thunder.

Father Jorgenson pushed open the steel door and made sure it was locked securely behind him as he entered the tower. He walked down the dark corridor toward the kitchen. "Ivan, it's Father Jorgenson," he shouted, his voice echoing against the cold stone.

He carried a basket, which he set on the kitchen table and began emptying. Among the contents were a small bag of flour, a packet of yeast, and a shaker of salt.

Ivan entered. He paused at the entrance to the kitchen, his head bowed.

Father Jorgenson noticed his distress. "What is it? What's wrong?" he asked.

Ivan walked over to a chair where the bundle of Hank's clothes were set. He carried them over to the table and set them down next to the bread ingredients.

Father Jorgenson sighed and shook his head. "Must have been whoever was driving the car I saw wrecked out on the road."

Ivan nodded.

"And he interfered with the ritual," the priest assumed.

Ivan nodded again.

Father Jorgenson issued another heavy sigh. He removed a bag of blood from the basket and set it down next to the flour, salt and yeast. "It wasn't your fault. I've told the diocese a hundred times that we need a lock on the outside, too." He stuffed the bundle of clothes into the empty basket. "Well, there's nothing to be done about it now. I'll see you next week, Ivan."

The priest headed back for the entrance, making sure Ivan remained in the kitchen. When he got there, he keyed in the eight-digit code that unlocked the door. It clicked and sprung open. He grabbed the door so he could slip through.

The nature of the beast's imprisonment was that as long as he was inside the tower, he was confined to the persona of Ivan, a monk who had long ago made the ultimate sacrifice to enable the demon's containment. It was only on the rooftop where he could assume his true form to accept the offering that kept him at bay.

The stones the building were made of were sacred, having come from an ancient cathedral in Turkey and blessed by the Pope himself. The creature was forever sealed within as long as the offerings were made—one way or another.

Father Jorgenson saw the movement out of the corner of his eye a second too late. He was struck on the back of the head by a heavy wooden stool and fell unconscious to the ground.

Hank placed the stool in such a way as to prevent the steel door from closing. Then he took the bundle of clothes from the basket, slipped out of the robe he was wearing and started putting on his own clothes.

Ivan peeked timidly from the kitchen door.

"It's okay," Hank assured him. "He's out cold."

The monk stared trepidatiously at the door.

"Hey, a deal's a deal," Hank said. "I told you if you let me live, I would get you out of here. So, let's go."

Hank padded the unconscious priest's pockets until he found a wallet with a bit of cash in it and a set of car keys. He smiled, then pulled open the door fully, letting in a flood of sunlight.

"Are you coming?"

Ivan walked slowly toward the open door, then more quickly, pausing to drag the body of the unconscious priest with him, until he was outside, staring up at the sun, his arms outstretched, reveling in his freedom.

Hank followed, removing the stool so the door could swing shut behind them. "Do you need a ride?" he asked, eyeing the old pickup parked nearby.

Ivan smiled at him, then transformed into his true form. A great set of wings unfolded from his back.

The demon picked up the priest in his enormous talons, then took off running and launched himself into the air.

Hank watched as the creature flew away, shrinking down to just a dot in the distance.

He got behind the wheel of the pickup, started the engine and began driving back toward the highway, suddenly realizing that he was still very, very hungry.

Tricked

Harrison Hardigan hated Halloween.

He hated the parade of costumed brats ringing his doorbell, the proliferation of skeletons and spiders and tombstones in his neighbors' yards, the ubiquity of pumpkin spice flavored everything everywhere he went. To be honest, that had more to do with Thanksgiving—which he also hated—but the plague of cinnamon, nutmeg and allspice, it seemed, was starting earlier and earlier every year.

Tomorrow was the cursed day. He had considered getting a hotel room, or just taking a long drive somewhere else, but he was not going to be driven from his home just because of the commercialized observation of some pagan celebration.

No, he would stand his ground. Let those trick-or-treaters come begging for candy and other treats. They'd get nothing from him. And if they were foolish enough to think a trick was an appropriate response, his garden hose was at the ready.

Harrison turned out the lights and climbed into his bed. It was a particularly cold late October, but would that stop the sniveling little beggars from traipsing up and down his front steps, their tiny feet thumping across his porch. They would just throw winter coats over their costumes so that only their masks were visible. It made the whole ritual even more ridiculous.

A strong wind howled outside his window. Maybe there would be a thunderstorm tomorrow. It wouldn't stop them, he knew, but it might slow them down a bit. He smiled at the prospect of a storm literally dumping cold water on their insipid plans as he closed his eyes, ready for sleep.

"Oh, Harrison," a female voice whispered in the dark. "Why does Halloween bother you so?"

Harrison's eyes sprung open, searching the dark for the source of the voice.

"Who's there?"

A shimmering shape took form at the foot of his bed, a woman who appeared translucent. She was older, a bit heavy, with thin hair flowing loosely over her shoulders. She was wearing an old, stained housecoat.

"Hello, Harrison," she said in a soothing voice.

"Who are you?" he asked.

"It's me, Beatrice," she replied.

"Beatrice?"

"Beatrice Kaminski."

Harrison sat up, scrutinizing her diaphanous features. "Doesn't ring a bell," he said.

"From school," she prompted.

He leaned closer and squinted at her. "No, sorry, can you be more specific?"

Beatrice rolled her eyes in frustration. "You took me to the fall Harvest Dance at Bedford Falls High School."

Harrison looked the apparition up and down, trying to connect the woman to his fifty-year-old memories.

"Bea," he said with a hint of recognition. "You really let yourself go."

"I'm not here to date you," she said. "I'm here to warn you."

"Warn me?"

"You must mend your ways, you must embrace Halloween in the spirit in which it should be appreciated. As an affirmation of life."

"Why?" Harrison asked.

"Why?" Beatrice asked back.

"What difference does it make?"

"Well, the path you're on will only lead to isolation and unhappiness."

"But I like being alone," Harrison asserted. "I hate people. They're so annoying. If I could afford to buy my neighbors' houses and demolish them, I would."

Beatrice appeared flummoxed. "Do not dismiss my warning," she admonished. "You will only have this one chance to redeem yourself. There will be three spirits who will visit you. Listen to them, learn from what they show you—"

"Wait a minute," Harrison interrupted. "Is this like 'A Christmas Carol' thing?"

"What?"

"This sounds a lot like the whole Ebenezer Scrooge story. 'Three spirits will visit you over three nights, blah blah blah…"

"No, this is nothing like that. This is about Halloween, not Christmas."

"Yes, yes, but aside from that, basically the same thing, right?"

Beatrice paused. She sighed, then nodded her agreement. "Yes, it's basically the same thing. But that doesn't mean you should—"

"Why you?" Harrison asked.

"Excuse me?" Beatrice asked back.

"Well, I haven't seen you in over half a century," he said. "As I recall, we broke up after that dance. You were flirting with Kevin Spassky. Isn't there someone more relevant to my life that should be giving me this warning?"

Beatrice looked behind her as if consulting some committee of ghosts in charge of such things.

"No," she replied. "Well, no one that wanted to come see you."

"So, why did you volunteer?"

"I was bored," Beatrice confessed.

"And now, so am I," Harrison said. He settled back into bed and closed his eyes.

"But I haven't finished the warning! The spirits, when they arrive, you must—"

"Listen to what they say, change my fate, yada yada. Good night," he said with an air of finality.

Beatrice shrugged and faded away.

Harrison awoke the next day with a faint recollection of his encounter with the geriatric version of his high school sweetheart in the back of his mind. He did some chores around his house, then settled down in front of his television with a TV dinner and a beer to watch C-SPAN. They seemed to be the only programming among the hundreds of channels on his cable service that wasn't centered around Halloween.

It was around three o'clock when his doorbell rang.

Harrison ignored it. Most of the time, after ten seconds or so, they would just give up and go away.

But this little goblin rang the bell a second time.

And when Harrison ignored that attempt, it rang a third and fourth time.

Harrison rose out of his easy chair and shuffled over to the front door. He opened it, ready to unleash a tirade about private property. "Listen, you little—"

But there was no one there.

He stepped out onto his porch and looked up and down the street, but there was no one in sight. He scratched the bald spot on the crown of his head and turned to head back into his house and came face to face with a skeleton standing in his doorway.

Not a costumed kid in a black bodysuit with bones painted on it. It was a full on human skeleton, hanging in the air, with a lit cigar clenched in its teeth.

"What the hell?" Harrison exclaimed.

The skeleton raised a hand to grip the cigar. Its tip glowed as smoke was drawn into the skull and expelled through the empty eye sockets.

"Hey, Harrison. Shall we get started?"

"Started on what?"

"I was under the impression you got the standard warning last night that I was coming? I'm your first spirit. Ringing any bells?"

Harrison thought back to the odd experience from the previous night that was hanging onto the edge of his consciousness.

"That was just a dream," he insisted.

"Do I look like a dream?" the skeleton asked.

"Well, frankly, yes," Harrison replied.

"Granted, that's a valid interpretation," the skeleton conceded. "But most people would think I was more of a bad acid trip."

"I don't do drugs."

"Of course not. Well, this is kinda what it would be like. Come on, let's get going. I have big plans later tonight, dancing around the cemetery with some friends."

"Go where?"

The skeleton reached out with a bony hand and placed it on Harrison's shoulder.

Suddenly, they were standing on the sidewalk of a city street, where densely packed bungalows stood should to shoulder with only a narrow passage between them. Throngs of costumed children ran up and down the sidewalk from door to door, chanting "Trick or treat," to the delight of the grinning home owners.

There was one boy who walked alone. He was dressed as a clown and clearly not happy about it.

Harrison realized the street they were on was the one he grew up on, and the boy standing in front of him was himself.

He had wanted to dress up as a devil. There was a costume at the Woolworths he had coveted for weeks. But in the end, his mother had decided he was going to be a clown, recycling a costume his older brother had worn years earlier.

He trudged up the steps to a nearby house, rang the bell, then held open the pillowcase he was using to collect candy in.

A smiling housewife opened the door. "Well, hello there," she said. "Is there something you wanted to say?"

Harrison remembered resenting having to utter those vapid words. He never understood that part of the ritual. Reluctantly, he said in a low voice, "Trick or treat."

A little girl in a princess costume peeked out from behind the woman.

The woman dropped a single Hershey's Kiss into the boy's sack. "What's your name?' she asked.

"Harrison," the boy replied.

"What kind of name is that?" the little girl asked.

"No, your first name," the woman said.

"That *is* my first name," the boy insisted.

The girl laughed at him. "He has his names backwards!"

The boy turned, walked away, and continued down the sidewalk, right toward Harrison and the skeleton. "That's a cool costume," the boy said to the skeleton.

"Is he supposed to be able to see us?" Harrison asked his bony guide.

"No, we should be invisible," the skeleton said, scratching his skull with his phalanges.

Harrison reached out and poked the boy with his finger, pushing the kid back a few inches.

"Shouldn't be able to do that, either," the skeleton confirmed.

"Don't worry, kid," Harrison said to his younger self. "You'll have the coolest name in school when *Star Wars* comes out."

"What's *Star Wars*?" the boy asked.

"You'll see," Harrison said.

The boy sighed and ambled off to the next house.

Harrison knew he would visit every home in the neighborhood

that night, gathering as much candy as he could. Then a few months later after the other kids had depleted their own supplies, he would start selling it off for a nickel a piece at school and buy himself a disappointing pair of X-ray specs from the back of a comic book.

Harrison turned to the skeleton. "So, what was I supposed to learn from that?" he asked.

The skeleton shrugged. "I don't know. It's one of those you'll know when you see it kind of situations. It doesn't raise any sad memories from your childhood? Any regrets? Lost opportunities?"

"Nope," Harrison replied, unmoved by the experience.

"Well, I'm sure it will come to you." He reached out again and place his bony hand on Harrison's shoulder.

Nothing happened.

"You're not very good at this," Harrison remarked.

"This has never happened before," the skeleton claimed.

"Yeah, well, while we're stuck in the sixties, do you mind if I buy some IBM stock?"

The skeleton tried the opposite hand on Harrison's other shoulder.

Again, nothing happened.

"Maybe you need to say something, too," Harrison suggested.

The skeleton took a step back, balled one hand into a solid knot of bones and struck Harrison square on the jaw.

He awoke sitting in his easy chair.

Some political analyst was droning on about the Federal Reserve on C-SPAN.

It was dark outside. He checked his watch. It was only about four o'clock. He looked out his front window and saw that the reason it was so dark was that black storm clouds filled the sky, lit up occasionally by distant flashes of lightning.

Unlike the dream from the previous night, his little day-mare was fresh in his mind. He picked up the can of beer he had been drinking and inspected the "best by" date.

The doorbell rang.

"What the hell?" Harrison exclaimed. Despite the oncoming storm, it appeared there still were little beggars hopeful to fill up their sacks with candy before it started to rain in earnest.

Harrison didn't wait for the costumed extortionists to ring again. He rose from his chair and strode toward the front door, throwing it open, ready to castigate the unaware little hobgoblins.

But the words never made it past his chapped lips.

Hanging in the air in front of him was a giant bee.

"Well," Harrison said, confused, "I didn't see this coming."

The bee buzzed.

"Okay, are you part of this whole Christmas Carol Halloween crossover? Or are you an independent random hallucination?" he asked.

The bee buzzed again.

"You know, I don't speak bee, so you're going to have to give me something other than just this meaningless buzzing."

The bee rose a bit, its wings fluttering madly as it bent its body so that its stinger was pointed directly at Harrison.

"Hey, watch it with that thing. I'm allerg—"

The bee stung him right in the middle of his chest.

But instead of a sharp pain followed by a swelling of his entire body and inability to breathe, Harrison found himself at a Halloween costume party.

He was dressed as Winnie-the-Pooh. Next to him was a young woman wearing a sexy bee costume. "Why didn't you just show up that way in the first place?"

"I like to do the sting. It's kinda my thing," Bee Girl replied.

"Whatever. Where are we?" Harrison asked, bored and anxious to get through this Dickensian hell he seemed to be stuck in.

"You don't recognize these people?"

"No, they're all wearing costumes," Harrison replied.

"Oh, right," Bee Girl replied. She scanned the guests to find someone Harrison might be able to identify. There was a woman wearing a Hogwarts cloak with a Ravenclaw scarf.

"Certainly you know who that is," Bee Girl said, pointing at the woman.

Harrison followed her finger toward the Harry Potter fan. "Laura," he said. "She works at my office—well, my old office. I'm retired, now."

"I know," Bee girl said. "If you hadn't taken that early retirement package, you would be at this party right now."

"I don't think so. I don't do parties."

"Well, if you were the boss, you kind of would have to be."

"Boss?"

"Yes, Laura took your job when you left, then was promoted to Branch Manager the following year."

"Huh," Harrison said.

"Because she participates in the company culture, attends branch outings, remembers people's birthdays."

"Yeah, that sounds like Laura. Nice to see she made manager. She always talked about that—whether you wanted her to or not."

Bee Girl looked at Harrison. "Aren't you filled with regret that your dislike for Halloween ultimately led you to not fulfilling your true potential?"

Harrison shrugged. "Not really. I'm not a people person. I was able to parlay that payout they gave me into a fixed annuity. Got a pretty sweet deal."

Bee Girl sighed, frustrated. "Seriously? No lesson learned here at all?"

Harrison shook his head. He spied a platter of stuffed dates on a nearby table. "Ooh, I love those," he said, reaching for the hors d'oeuvres. His hand passed right through them. "Great, now it works the way it's supposed to."

"You know, you don't deserve this chance to change your life," Bee Girl said.

"Never asked for it," Harrison replied. "Are we done here?"

Bee Girl transformed back into a giant flying bee and jammed her stinger into his chest.

Harrison awoke in his easy chair. He rubbed at his chest where he could still feel the sting of his most recent visitor.

"Aw, jeez. Whatever happened to the ghosts who were just sheets with two eyeholes?" he wondered aloud.

The doorbell rang.

Harrison rolled up out of his chair and shuffled toward the door. "Coming," he said. "Keep your pants on—or whatever it is you're wearing."

He opened the door.

Standing on the porch as it started to rain was a man in a Batman costume. Well, not really an official Batman suit, it was obviously some unlicensed rip off. "Harrison Hardigan," he said in an imitation of Christian Bale's version of the superhero, "I am the spirit of Halloween yet to come—"

"Right, got it," Harrison said. "Let me save you some time. No matter what you show me, I'm not going to embrace Halloween. I just don't like it. I don't like the themes, the excuse for kids to extort their neighbors for candy, adults who use it as an opportunity to wear wildly inappropriate or sexualized costumes. I just don't get it. Never will. Don't want to. So, thanks for the effort, but I'm going to go back to my chair and watch C-SPAN."

He closed the door on the dime store superhero and turned around to head back to his chair.

The doorbell rang again.

He opened the door. "Listen, really, you can stop with the whole—"

But there was no one there to talk to. The ghost had disappeared. Harrison leaned out to peek up and down the street, but the spirit of Halloween yet to come… had gone.

Lightning lit up the horizon, and a clap of thunder rolled in a second later.

"I'm never drinking year old beer again," Harrison promised himself.

Then there was a sound that was wholly unexpected.

"Boo!" said a small voice from below.

The shout surprised Harrison.

He looked down and saw a small child in a classic ghost costume, simply a sheet with two eyeholes cut into it.

The old man stumbled backwards, tripping over the area rug at his feet just inside the door, and fell heavily, banging his head on the corner of the small table where he kept his keys and unopened mail.

The impact dented his skull deeply, and turned his head in such a way as to twist his neck in just the right fashion to snap his spinal cord, killing him instantly.

It took a moment for Harrison to realize what he was looking at. He looked so unnatural, with his body facing one way and his head another. But there was his dead body, laying lifeless at his feet.

"That's what I came here to warn you about," the fake Batman said.

Harrison looked over and saw the ghost standing next to him.

"If you had just let me finish."

"Yeah, well, I was always stubborn like that."

"Tell me about it," the ghost Batman said.

The young kid in the ghost costume walked tentatively up to Harrison's body. "Are you all right, mister?" he asked.

"No, kid, can't you see my head is halfway twisted off?" Harrison replied.

The child evidently heard him, because he ran out of the house screaming and kept on running down the street until he was out of sight.

"I didn't think he would be able to hear me," Harrison said to Ghost Batman.

"He shouldn't have. Things have been wonky all night, though," the ghost explained.

"Well, what's next?"

"You know, the afterlife. It's not too bad if you can find something to do."

"Any recommendations?" Harrison asked.

"Well, there is an opening, if you're interested. Our ghost of Halloween present quit tonight."

Firefly

Barbara and Amanda were twins, but Amanda was technically the older of the two since she came into the world first.

She made a dramatic entrance, specifically because she was born with a full head of golden locks that seemed to have an almost electric glow even through the mess of birth.

The doctor and nurses and Amanda's parents were so enthralled by her angelic appearance, they almost forgot there was another girl waiting to be born.

Barbara seemed reluctant to follow her sister. The doctor was on the verge of performing a C-section when she finally decided it was time.

Everyone expected the second child to be like the first, a plump cherub with a bright yellow mane. But Barbara was pale and tiny, with thin wisps of stringy black hair pasted against her head.

Their parents never consciously meant to favor one daughter over the other, but it happened, nonetheless.

Others were even more egregious in displaying a preference—

especially Amanda and Barbara's grandfather, who gave Amanda a nickname she went by for all of her short life.

Firefly.

She was Grandpa's firefly, her hair lighting up a room like the glow of the nocturnal insects that dotted the mid-summer skies.

Barbara did not receive a nickname. She was always Barbara. Never Barb, or even Babs. She actually detested those abbreviated versions of her name, but still resented the fact that no one—especially Grandpa—thought her worthy of any sort of sobriquet.

She made the mistake of confiding her feelings to Firefly, who instantly took to calling Barbara Babs whenever she wanted to get under her skin, like sisters—especially twins—are wont to do.

As they grew up together, people sometimes forgot that Firefly even had a sister. She was every teacher's pet, the star of all the school plays, the object of every boy's infatuation.

Barbara was often relegated to the background in Firefly's presence. Her parents did make an effort to treat each girl equally. For birthdays, they each received their favorite cakes—angel food for Firefly, devil's food for Barbara. But one year, the family was so caught up in the celebration of Firefly's birthday coinciding with her acceptance to a special high school for artistically gifted students, that they forgot to light the candles on Barbara's cake and neglected to sing "Happy Birthday" to her.

That was the night of Firefly's accident.

At least everyone believed it had been an accident.

They wanted to believe that.

They had to believe.

The alternative—that she had been pushed or otherwise caused to fall down the staircase—was too horrible to imagine.

Particularly because the only other person on the landing at the top of the stairs had been Barbara.

The funeral was a grand and momentous ceremony, attended by hundreds of people. She was buried in a yellow casket that matched her lustrous hair, wearing a yellow dress, her nails painted yellow, with gold jewelry around her neck and attached to her pierced ears. The cost of all these luxuries was paid for by Grandpa, who seemed the most despondent by her loss. Even more so than her own mother. And certainly exceeding the grief expressed by her sister.

Barbara didn't fool herself into thinking that in Firefly's absence, she would receive the attention that had once been lavished on her sister. At best, people found Barbara's presence a heartbreaking reminder that Firefly was gone. At worst, she received glares of disdain and blame, even silent accusations.

Barbara didn't care.

The girls had shared a bedroom their whole lives. The decor was dominated by Firefly's tastes. But after she was gone, Barbara packed all of her sister's belongings into cardboard boxes and stacked them in the back of her closet. She painted the walls black, covering the giant yellow caricature of a firefly grandpa had painted over her sister's bed. It had a cheerful face with a broad smile and big eyes and a glowing yellow butt the color of Firefly's hair.

Barbara hated it, and it was the first thing she rolled dark pigment over.

Her parents assumed she was so grief stricken that she couldn't stand to be reminded of her loss. But the truth was, Barbara had lived so long in her sister's shadow that she couldn't bear to be around any reminders of her existence.

Shortly after Firefly's death, her grandfather passed on as well. Her parents' relationship fell into a constant conflict that set the tone in the house throughout her high school years. After Barbara graduated from college, she decided to move as far away from her family as possible.

A small inheritance from her grandfather—initially meant for Firefly, but passed on to Barbara since Amanda was dead—allowed her to purchase an old farmhouse in the country.

She worked as a freelance web developer, something she could do remotely and alone, which suited her just fine.

One day, a shipment arrived from her parents. It was the collection of boxes she had packed all of Firefly's belongings into all those years earlier. They must've assumed Barbara had wanted to save them.

She lit a fire in the fireplace—which she rarely did because she didn't care for the smell. But in this case, she wanted to destroy the last remnants of her sister's existence, and fire was the best tool for the job.

She tossed dolls and stuffed animals, books and small figurines onto the flames. Occasionally, the thick smoke was so voluminous it escaped the draft of the chimney into the room.

Barbara ignored it. She burned all the clothing and shoes, photographs and programs from school plays and concerts.

Eventually she was left with a single small box in which were Firefly's journals.

Curious, Barbara opened one and started reading what her sister had written.

It was a story.

And quite frankly, it was really good.

She sat down and continued reading, discovering that the journals had several dozen such tales. To be sure, they weren't anything that Barbara normally would read, but she was smart enough to realize that there indeed had been some talent behind those irritatingly golden locks.

On a whim, Barbara typed up one of the stories on her computer and then looked up magazines that were open to submissions. She chose a few of the larger ones she recognized and emailed them the story under her own name.

To her surprise, they accepted it.

All of them.

Just to see what would happen, she wrote a note to each of the editors explaining that the story was desired by their competitors, and she would sell it to the highest bidder.

And each of them made higher and higher offers until one of them had overbid them all with an outrageous sum, one that she knew was only afforded to the most accomplished and popular of writers.

She accepted, and her story—Firefly's story—was met with critical acclaim.

So, she sent out another one.

And the same thing happened.

Critics were hailing her as the next literary giant of her time. After only two stories.

Thereafter, she no longer had to submit Firefly's stories, offers came to her for anything she might deign to write from all the major literary publications.

She was careful to meter out the stories, one every two or three months. The income she generated was more than enough for her to quit her IT job and live off the fruits of her sister's long forgotten labors.

Then a publisher offered to assemble a collection of her stories. It made the bestseller lists. Hollywood producers optioned some of them to be adapted into films.

Despite the fame Firefly's stories were accruing for Barbara, she remained reclusive, shunning the spotlight—which made her an even more intriguing figure and drove sales higher.

She engaged the services of a literary agent and a business manager. The two men, quartered in New York, took on the responsibility of soliciting, marketing and promoting her work.

But there was a problem.

Firefly had only written so many stories, and Barbara had nearly exhausted her literary glory hole.

She tried her hand at imitating Firefly's style, the floweriness of her prose, the voices of her characters, the universal appeal of her themes—but her efforts fell short. No one would mistake her uninspired imitations for the real thing.

Then she had an idea. When she had been working as a software engineer, she had dabbled with expert systems, machine learning and artificial intelligence. What if, she wondered, she fed Firefly's stories into an algorithm that would endeavor to create new stories based on the patterns it could discern from her previous works?

When she tried it, it exceeded her most optimistic expectations. She was nervous sending the programmatically generated tale to her agent, but he and the rest of the literary world accepted it as another example of the author's brilliance.

What about a novel? She set her Firefly AI to the task.

The book was a number one bestseller for almost a year and was nominated for the Pulitzer prize.

People wanted more.

Publishers offered outrageous advances, and Hollywood A-Listers were battling to star in the film versions of her work.

Then, one day, something wholly unexpected happened.

Firefly sent her an email.

Dear Babs, it began. *I'm so glad you published my stories, even if it was under your name, I've always believed the proof of the writer is in the reader, and you have give me more of them than I could ever have imagined. But I've told my stories, and I'll tell no more. Yours always, Firefly.*

At first she thought it was a joke, someone pranking her. But who knew about Firefly's journals but herself? Her parents? They had long since divorced. Her father had made subtle inquiries about obtaining some financial assistance from his famous daughter, but Barbara had ignore his request and sent back any further letters unopened.

Could it be him? Did he know about the journals? Had he read them? Did his subsequent unopened letters lead him to resort to blackmail of his own daughter?

Barbara thought not. It was her mother who had written the note that accompanied the shipment of Firefly's belongings. And she had always thought her father to be somewhat of a dullard.

Her agent? That didn't make any sense. He had become rich himself off of his commissions and the packaging deals he had set up for the movie adaptations of her work.

Then who? Maybe a childhood friend? Someone Firefly had shared her stories with in school, and recognized them when Barbara had published them under her own name?

But Barbara thought that unlikely. Firefly had been very secretive about her journals, writing in them only late at night when she thought her sister was asleep.

Maybe a fan who had dug into her past and pieced things together? That seemed a stretch as well.

Besides, all her life, she was known exclusively as Barbara. Who would think to call her Babs?

So, she did a little detective work using her IT knowledge to trace the origins of the email and discovered it had been sent from the same IP address as the server that was home to the software for her Firefly AI.

The thought of her creation spontaneously sending her such a message was both disturbing and intriguing. Did the AI actually think it was Firefly? She had heard stories of artificial intelligences becoming—or at least seeming to become—self-aware. But the input into this one was merely the collected writing of a teenage girl.

Barbara stared at the email on her screen for a while, then hit the reply button and typed, "Sorry, sis, I have contracts for three more novels and my agent says he can get crazy money for any more shorts, so shut up and keep writing."

Then she clicked send.

She stared at the screen for a moment, part of her expecting a reply, but none was forthcoming. She turned off the computer and went upstairs to get ready for bed.

Thunder rumbled in the distance as she donned her gray flannel nightgown, turned off the lights, and crawled under the comforter.

Her bedroom was a bit drafty, and it creaked whenever there was a strong wind as there was tonight. Its vehemence and volume presaged a big storm. She had plans to use some of her writing money to remodel and expand the house—maybe she would tear the whole thing down and start from scratch. But for tonight, she was at the mercy of the craftsmanship of whomever had built the farmhouse over a hundred years earlier.

Lightning struck nearby, so close that the blast of thunder that shook her house followed the bright flash almost instantly. It lit up her room in an eerie glow that had a slightly yellow cast to it.

Then the room was completely dark. Barbara looked to her night table where the glowing red numerals of her alarm clock usually cast their dull glow, but it was off. The power was out. She hoped her refrigerator would stay cool until it came back, but out where she lived she knew it could be days before crews from the electric company made their way this far from civilization.

Well, there was nothing she could do about it now. She closed her eyes, listening to the downpour of rain that was let loose from the crack in the heavens the lightning had opened up.

Something, however, not the sounds of the storm, kept her from falling asleep. A nagging feeling at the back of her mind, and a barely perceptible glow pushing past the barrier of her eyelids.

She opened her eyes.

There, hovering just in front of her face, was the luminous glow of a firefly.

Barbara reached out to grab it, but it flew out of her reach, dancing around the room, blinking at her with that annoying yellow light.

She closed her eyes again, but somehow those dim flashes made their way to the back of her eyes. Even when she turned around and buried her face in her pillow, she saw pulses of yellow dancing around.

Then, on the wind that was blowing through the trees outside her bedroom window, she thought she heard a voice.

"Babs..." it called.

No, that couldn't be. The nearest house was hundreds of yards away, and it wasn't the television or a radio she left on. The power was out.

"Oh, Babs..."

She sat up in her bed, wielding one of her pillows as a muted weapon. She saw the twinkle of the firefly across the room and hurled the pillow at it. The feather-filled cushion landed on her dresser, knocking various items off its surface. She heard a bottle break and could smell the scent of her favorite perfume.

"You damn, bug, I'm going to kill you for that!" she promised.

She slid carefully out of the bed. With the storm clouds blocking any moonlight, her room was truly pitch black, except for the moments when a bolt of lightning sent its illumination her way. It was enough for her to make her way to the dresser and reclaim her pillow, but when she turned to get back into her bed, her foot found a shard of the broken perfume bottle, and it cut her deeply.

"Dammit!" she exclaimed, lifting the injured foot up off the ground with one hand while she braced herself against the dresser with the other.

The next flare from the storm revealed an inch and a half long sliver of glass embedded deeply in the ball of her foot. She carefully pulled it free. But it was even more painful coming out than it had been going in.

Blood seeped from the wound.

She had no choice but to try to navigate to the bathroom, walking on the heel of that foot. She'd worry about cleaning up the blood later.

The firefly danced in the far corner of the room.

"How many of you cursed insects are there?" Barbara asked the dark.

Just me, the firefly seemed to answer with a yellow wink, before it silently flew toward her.

Barbara waited. She had been very good at catching fireflies when she was a child, able to anticipate where they would be between flashes. She would take the bugs and hold them down. Then, when they lit up their butts, smash them with a stick.

The bioluminescent glow would persist for several minutes. And she delighted in waving the branches in front of her sister, who thought the practice was cruel.

Barbara watched the firefly carefully until she detected a pattern, then she made her move. But the firefly wasn't quite where she expected it would be. She tried to adjust, but ended up putting weight on the ball of her injured foot, and the wet film of blood covering it caused her to slip and slam her shoulder into the wall.

She thought she had heard a crack. And when she tried to move her left arm, fingers of pain grabbed her collarbone. She carefully lowered that arm to her side and held it as still as possible.

The firefly mocked her from the hallway.

Barbara put the pain aside. She stood and walked carefully toward the doorway of her bedroom, holding her left arm motionless while she used her right to reach out for obstacles in front of her like a blind woman.

She ignored the injury to her foot. The bleeding seemed to have slowed, and she suffered the agony of putting pressure on the wound for sure footing.

The firefly seemed to be leading her out into the hallway, onto the landing at the top of the staircase. Its faint yellow light was just bright enough to illuminate the edge of the banister.

Barbara grabbed hold of the wooden railing as she cautiously stepped forward. She could feel the coarse fabric of the carpet runner that ran the length of the landing underfoot.

She closed the distance between herself and the firefly, watching and waiting.

Then a nearby lighting strike lit up the whole house.

In that brief moment, she saw the dark speck of the unlit firefly hovering just in front of her. She reached out and snatched at it with her right hand.

Did she get it?

She waited, watching to see if there were any indications it had evaded her, any taunting flashes in the dark.

But she didn't see any.

She squeezed her closed hand tight, unsure if there was anything inside to crush, but if there was, she made sure it wouldn't escape unharmed. Then she smashed her hand against her bare thigh and rubbed it back and forth in an effort to obliterate anything that remained.

She turned in the direction of the bathroom, so she could clean up her foot and put on a bandage, but out of the corner of her eye she caught a glimpse of a brief, dim flicker of yellow light.

Barbara howled. She turned toward it and charged, not realizing she was heading for the top of the staircase. And when she thought she was placing her foot on solid floor, she instead stepped onto unsubstantial air.

She grabbed wildly around her, her fingers brushing past, then reaching for the banister. As her body started to tip over the top step, she got hold of the polished wood, then swung her left arm around to reinforce her purchase.

The pain in her broken collarbone erupted once more, and she screamed.

But she did not fall.

Right away.

The fingers of her left hand spasmed.

She tried to get her feet underneath her, but the bleeding had resumed in force, and her efforts to climb back up onto the landing failed. Her right hand lost its grip, and she fell, smacking her skull on the edge of one of the hardwood steps, then tumbled down, ass over teakettle.

Her mind flashed back to the night her sister had died. She could still see the look on Firefly's face when she realized Barbara had pushed her, and she was going to fall to her death.

Barbara's body landed in a heap at the bottom of steps.

But she wasn't dead.

Her head hurt, and her collarbone was aflame, but as far as she could tell, she could still feel and move her arms and legs, and open her eyes onto the darkness of her living room.

Slowly, she got to her feet, testing her limbs, making sure there was nothing else broken or cut. But aside from the bump rising on the back of her head, she was fine.

The firefly glowed smugly in the center of the room.

Barbara smiled. "Is that you, Firefly? Have you come back to try to kill me? To get back at me for what I did to you all those years ago? Or are you just jealous that I'm getting all the praise and glory for your vapid little stories?"

The firefly blinked.

A long flash of lightning lit up the room.

Barbara spied the iron shovel next to the fireplace used to scoop out ashes. Before the room dimmed, she grabbed it, then swung around to see where the firefly had gotten to.

It was floating near the front door.

Barbara swung at the air, but her blows missed, and the firefly kept on bobbing and weaving like a boxing contender wearing out the champ as he forced him to launch blows that never landed.

In the next flash of lightning, she reached for the front door and opened it. If she couldn't kill the pest, maybe she could get it out of the house.

To her surprise, the firefly flew toward the door and out into the storm.

Barbara watched in amazement, waiting for a raindrop to knock it out of the sky, but it seemed to be able to fly around them.

"Babs..." the wind whispered.

She stepped out into the downpour and was instantly soaked. But that didn't slow her down as she strode barefoot through the muddy grass, her eyes fixed on the tiny dot of light bobbing through the storm.

Barbara reared the shovel back and swung at the firefly, her blow carrying through and landing in the mud. She fell to her knees and lifted the fireplace implement away.

There was nothing there.

But then she noticed a faint glow coming from the back of the shovel. It was the crushed remains of the firefly in mid light, still glimmering.

She laughed.

Slowly, she got to her feet, staring at the smear of glowing yellow already starting to fade. "I got you!" she said triumphantly. "I win. Again."

Barbara raised the shovel to the sky in victory.

A yellow bolt of lightning snaked down from the black cloud above, striking the iron tool and sending hundreds of millions of volts through Barbara's body into the wet ground at her feet.

The agent saw the business manager waiting for him at their usual table in the center of the fancy dining room. "Sorry I'm late," he said.

"No matter. I don't mind taking extra time away from all this sordid business. Such a waste that she died just as she was hitting her prime," the manager replied.

"Yes, but it was a good ride while it lasted. And it's not completely over."

"Oh?"

"I got an email with another story this morning."

"How is that possible? She died a week ago."

The agent shrugged. "Maybe she scheduled it in advance. She was very clever with computers."

"Any good?"

"Very good. A bit dark. It's about a woman who is haunted by the ghost of her sister. Coincidentally, it ends with the main character dying by a lighting strike."

"That is quite a coincidence."

"There was one odd thing, though."

"Really? Odder than her having written about her exact manner of death? What was that?"

"Just something that struck me as so out of character. She signed it, 'Babs.'"

If you enjoyed this book, please consider leaving a short review on Amazon, Goodreads or Audible.

Amazon

Goodreads

Audible

Everyman Thrillers ...
ordinary people in
extraordinary circumstances.

www.ingramcontent.com/pod-product-compliance
Lightning Source LLC
Chambersburg PA
CBHW020539020726
47494CB00006B/1831

* 9 7 8 1 9 5 3 5 6 6 1 7 1 *